"Very engaging. Hard to put down."
— BILLY ALLMON, U.S. Navy SEAL (Retired)

"Sweetly sentimental and moving… An endearing page-turner."
— PUBLISHERS WEEKLY

"A tapestry of emotion deeply set inside the bravest of Americans: the soldier."
— MILITARY WRITERS SOCIETY of AMERICA

"Reminds me of *American Sniper* and *Lone Survivor*, but accompanied with a beautiful and epic romance that is completely unforgettable."
— LAUREN HOFF, United States Air Force

"Spot on with characters and descriptions. Strong women. Larger than life men. Well done."
— LYNNETTE BUKOWSKI, Founder/CEO of LZ-Grace Warriors Retreat Foundation and Ombudsman to Special Operation NSW Commands

"A heart-rending, white-knuckle journey into the courageous lives of our nation's heroes. Shows us the meaning of commitment—to country, and to love."
— JOCELYN GREEN, Award-winning author

Other Books by Jessica James

Suspense:
MEANT TO BE

Historical Fiction:
SHADES OF GRAY
NOBLE CAUSE (An alternative ending to Shades of Gray)
ABOVE AND BEYOND
LIBERTY AND DESTINY

Non-Fiction
THE GRAY GHOST OF CIVIL WAR VIRGINIA
FROM THE HEART: Love Letters and Stories from the Civil War

www.jessicajamesbooks.com

JESSICA JAMES
HONOR COURAGE LOVE

DEADLINE

A Novel

Jessica James

PATRIOT PRESS
Gettysburg, Pa.

We hope you enjoy this book from Patriot Press. Our goal is to provide high-quali-
ty, thought-provoking books that honor the spirit, courage, and devotion of American heroes, past and present.

www.patriotpressbooks.com

ISBN 978-1-941020-09-8
Library of Congress Control Number: 2016900048

Cover Design by Kari Ayasha of Cover to Cover Designs
Edited by Elizabeth White
Interior Design: Patriot Press

May 2016

Proudly Printed in the United States of America

Dedicated to the warriors who put country before self,
and to those who have sacrificed without recognition.

———————————

Before there can be peace, there must be justice.

Chapter 1

The wail of a siren jolted Caitlin Sparks from her thoughts an instant before the flashing red and blue lights barreled out of the fog in front of her. Clutching the steering wheel more from surprise than fright, she watched the swirling beams pass her, then shifted her gaze to the rear-view mirror for the brief moment it took the fast-moving vehicle to vanish again into the darkness.

Wow. They're sure in a hurry. Caitlin concentrated on the otherwise-empty road, trying to distinguish landmarks through the heavy rain and curtain of fog. Despite her best efforts, anything not lying directly in the path of her headlights was indistinguishable.

Reaching to turn up the radio, Caitlin's stomach leaped as a second, then a third, police cruiser barreled out of the haze before disappearing into the darkness behind her. She cursed the broken emergency scanner sitting on the seat, and then made a split-second decision when her headlights glanced off a red reflector marking a wide driveway. Slamming on her brakes, she executed a quick U-turn, sending everything on the seat beside her crashing to the floor.

So much for a quiet night at the office.

Her eyes flicked to the dashboard just as the clock turned to eleven fifty—almost midnight. Her newspaper shift didn't start for another six hours, but insomnia had driven her out of bed. She had hoped a night of research and writing in an empty newsroom would help quiet her over-active mind. Though she hated to admit it, the familiar glow of her computer terminal and the warmth from the hot thermos of coffee she'd brought along provided comforting solace.

Leaning forward and holding the steering wheel with a white-knuckle grip, she struggled to see flashing lights—or anything—in front of her headlights.

"I really am insane," Caitlin said out loud as she swung onto a narrow road, hoping the cops had turned here too. She thought she had seen the slightest trace of a roadside flare, but maybe it was her imagination. Banging her dashboard in an attempt to get the defroster to work, she peered determinedly into the inky darkness for the familiar sign of emergency vehicles.

Even though a simple outing to do some late-night writing had turned into a miserable drive through the rain stalking police cars, Caitlin was more excited than disheartened. As a seasoned reporter, she couldn't resist the temptation of a good story. They didn't come around that often at a small daily paper.

Turning the windshield wipers on high, as if that would clear the fog from the road in front of her, Caitlin thought about the last time she'd chased down a story on a night such as this—and then tried to think of something else. The memories from that occasion crashed down upon her almost like a physical weight, causing a surge of apprehension she forced away.

One more mile and I'm turning around. The road had long since turned to gravel, pretty common in that part of Virginia, but it had narrowed substantially to a single lane—a deeply rutted and potholed single lane at that. Caitlin clenched her teeth as one tire fell into a seemingly bottomless pothole that whipped her head forward.

She hoped to find a place to turn around, but the high banks on each side of the narrow road made a U-turn almost impossible. When her headlights caught the reflection of something up ahead, she breathed a huge sigh of relief. *A road flare.* She rounded a curve and came upon a policeman motioning with his flashlight for her to stop. His dark rain slicker shimmered in her headlights, creating an eerie-looking apparition that made her heart skip a beat.

"Can't go no further, miss," the man said gruffly, once she'd stopped and lowered her window.

Caitlin flipped out her press pass and smiled with relief. "Hey, Olson. How's it going?"

"Caitlin. How the hell are ya?" The robust officer leaned in the window. "Why, I haven't seen you since…" A look of discomfort and then sympathy crossed his face.

Caitlin just nodded, glad he didn't finish his sentence. With his rough, tough-guy exterior, Olson used to intimidate her. But once she got to know him, she discovered what a kindhearted, gentle soul he was. After more than thirty years on the job he had seen just about everything, and was always willing to share information with her—even if most of it was off the record. She didn't run into him much anymore, but always enjoyed the reunion when she did.

"What's going on?" Caitlin pulled forward and steered as far off the road as she could as another cruiser passed by with lights flashing.

"Homicide," Olson said, taking off his wet hat and giving it a shake. "Maybe a double from what I'm hearing."

Caitlin's heart started to pound with a little adrenalin. Her hunch had paid off.

"Anyone else here?"

The officer grinned, knowing exactly what she meant. "Are you crazy? Ain't no other reporters dumb enough to be out on a night like this. Anyway, it might be you're the last one that gets through." He gave her a wink.

Caitlin shot him a look of appreciation. "Thanks, Olson." She reached out and touched his arm. "You getting relieved soon? You look cold and wet."

"Who knows? Everyone wants to be up at the scene, not stuck down here on the road keeping nosy reporters out." He lifted a hand and motioned in the direction of the crime. "I've seen enough of that stuff. They can have it."

"Well thanks for passing me through. Good to see you again."

"Well, it might be the last time."

"What?" Caitlin moved her foot back to the brake.

He bent down to the window again. "You didn't hear? I'm retiring. End of the month is my last day."

"Congratulations." The news made Caitlin both happy and regretful at the same time. "I'm sure going to miss you." She put her hand on his wet arm and gave it a heartfelt squeeze. "Who's going to teach the new reporters the ropes now?"

Unlike other veteran cops, Olson had taken the time to show her the ropes when she was a rookie reporter a dozen years ago. From police lingo and protocol to local politics and personalities, he'd taught her more through his patient answering of questions than she could have learned in a year of schooling.

"Aw." He pushed away from the car. "They don't need me. They got this." He used his thumbs on a make-believe cell phone.

"You got that right. Well, enjoy your retirement if I don't see you." Caitlin started to drive away, but then hit the brakes and yelled out the window. "Who's the investigating officer?"

"Madison," Olson said, with what looked like a frown. "You best stay out of the way."

Caitlin's heart sank as she waved a thank you and then closed her window. Of course her luck had to run out sometime. She had never worked with Detective Madison—*Mad Dog* Madison, as he was affectionately known in the newsroom. But then again, neither had any other reporter. The only interviews he gave began and ended with "no comment."

All she really knew about him was he had served in the military and moved quickly up the career ladder in the police department to the rank of detective. Even though he hadn't been on the force that long, he was well known in law enforcement circles— almost a legend to those who aspired to work with him—and was reputed to be one of the best interrogators in the region.

But his no-nonsense approach and abrupt retorts in dealing with the media didn't give him many fans among journalists. They preferred working with flamboyant police officials who would hold press conferences and pose for photographs at a crime scene.

As for Caitlin, she didn't blame the detective for avoiding reporters and not trusting the media. In many ways, she had the same distrust of cops as he did for journalists. The corruption in Washington, D.C., did not end with politicians and did not stop at its geographical boundaries. The desire for power and influence had crept into the very fabric of the local culture, including those who were charged with enforcing the laws and protecting the citizens. Her job required her to work with law enforcement officers, but that didn't mean she had to like it.

After driving up a dirt lane that inclined steeply, Caitlin pulled in behind an unmarked cruiser and sat in her car to take in the scene. What appeared to be a large, extravagant retreat-type home loomed eerily out of the darkness, offset by flashing lights from perhaps a half-dozen police vehicles. The squawking of radios created a sense of chaos as Caitlin watched officers scurry around and then disappear into the shadows.

Despite the misty gloom surrounding the scene, Caitlin surmised from the incline that she now sat on top of a hill. The home was constructed on high stilts and the wooden deck that wrapped around it probably provided a breathtaking view, making it a prime piece of real estate.

Caitlin studied the site but could find no mailbox to provide a house number. *Maybe a rental house?* Even though the chalet was constructed of log and located in the middle of nowhere, its size and prominence suggested a luxurious and lavish lifestyle—not a rustic one. The short distance to downtown D.C. boosted her belief this was a weekend retreat for those who ran in the elite circles of Washington's political class.

She examined the scene again, questioning the heavy response and urgency. Judging by the number of police cars, she made the assumption this was not a cut-and-dried domestic dispute or even a murder-suicide. This appeared to be a full-fledged murder investigation—and no police tape restricted her from taking a closer look. She had to at least get close enough to see if she could find a house number so she could cross-reference the location on a map and track down an owner's name.

Caitlin grabbed her notebook and was greeted with a loud splash as soon as her foot hit the ground. *Way to park in the middle of a mud puddle, Caitlin.*

Shaking her foot, she was glad she'd had the sense to wear work boots and a heavy barn coat. A hat and gloves would be nice, but she hadn't known she was going to be traipsing around in the rain so didn't have them with her.

After looking around to make sure no one had noticed her presence, Caitlin decided to head to the back of the house where there seemed to be less activity.

But maneuvering across unfamiliar, uneven terrain proved difficult. The heavy cloud cover blotted out all illumination from above, while the flashing beams of the police cruisers created a disorienting array of colored lights and shadows. She had to practically feel her way up the stone path of steps through the trees, which were slippery from the rain.

When she reached the back of the house, Caitlin found it was much quieter; just the sound of the wind in the trees and the occasional squawk of a police radio emanating from inside. The darkness was oppressive, but she now stood at the bottom of a set of wooden stairs that led to the wide deck on the first floor.

Here we go. Caitlin gripped the wet handrail and tiptoed up the steps, surprised she had made it this far without being stopped. When she reached the top, she noticed most of the blinds were drawn, making the house appear empty. But as she proceeded along the wrap-around deck toward the front, a soft glow of light punched a hole in the darkness, lighting a short span of the wooden planks. *Good. No curtains.*

Creeping in the shadows, she stopped beside the window and bent cautiously forward to get a glimpse inside. The sight that greeted her seemed like a scene from a movie. About a half-dozen cops filled the room—some taking prints, others snapping photographs or writing notes. A table obstructed her view, but their general focus appeared to be something on the floor.

Most notable among the officers busy at their jobs was a

broad-shouldered man with an unlit cigarette dangling out of his mouth. The way he commanded attention and directed the others in the room made Detective Madison easy to recognize. Although she'd only ever seen him from a distance and in passing, he was not the type of man one could forget.

Caitlin shivered in the rain, but couldn't tell if it was from the chill of the night, the great story she was on the verge of getting... or intimidation as she stared at the officer in charge of the investigation. To help renew her courage, she closed her eyes and pictured her editor's face when he saw the headline for this story in the file for tomorrow's paper.

Heavy footsteps moving out of the house nudged Caitlin from her thoughts, and before she even opened her eyes, she knew it was Detective Madison. Holding her breath, she stood perfectly still as he walked to the corner of the deck with long, brisk strides that suggested boundless impatience. Luckily, he was facing the opposite direction as he stopped and attempted to light a cigarette just a few feet away.

Caitlin prepared to take a step back into the shadows, but before she had time to move, the detective cursed. Cupping his hands, he turned completely around to put his back to the wind that had extinguished his lighter. Just as the cigarette sparked red, his expression changed and Caitlin knew he had spotted the tip of her boots. She held her breath as he slowly raised his head, taking in every inch of her, until he stared straight into her startled eyes.

Without saying a word he lowered his gaze from her face to the small notebook she held, and then raised it again. Disapproval and displeasure radiated from him in a palpable wave.

"I hope you're not a reporter." His voice was low and calm... hostile. "This is a secure crime scene."

Though her heart pounded at his tone, Caitlin found herself

momentarily flustered by the color and depth of his eyes. Even in the dim light she could see they were a deep shade of blue— the type of eyes that drew you in and made you pause. The type that missed nothing and announced to anyone who looked close enough that this was not a man to be messed with.

Caitlin turned her palms up, feigning calmness and innocence. "I'm sorry, I didn't notice any tape or signs that it was secure." She regretted the words almost before they had left her lips, but there was no way to take them back. *Dammit. Think before you speak.*

When she mustered the courage to look back at the detective, Caitlin could not interpret the emotion on his face—but it did not appear to be anger. Taking a long draw on his cigarette, he simply cocked his head to the side and stared at her through half-opened lids as if trying to read her mind, thought by thought.

"Okay, Scoop," he said, casually relaxing against the porch railing. "I'll level with you." He took another drag from the cigarette and looked down at her. "I don't like reporters."

Thanks for the newsflash.

"But…" He paused and peered at the dark sky above him. "Since you obviously took the time to come all the way out here on a less than agreeable night, I'll give you the lowdown."

Caitlin waited for him to continue, biting her lip to keep from saying anything stupid again. She could tell from his condescending tone there would be no information forthcoming.

"I'm investigating an *incident.*" He tilted his head again and stared at her, gauging her reaction to that revelation.

An incident? Wow. Should I write that down and pretend that's helpful? She shot him a look of aggravation that she was sure he noticed, but did not acknowledge.

"And you're in my way. That makes me irritable, you know? I

mean, here I am chilled to the bone. Tired. Frankly, I don't want to be here."

Caitlin nodded like a first-grader getting a lecture from her teacher.

"I sure as hell can't figure out why *you* would want to be here." He brought the cigarette up to his lips with a slow, even motion, inhaled, and then let it drop to rest at his side.

"Actually, I left a warm house to be here."

The detective stared at her intently with those slate-blue eyes again, as if surprised to hear her speak. "I hope you're not going to blame me for that bad decision."

His tone and expression should have made Caitlin turn and leave, but she ignored them both and decided to push on. What did she have to lose at this point? "Well, since I'm here and we ran into each other, maybe you could give me some information... I mean, so I don't have to go back completely empty-handed on such a cold, miserable night."

The detective's eyes flashed a little this time, but his face remained like stone. "Tell you what. I'm going to be a nice guy and give you the courtesy of a warning." He took a step forward and stared down at Caitlin. "You get out of here before I lose my temper, and I'll *try* to forget this ever happened."

He took one last draw on his cigarette, crushed it between his fingers, and stuck it in his coat pocket. Without another word, he turned and disappeared around the corner of the porch. It wasn't until Caitlin heard the door slam shut that she remembered to breathe again. And it wasn't until she remembered to breathe again that she noticed the light drizzle had turned to a steady rain during her conversation with Detective Madison. Large, icy drops were hanging on her eyelashes, sliding down her face, and dripping from her hair.

I guess I'll take that as a no comment.

As she made her way back to her Jeep, Caitlin tried to find some humor in the situation. But wet and weary and chilled to the bone, it didn't take long to come to the conclusion that her first meeting with Mad Dog could really not have gone any worse.

Chapter 2

Dripping wet, cold and tired, Caitlin tried to find one good thing that had come from driving to the middle of nowhere in the middle of the night in the pouring rain—she couldn't. Not only was she leaving with no information, she had pissed off the investigating officer.

My reputation would be better off if I had spent the night in a warm bed or at the office and picked up the press release from police headquarters in the morning.

Opening the door to her Jeep and sliding into the seat, she decided she had two options. She could leave and pretend this night had never happened, or she could hang around and see if one of the other officers would talk. If she targeted one of the younger, inexperienced guys she might be able to get something.

Like in more trouble, her conscience told her.

And what good would it do? If she couldn't get it confirmed by the investigating officer she wouldn't use it anyway. And not that it mattered in the grand scheme of things, but she didn't want to piss Mad Dog off any more than she already had. She liked to build relationships—not destroy them on the first meeting.

Then again, how do you destroy something you never had?

Throwing her unused notebook on the seat beside her, Caitlin spied the thermos of coffee lying on the floor. She stared at it as her mind kicked into a new gear. The nearest store had to be at least five miles away—and Detective Madison sure did look cold.

Caitlin held onto the steering wheel and tried to talk herself out of what she was thinking. As it stood, the most she would get from her time out in this nasty weather was a runny nose and sore throat. She had no information to go back to the office with—not even confirmation this was a murder scene. Yes, it would be an act of desperation, but that didn't mean it wasn't worth a try.

Desperate times call for desperate measures… right?

Caitlin sat back and noticed her face in the rear-view mirror, then moved in closer to get a better look. Holy cow. No makeup. Hair dripping wet. Cheeks and nose red from the cold. *Nice first impression, Caitlin.* Seriously. A little lipstick would have done wonders if she'd only remembered to put some on.

She turned her head and squeezed the water out of her pony-tail, then blew on her freezing hands. The air temperature wasn't just cold. It was wet and damp. The kind of pure discomfort that goes straight to the bones. Detective Madison had the whole night ahead of him. He had to be perfectly miserable, even though he'd shown no sign of it.

Without analyzing the situation any longer, Caitlin scooped up the thermos and the coffee mug she had tossed on the seat as an afterthought, knowing it would only be moments before Madison would order the area secured with police tape—if indeed he hadn't done so already.

As she headed back to the house, she spied the detective on the porch in deep conversation with another plain-clothed officer.

"Detective." Caitlin hurried up the front steps, trying to muster her courage as she walked. The man had an intensity about him she could feel even from this distance.

Madison put an unlit cigarette back into his pocket and strode toward her with a look of displeasure written clearly on his face. He reached her before she had made it halfway up, and didn't give her a chance to explain. "I thought I made myself clear earlier, but maybe you didn't understand. Would a trip to jail help?"

"No. I'm leaving, but I-I just thought you could use a cup of coffee." Caitlin twisted the top off the thermos. "I mean, I brought it and I thought it may as well not go to waste."

"That's nice of you, Miss—"

"Sparks. Caitlin Sparks." Caitlin finished the name for him even though the sarcasm in his voice made it clear he knew what she was up to and wasn't going to fall for it.

"Thanks for the offer, Scoop," he said, ignoring her real name, "but I have men bringing food and coffee right now."

Whether it was the gust of bone-chilling wind that kicked up at that moment or the aroma of the hot brew, Caitlin didn't know, but the detective suddenly had a change of mind and reached out for the large mug.

"On second thought, you're right. No sense in it going to waste." He regarded her with an expression that had the same effect as another blast of cold wind, causing a shiver of discomfort to run up her spine. "It's going to be a long night."

Caitlin poured the dark liquid into the mug and watched Madison's eyes turn almost soft as he took a large swallow. He lifted his gaze to hers as he brought the mug back down. "You're not planning on staying out in this weather all night, I hope."

"No." Caitlin stamped her feet to get the feeling back into them. "I'm taking off as soon as I get some information."

The detective tilted his head and gave her that look again, as if he couldn't quite figure her out. Caitlin, on the other hand, had figured *him* out completely. He was a man not accustomed to being pushed, or even questioned, and reflected an intensity that made him come off as unshakable and tough. If not for his occupation and menacing reputation, Detective Madison *might* be someone she'd want to know better.

"Okay." He wrapped both hands around the mug. "Don't ask me why I'm doing this, but I'll give you three questions. Shoot."

Caitlin's gaze darted back to his, stunned that he'd even spoken to her. Three questions? She wasn't ready for this. She had about a hundred. "Well, I don't even know the basics—like what you're investigating and the sex of the victims."

"Is that your first question?"

"No, that was a statement."

"It's two questions, but I'll only deduct one. Possible homicide. One male. One female."

So Olson was right. "What was the murder weapon?"

"I can't release that." He sounded grave.

"Does that mean you haven't found a murder weapon yet?"

"Is that your third question?"

Caitlin frowned. She didn't want to waste another question on something that should be available by morning. "No." *Damn it.* She cleared her throat. "My next question is, where were they found and by whom?"

"That's two questions."

"Well, it's only one sentence." She glanced up and made a half-hearted effort to smile, but the intense look of his expression almost caused her to waver. She knew she was pressing her luck, but needed to make the most of her limited situation.

"I can't answer that one at this point in the investigation."

"Do you mean the person who found them is a possible suspect?"

"I mean it's too early to rule anyone out."

Her questions seemed to be irritating him, as if he hadn't expected them to be quite so intuitive.

"I gotta get back. I've given you enough." He shot her a look that made it clear he had reached his limit.

"More coffee?" Caitlin held out the thermos.

"Thanks. That sure hit the spot."

Caitlin tried to keep her own cold hands from shaking as she poured another cupful into the outstretched mug. "I get the feeling you thought I would blow a question on the actual cause of death." Caitlin attempted to make conversation, just in case she could get him to reveal anything else. She was beyond intimidation at this point.

Madison looked at her from over the mug. "I guess I kind of assumed you would do that."

"This isn't my first investigation, Detective." Caitlin shot him the same sideways glare he had used on her. "I don't need you for that. I can get it from the coroner."

"Thanks again for the coffee." Madison turned abruptly and headed back to the house.

Goodbye to you, too. Caitlin scrutinized him as he walked away, his long, confident strides showing no signs of discomfort from the weather or weariness from the lateness of the hour. He was quite a commanding and imposing-looking man. *But he could sure use some people skills.*

Madison stopped at the top of the steps to say a few words to a young officer now guarding the front door. Caitlin assumed it had something to do with securing the area with police tape since he nodded in her direction and then pointed toward the road. She knew he was going to disappear, knew he wasn't going to tell her anything more, but for some reason she just stood there, awkwardly holding a half-empty thermos of coffee.

It wasn't until the front door slammed shut that Caitlin turned back toward her vehicle to leave.

Chapter 3

Detective Madison entered the police station and headed toward his office. It had started raining hard again about fifteen minutes earlier, and hadn't let up.

The short walk from his truck into the building had left him soaked again, and the night on the scene had left him cold to the bone and sleep-deprived. He looked forward to a strong pot of coffee to help cover the exhaustion and relieve the chill that left his bones aching.

"Phone calls for you, sir." The front desk clerk reached over the counter and handed him two pink slips as he walked by without stopping. "A Caitlin Sparks has been calling for you," she said in a loud voice as he disappeared around the corner.

Madison took the notes, crumbled them in his hand without looking at them, and tossed them in the next trash can he passed.

Six o'clock in the morning

Caitlin had been pacing nervously in front of her desk for the past half-hour, trying to decide if she should try calling Detective Madison's direct line. She didn't like using the individual office numbers she'd been given by a source at the police station unless it was absolutely necessary, but it was beginning to appear like he wasn't going to return the calls she'd made through the front desk.

She paced some more and then moved toward the phone. *Good heavens, Caitlin. What are you afraid of? The worst thing he can do is hang up on you.* Deciding it was now or never if she was going to make deadline, she dialed the number. *One ring. Two rings.*

"Madison."

Caitlin's heart did a flip. Whoa. She hadn't really expected him to be there—or to answer the phone if he were.

"Oh, hi… Detective Madison. This is Caitlin Sparks. We met last night and—"

He didn't let her finish. "How did you get this number?"

"Oh, well I called through the front desk twice but you didn't return my calls." Caitlin tried to defend herself. "So I—"

"That doesn't answer my question."

Annoyance and impatience radiated through the phone line, causing Caitlin to hurriedly defend herself.

"I needed to get hold of you, so I—"

"Are you going to answer the question?"

"No," she answered frankly. "My sources are confidential. I extended the courtesy of going through the proper channels… twice." She tapped a pen on the desk nervously and then continued. "You don't think much of me, do you?"

"Actually not at all—unless I'm forced to through a phone call I inadvertently answer at six in the morning thinking it's important." She heard an exacerbated sigh that sounded almost like a growl. "Look, I have a stack of paperwork sitting in front of me, what do you want?"

His quick retorts and unsympathetic tone threw Caitlin off balance. She answered without thinking. "I wanted to see if you were done with my coffee mug yet." She grimaced, both at what had come out of her mouth—unplanned—and at the sudden silence on the other end of the line. *Why hadn't she prepared a little better?*

But the silence was followed by a short, forced laugh. "Really? You're calling for a coffee mug?"

Caitlin heard what sounded like creaking wood followed by a *thunk*, and she imagined him reclining back in his chair and placing his feet on his desk.

"Or do you have a hole in your story right before deadline you desperately need me to fill?"

Caitlin exhaled the breath she didn't even know she'd been holding. "I think maybe the *desperately* part is a bit of a stretch." She drummed the desk with nervous fingers. "But now that you mention it, since you're on the phone and so agreeable, I guess there are some things you could help fill in."

She plunged on, deciding not to give him time to argue. "I wanted to see if I could possibly find out the official cause of death."

This time the laugh was a real one. "You can't get that out of the coroner's office?"

"No." Caitlin could not keep the irritation out of her voice. "For some reason there is a *new* rule that all information has to be approved by the investigating officer—which in this case is *you*." She paused. "I thought I could trust releasing my trade secrets to a cop, but I guess I was wrong."

"And I guess you think offering coffee to a cold detective in the middle of the night and then calling him the next morning on the pretense of getting a mug back is completely trustworthy behavior?"

"Okay. You win." Caitlin stabbed a piece of paper with a pen. "But how about a truce… or at least a compromise? You don't have to give it to me on the record. I'll use it to get the coroner's office to confirm it."

"That's not how I do things."

"It's not how I do things either, to be honest with you."

"Oh, so now we're being *honest*?"

"I'm on deadline. Are you going to give it to me or not?" Caitlin waited for an answer, but feared she had pushed too far. She fully expected to hear the sound of the phone disconnecting. Instead, she heard some papers rustling.

"Cause of death... *off* the record ... is lateral gunshot wounds to the cephalic region caused by a high-velocity, large-caliber projectile that resulted in perforating and penetrating wounds."

"So in English, that means someone blew their brains out with a gun of some sort. Is that what you're saying?" Caitlin held the phone tightly against her ear so she wouldn't miss anything.

"Very astute." Madison spoke in a voice barely audible. "I don't know why I'm doing this."

"Cause you're a nice guy." She corrected herself almost immediately. "No, I take that back."

Caitlin thought she heard him laugh again, but chalked it up to his exhaustion rather than her comic ability or his sense of humor.

"So the obvious question is, is this a murder-suicide or is there a murderer on the loose?" She held her breath waiting for the answer.

"No comment," he finally said. "I gotta go."

"Wait. I have one more question." She didn't wait to see if he'd hung up. "I'm hearing that these were two employees of the State Department."

"That's not a question." His response was immediate and his voice had a sudden edge that could be felt through the phone.

Caitlin grunted. "Are they?" She knew she was pushing it,

but a source had told her that two employees who had gone on a weekend retreat had not returned. It might be a stretch, but the silence on the other end of the phone somewhat validated her suspicions. If he would just confirm it, maybe she could find someone else to verify the information and go on the record.

She waited, but after hearing nothing for a few long seconds, feared he had hung up. "Hello?"

"I'm still here. I can't confirm or deny that at this point."

"Okay. This afternoon then for tomorrow's paper?" If she couldn't find anyone to go on the record, she couldn't use the information in print. Beating the competition by getting a story *first* was always her goal, but getting it *right* was even more important.

"Are you trying to push my buttons?"

"I'm trying to do my job."

He exhaled loudly. "I don't know what you're hearing and who you're hearing it from, but that's not something that can be released right now."

"You're not going to use the *notifying next of kin* line on me, I hope."

"There's more to it than that. Trust me."

"My job is to inform the public—good news or bad—but if you're telling me to hold off on certain things for *now* for the greater good, then that's what I'll do."

"That's what I'm telling you."

"Okay. I'll stop by the police station on my way home to see if there's anything new."

"Thanks for the warning."

Caitlin rolled her eyes, but then she heard the detective take a deep breath, as if trying to figure out how to say something.

"I can't give you any more than I did, and I probably gave more than I should have." He sounded more frustrated with himself than irritated with her.

"Can't? Or won't?"

"Actually, I can't. It's out of my hands."

"What's that supposed to mean?"

"This is off the record." His voice was low and threatening. "You understand?"

"Of course."

"The Feds rolled in shortly after you left."

"The Feds? Who exactly?"

"FBI mostly."

"Why?"

"I'm just telling you it's not my investigation anymore. That's all."

Caitlin's head was spinning with more unanswered questions. "You're saying they're assisting you, right? I mean, it *is* your jurisdiction."

"I'm saying it's their investigation." He sounded angry, and frustrated. "I gotta go. That was off the record. Remember that."

"Absolutely. Thanks."

"Scoop?"

"Yes?" Caitlin answered to her new nickname.

"If you burn me, you'll be sorry. I can promise you that."

"You can trust me," she practically whispered into the phone *Click.*

Chapter 4

Caitlin pulled an early-run paper off the press and took it back to her desk to read. With her eyes cast downward on her story, she almost ran into a handful of people gathered around the newsroom television.

Glancing up, she saw they were engrossed in watching a correspondent deliver a report from the middle of a familiar-looking dirt road. The banner at the bottom read "Hillside crime scene," but Caitlin could see the news crew had not even gotten close enough to get a shot of the exterior of the house where last night's crime had taken place.

She looked down at the paper in her hands and studied the large photo that went along with her story. It was dark—she had snapped it as an afterthought—but it clearly showed the house and the police activity surrounding it. She had beat everyone on this one.

Turning her attention back to the television, she smiled at what she saw. Yellow tape sparkled in the morning sunlight behind the reporter—and she had to be at least a half a mile away from the house. Detective Madison had definitely secured the scene after she'd left.

"Officials are being tight-lipped about what transpired here," the reporter said, causing Caitlin to shake her head. *Really?*

"All we know at this point is that a major police incident took place."

Even if he was now off the case, that comment had Mad Dog Madison written all over it. A police *incident?* Can you be any more vague? What she wouldn't give to have watched that interview.

As the camera zoomed in on the reporter, Caitlin's thoughts wandered back to a city hall press conference about ten months earlier. Shelley Lee, as this correspondent was known on the air, had been new at the time, and had asked Caitlin for a rundown on the backgrounds and personalities of some of the officials she might meet while covering her beat.

When they had gotten to Detective Madison, Caitlin had explained she'd never worked with him and didn't know him—which had not bothered Shelley in the least. She'd laughed and said she'd rather find a way to get handcuffed by him than get information out of him anyway.

Caitlin's eyebrows rose at the memory. Judging from the lack of information Shelley had acquired from Madison about the crime, it didn't appear she had been successful at either one. The competitive nature of the opposing fields of journalism, caused print and broadcast reporters to distrust and dislike each other, but Caitlin felt a pang of sympathy for Shelley. She'd thought *her* first meeting with the detective had gone as badly as it could—but it seemed like this correspondent had struck out even worse.

Although Shelley Lee was blonde, good-looking and already a bit of a local celebrity, she apparently hadn't made much of an impression on Madison. Caitlin pegged him as the type of guy not easily impressed by status or appearance, and Shelley Lee proved her assumption. Of course, he didn't seem like a guy much impressed by anything. He was detached and unemotional—probably good traits to have considering his profession.

As she stood there trying to picture Shelley Lee flirting with a cold, wet, and tired Detective Madison in order to get information out of him—or trying to persuade him to show her his handcuffs—Caitlin shook her head. *That would have been a sight worth seeing.*

"We need to get on this, people." The urgency in the speaker's tone startled Caitlin and made her turn around. Fred, one of the news editors had just arrived. He raced across the room to his desk. "We need a story."

Caitlin held up the paper. "Like this?"

Fred stopped and stared. "How'd we get that?"

"*We* didn't get it." Caitlin corrected him. "*I* did. By freezing my ass off."

He grabbed the paper out of her hand and looked at the picture, and then up at the television. "I listened to the radio on the way in. They're not letting anyone anywhere near that scene. How'd you manage this?"

Caitlin snatched the paper back. "Believe it or not, this is what I do for a living. It's called reporting the news." She emphasized the words for him, and then turned back to her desk. She didn't owe Fred any more of an explanation than that. He was one of the editors who enjoyed making her life miserable by assigning her to cover non-stories like new business openings or street festivals.

Even though she had earned the title of 'Head Investigative Reporter' under former supervisors, a new slate of editors had been brought on board who did not assign stories based on assets. The meatier stories were assigned to young reporters who never left their desks and did their research and interviews via the Internet and email. Face-to-face communication was old-fashioned and out of style—fingertips on phones and tablets now did the talking... and walking.

No wonder the paper's readership was dwindling.

After getting a cup of coffee, Caitlin sat down and began scanning the front page. In addition to the double murder story, there was a feel-good piece about an annual festival running across the top, and an article about a Hollywood actress putting her local twenty-five acre estate up for sale for three million dollars as a centerpiece article.

Interesting reads maybe, but not her idea of news. Having worked under the tutelage of old-school, hard-edged editors, Caitlin didn't understand this new trend. It wasn't really reporting anymore. It was a public relations job. "Don't make waves with readers," they told her. "Don't piss off advertisers or they'll pull their money." "Don't irritate government officials or they'll stop talking."

None of the warnings caused Caitlin to change her tactics. She wrote every story with two goals in mind: accuracy and fairness. If someone was upset about a story—which they often were—she advised them to write a letter to the editor to correct the record. They seldom did. Facts were facts.

"You should have given me a call last night."

The paper's chief photographer—or as they now called him, visual art director—flopped down in a chair beside Caitlin's desk. "I could have gotten a better shot than that." He nodded toward the front page.

Caitlin couldn't help it. Her eyes drifted from the wool hat on his head to the sagging jeans and dirty shoes. This was a representative of the newspaper who interacted with the public more than most reporters, and they allowed him to dress like a hippy. She shuddered to think what kind of impression his cocky attitude would have made on Detective Madison. It certainly wouldn't have improved the officer's feelings toward the media in general, or the newspaper itself.

"It was late," is all she said.

"I'm sure I was up." He moved forward, resting his arm casually on her desk. "I wish some of your luck would rub off on me. I'd love to get tipped off on a big story like that."

Caitlin did a slow burn, but didn't say out loud what she was thinking. "No one tipped me off, Bart. And there was definitely no *luck* involved."

"Oh? You just happened upon it?" He sat back and crossed his arms. "S-u-u-r-e."

"I didn't say I just happened upon it." Caitlin wrapped her fingers around her coffee mug to keep from wrapping them around his neck. "I followed a hunch."

She glared at him, comparing him to other twenty-something millennials who worked as reporters. They attended Ivy League schools. Interned at *The Washington Post.* Then walked into their first job thinking they knew more about reporting than those who had worked in the trenches for decades. It never occurred to them they should actually try writing something worth reading or do the boring, tedious work it takes to properly research a story. Click your fingers. Instant news. That's how they thought it worked.

Bart laughed. "Sure. Right. Followed a *hunch* in the middle of the night that took you to the scene of a double murder." He stood and turned to leave. "You can call it a hunch, Sparks. We'll call it luck."

"Who's *we?*" Caitlin brows knitted in confusion and alarm.

"The newsroom," he said over his shoulder as he walked away. "There's an office pool to figure out who contacted you."

Caitlin closed her eyes to calm herself, and then turned back to the paper. Bart and the others would never understand the time and energy it took to cultivate good sources—so even if someone *had* contacted her, she wouldn't exactly call it luck. And was it luck that she had turned her vehicle around on a cold, rainy night to follow police cruisers? Would any of them have done that?

Stopping only to take a slug of coffee, Caitlin bent over her computer, typing every question that came into her mind about the murders. She didn't want to be caught off guard if she had the chance to talk to Detective Madison again—and she needed to get everything straight before she called the FBI.

"Hey, good job last night."

It surprised Caitlin to find Fred standing beside her desk, but she didn't bother to respond. She knew he didn't stop by to compliment her. There was something more coming.

"I'm sending Linda out to the scene for a follow-up."

Caitlin blinked repeatedly, like she had something in her eye. "Linda?"

"Yes. She's got some good contacts in the police department."

"She does?" Caitlin could hardly believe her ears. *Does he think calling the police department to get a daily log means she has good contacts?* "Okay. Whatever. Good luck with that." She turned back to her computer, but Fred didn't leave.

"What's *that* supposed to mean?"

Caitlin shrugged. "I'm sure Linda's police sources will tell her."

"Look." Fred didn't try to control the anger in his voice. "You need to be a team player and share any information you have."

"All of the information I have is in the story. Maybe you should read it."

"No, I know you. You always come back with off-the-record

stuff, and you're withholding it."

Caitlin's head jerked up. "You think I'm going to share something a source told me off the record with *you?*"

After more than a dozen years at this job, Caitlin had no shortage of connections—informants who trusted her with the information divulged, no matter how sensitive.

As a result, she had earned the reputation of being well-armed with facts, which caused a healthy mix of fear and respect from those in high places. Officials knew there was no way to wiggle out of a direct question from Caitlin Sparks to confirm or deny a fact she had already been told was true by one of her sources.

She'd taught them to believe it was better to come clean and get the story out rather than give her the time or incentive to find even more ammunition. "It won't get into print. We just need it for background."

She snorted. "That's what you told me last time."

Fred had burned Caitlin when he'd let another reporter print something an informant had told her confidentially. She had a personal rule of never using "unnamed sources" in her stories, but the paper had no such edict. Even though the source had not been named, it had taken a long time for her to get that person's trust back.

"I'll send Linda over before she heads out. You can brief her."

"You can save her some time by telling her to read my article. I don't have anything else to share." Caitlin picked up her phone to make a call, and then paused as if waiting for him to leave. "Our conversation is over, right?"

Fred didn't answer, but turned and stormed across the newsroom toward the office of the managing editor. Caitlin knew that between them they would attempt to make her life miserable over the next few weeks, but she had to stick by her principles. Nothing on God's green earth was going to make her share what Detective Madison had given her off the record. Linda would find out soon enough her local police contacts weren't going to be of any use.

Once Fred had disappeared, she replaced the phone in its cradle and tipped back in her chair to think. Even though she was officially off the story, that didn't mean she wanted to stop digging. She had a strange feeling about this case. The kind of feeling that made the hair on the back of her neck stand up when she thought about it.

Was she being overly skeptical? Distrustful? The fact that the State Department was indirectly linked to the last suspicious death she'd covered seemed a little too coincidental for her to just brush aside. Her gut told her something wasn't right—and the fact the FBI had taken over the case only added to her suspicions.

When her phone rang, she said a quick prayer that it would be someone telling her something useful about the case. "Sparks."

"Hey Caitlin. It's Mary Barto." There was a long pause, as if the woman was waiting for a reaction or wasn't sure what to say next. "I don't know if you remember me—"

"Hi Mary," Caitlin interrupted her and looked upward. *Thank you, God.* "Yes, I remember you. How's it going?"

Caitlin kept her voice calm and conversational even though she could hear her heartbeat drumming in her ears. She barely knew Mary—had met her only once at the State Department—but she could tell from the tone of the woman's voice this was important. She sounded strained, stressed... nervous.

"You heading into the city today by any chance?" Mary asked.

"I can be."

"You know where the Casey's Coffee is? It's not great, but it's convenient to the Metro."

"Yes. I know where it is." Caitlin's senses were hyper-alert.

That would place it within walking distance of the State Department building.

"I'd love to buy you a coffee."

"Sounds good. What time?"

"How about eleven?"

"I can do that. I'll see you there."

Caitlin glanced at the clock as she hung up the phone. She'd have to leave right now and hurry if she was going to get there on time.

Chapter 5

Caitlin walked the short distance from the Metro to the coffee shop and arrived just as Mary was sitting down at a table in the far corner. With striking red hair and beautiful green eyes, she was easy to recognize. Caitlin slung her purse over the chair and joined her.

"Hey. Hope I'm not late."

"Right on time." Mary smiled shyly. "I wasn't sure you would remember me. We only met once when Vince—"

"I remember." Caitlin didn't give her a chance to finish.

"Well, thanks for coming on such short notice."

"It sounded important."

Mary shifted in her seat nervously, but didn't say anything.

Afraid the woman was losing her nerve, Caitlin moved her chair closer and talked in a low voice. "You can tell me anything. You have to trust me."

"Can I help you ladies?"

Both of them were startled by the sound of the waitress's voice right beside them. Caitlin recovered first. "Just a regular coffee with two creams for me."

"Black for me."

As soon as the waitress left, Mary started the conversation again. "You won't print my name in any stories. Right? I've been told I can trust you, even if you are a reporter."

"Absolutely." Caitlin ignored the jab at journalists.

"I don't know if you heard yet who the victims of the Hillside murders are."

"Not any names." Caitlin felt a small tremor of excitement mixed with a vague sense of dread about what she was going to hear. "I heard a rumor they might have worked for the State Department."

"They did." Mary's eyes welled with tears. "Jay Brown and Sandra Wentz. The things they are saying about them are terrible. I can't believe what they're doing."

"Who's saying what about them?"

"The State Department press office. They're saying they went to that chalet on a lover's retreat."

"And you don't think they did?" Caitlin's brow creased as she tried to understand what she was being told.

"I know they didn't. They were good friends, but they weren't messing around."

"You're sure?"

"Positive. I know both of them and their spouses. It's ludicrous."

"Then why is the State Department doing that?"

"To cover up the real reason they went there."

"Which is?" Caitlin couldn't help it. She found herself almost sitting on the edge of her chair as she waited in breathless anticipation for the answer.

Mary fiddled with her long red hair and said nothing for a few long moments.

"You can tell me. I promise, it's safe with me."

"They were planning to blow the whistle on what's going on," she blurted out.

Caitlin's heart started pumping with such violence she had to concentrate so she could hear, but she kept her speech slow and her voice calm. "And what is going on?"

Mary put her head in her hands. "Good heavens, I don't even know. I just know it isn't right."

"Why? Why do you know it isn't right?"

"First Vince, and now Jay and Sandra."

The waitress appeared again with big mugs of steaming coffee and set them down. "Anything else ladies?"

"No. Thank you." Caitlin tried to smile and appear relaxed, but at the mere mention of Vince's name her leg started bouncing with nervous energy. She slid her hand under the table and rested it on her knee to hold it still.

"How are the Hillside murders related to Vince's death?" Caitlin picked up her coffee, but her hand shook so much she set it back down.

"You don't believe Vince committed suicide, right?"

"Of course not." *How did Vince become the focus of this conversation?* She concentrated with every ounce of her being to will away the moisture that formed in her eyes.

"And you know he was going to testify about the Kessler Affair. Right?"

Caitlin nodded. The Kessler Affair, as it was commonly referred to now, was named after Randy Kessler, an investigative reporter who'd been taken hostage while covering a story in a foreign country. His death, and the deaths of two former SEALs during a rescue attempt, had created a major scandal because of the secretive circumstances surrounding it. "How'd you know that?"

"It's pretty common knowledge on our floor. I know Vince

didn't feel right about what was going on even though they threatened him to keep his mouth shut."

"I didn't know he received any threats." Caitlin tried to control her heart rate and the whooshing sound in her ears, but every minute seemed to bring new revelations that overwhelmed her.

"Oh, it wasn't threats on his life or anything like that. They told him—and most everyone else—that if we didn't keep our heads down and do what we were told to do our lives would become… difficult."

"Like they've made it for me," Caitlin said, referring to the runaround and insults she'd received from the State Department while trying to uncover the truth about the supposed suicide.

Truth be told, she took heat on a lot of stories—but the pushback on that story had been especially brutal. Politicians and federal officials had a habit of leaking their version of events to select members of the media as a way to manipulate and control the way the message was told. They did not react favorably when reporters questioned the narrative or did stories outside the established perimeters.

Mary nodded. "Exactly."

"So you don't believe those two at the chalet were having an affair?"

"Absolutely not." She took a sip of coffee and glanced around to see if anyone was watching. "Sandra sent me a text message the afternoon they left."

The whooshing in Caitlin's ears grew louder. "And?"

"She said they had contacted Senator Wiley about testifying, putting it all out there. They wanted to get out of town to go over their testimony."

Caitlin sat back in her chair. "Do you know what they knew?"

"Not for sure." Mary took a deep breath and tapped her fingernails on the table.

"But?"

"They were in Renoviah during the Kessler Affair." She stared at her coffee cup. "They were there."

Caitlin had to clench her teeth to keep her jaw from dropping. A half-dozen State Department employees had been rescued in Renoviah during the Kessler Affair, but she'd never been able to get their names or track them down. Nobody had. The State Department had made sure of that.

They'd not only refused to provide any information on their end, they'd called her editors and bullied them into changing the story, and then attempted to intimidate the publisher and get him to drop it altogether.

"Are you sure?"

She nodded while staring straight ahead.

"So they were going to testify, even though they'd signed a document to keep quiet?"

"That's why they called the senator. To make sure it would be legal under the whistleblower statute."

Caitlin was finally able to take a sip of her coffee without spilling it. "They must have had something concrete to have made that decision. They must have known they were doing the right thing even though it was putting their careers in jeopardy."

"Too bad they didn't know they were putting their *lives* in jeopardy." Mary's chin trembled. "And their reputations after they were dead."

"So what do you think is going on?" Caitlin decided to put her on the spot. "Who do you think is responsible?"

"I don't know." Mary shook her head. "I don't even want to know. I just wanted to make sure you knew they weren't having an affair. This is a smear campaign to get people off the right track. That's all I know."

Does she know more than she is saying? Caitlin studied the woman, but couldn't tell. No doubt her bosses at the State Department had told her not to talk. And having your co-workers found dead would provide more than enough incentive to keep your mouth shut.

"It's pretty big coincidence, don't you think? I can't say I know why or how, but it just doesn't add up to me."

Caitlin decided she would have to be content with what she'd been given. At least she knew she needed to keep going now, that her hunch was correct. Something wasn't right.

Both women were quiet for a moment, but finally Mary spoke again. "Vince was a good friend of mine." Her attractive green eyes glistened unnaturally. "I really admired him. I'm sorry for your loss."

Caitlin tried to look cheerful, even though the emotions washing over her made her want to burst into tears instead. "Thanks. He spoke highly of you."

Mary's face brightened a little. "He did?" Then her expression turned sympathetic and mournful. "I wish I could be of more help."

"You've been a great help—by letting me know my gut feeling is correct."

A few minutes passed with an awkward silence. When Caitlin looked at Mary, she got the feeling something was still bothering her. "I hope you don't get in any trouble by meeting with me."

"No, I won't." She cleared her throat, and talked in a hushed tone. "To be honest, my supervisor told me to meet with you."

Caitlin gave Mary a questioning look.

"She told me I should warn you to stay away from this story. That there's nothing to it."

Caitlin was too flabbergasted to speak.

"I told her you were only doing your job, but she said it's not your job to dig up things better left alone." Mary finished her coffee. "They aren't kidding, Caitlin. I'm scared—and you should be too."

"So she was there when you made the phone call to me?"

Mary nodded. "She wanted to make sure I talked to you."

The hairs on the back of Caitlin's neck started to rise, and she wondered if they were being watched while they talked. "I appreciate you telling me all of this—rather than what you were supposed to tell me. I know it's risky for you."

Mary nodded absently, as if she was thinking about something else.

Caitlin scrutinized her face. "Is that all? Did you think of something else?"

"No." She shook her head, fingering her mug broodingly. "Well, maybe. How well do you know the detective working on the Hillside case?"

"Madison? Detective Madison?"

"Yes. That's the name."

"Not very well, why?"

"Oh." Mary seemed disappointed. "I was hoping you could warn him too."

"*Warn* him?"

Mary toyed with her napkin. "I overheard a conversation in the next office I probably shouldn't have. I think they were talking about Detective Madison."

"And?"

"I mean, it's probably nothing—I only heard one side of what was being discussed. But it sounded like someone on the other end of the line was upset about where he was going with the investigation."

"What did the side you heard say?"

"She told the person not to worry, that he wouldn't be on the investigation anymore."

Caitlin let her breath out slowly. That backed up everything Madison had told her—and proved he had been taken off the investigation by the State Department, not the FBI.

"Please don't give up. No matter what they do to you."

"Believe me, I'm not." Caitlin's thoughts drifted back to the night of the Hillside murders. How much of the scene had Detective Madison been able to process before being kicked out by the feds? She hadn't completely believed him when he said he was off the case. Now it was clear he'd been honest with her.

Mary glanced at her watch. "I have to get back to work." She stood and bent down to pick up the bill the waitress had left on the table. "Thanks again for meeting with me. I feel better knowing you understand the danger, and that you won't stop searching for the truth."

"I'll get it." Caitlin put her hand on the bill, and at the same time, lay her business card on the table. "If you hear or think of anything else, don't hesitate to call. Okay?"

Mary picked up the card and nodded. "Thanks, Caitlin."

As Caitlin watched her walk away, the emotions that had been sitting at the surface almost got the best of her. She choked back a sob as her mind wandered back to the recent past. If she could only go back in time, knowing what she knew now, and somehow change the outcome. Just last summer she had been head over heels in love with Vince Chandler at the State Department. Now he was dead, and so were two other people who worked in the same building—and that was not even counting the Kessler Affair.

She brushed a tear from her cheek as she stood.

Coincidence? Caitlin didn't think so.

But she sure didn't know how she was going to prove it.

Chapter 6

Caitlin rubbed the back of her neck, trying to release the kink that had resulted from bending over files and staring at her computer. She'd been reading for hours, but she didn't want to stop until she discovered the piece of the puzzle that would link the murders of the two State Department workers with the supposed suicide of Vince Chandler—and possibly link them all to the Kessler Affair. She had to be missing something. But what?

Every phone call she'd made and every tip she'd followed up on so far had led to a dead end. No one was talking at the FBI or the State Department, and the local officials were being kept out of the loop. "Read the official press release," they would tell her, as if that contained anything of value.

Even her usually reliable sources were of no help. She had hit a wall and didn't know which way to turn. She needed hard evidence, and it would take a lot of it to undo the storyline the State Department and FBI were pushing about the latest murders. Just as Mary had warned, the press release indicated the two dead workers were having an affair—but they went even further. Within a few days of the killings, work records were leaked to the press that implied the two were rogue employees and troublemakers. Certain co-workers—ones who had apparently promised to do as they were told—were interviewed by select media. They further maligned and smeared the victims by recounting how unreliable the two had become over the past few months.

Caitlin shook her head while reading one of the news reports. The strategy had worked. No one seemed to care about the two dead federal employees. The way the media had depicted the deceased, most people believed the couple had somehow deserved what they got. For the most part, the murders were already forgotten news.

Not to Caitlin. The official cause of death for both was gunshot wounds to the head. The press releases implied a murder-suicide took place, but no evidence for that arbitrary theory was ever released. The FBI insisted there was no reason for alarm and maintained no killer was on the loose, so people had gone back to their work places and their soccer games and dismissed the crime from their minds.

Although Caitlin had filed a Freedom of Information Act request to see the evidence supporting their claim, she had not yet received a response.

"What are you working on?"

Caitlin jerked in surprise and turned her head, grimacing at the pain it caused. "Um…"

"Not the Hillside murders again."

"Just looking for something I might have missed the first time." Caitlin's heart sank a little at the sight of the managing editor, Stan.

"I'm not paying you to solve crimes, Sparks. I pay you to cover the news. There's a barn fire over on Kindig. Go check it out."

"A barn fire? On Kindig? That's barely in our readership area."

"You heard me."

Caitlin knew there was no sense in arguing. Stan had only been the managing editor for two months, but already she'd had more than one run-in with him. Ordering her to cover barn fires on the other side of the county was his way of showing her who was boss. If she argued any more, she might end up taking obits over the phone or putting together the special events column.

"Sure, I'm on my way." She said the words out loud, but there was no need. Stan had already turned his back and was walking away.

Grabbing her purse, Caitlin headed for the door, pulling her phone out as she walked and trying to decide who to call about the Hillside murders while out of the office. She was tempted to call Detective Madison, but abandoned the idea almost immediately. He was no longer on the case, and even if he were, the chance he would talk to her was not very good.

Her cell phone vibrated before she'd even made it out of the building.

"Hey, Caitlin. It's Louie."

Caitlin continued walking despite her surprise. "What a co-incidence," she said. "I'm heading toward a fire down your way."

"Really?" There was a slight pause. "Why don't you stop by?"

"You sure?"

"Of course. Since you're going to be in the area. Haven't chatted with you for a while."

"Well there just happens to be something I'd like to talk to you about."

"Oh, really?"

Caitlin lifted her eyebrows at the tone of his voice, but hesitated to say anything more over the cell phone. "Just something I'm working on."

"Okay. Well, I'll see you when you get here."

Caitlin checked the time. "It'll take me at least a half hour to get to the fire. Half hour on the scene. So say about two?"

"Perfect."

She could hear him putting ice cubes in a glass, and he sounded pleased.

"I'll be waiting."

The next thing Caitlin heard was the click of the phone as he hung up. Oh well. Louie never was one for many words. What could you expect from a former CIA operative?

Glancing at the address of the barn fire she had put into her phone, Caitlin pulled out of the parking lot and headed north, not waiting for the map to load. She finally had a chance to study the directions while stopped at the last traffic light in town. *Terrific.* No direct route, so she would have to zigzag her way across the county on narrow back roads. On the bright side, it appeared to be only three or four miles from Louie's farmhouse, so she wouldn't be going out of her way for a visit. She'd make a quick appearance at the fire scene, get some quotes from the chief, and head over to Louie's place for a quick chat.

It had never entered her mind to call him, but maybe he was just the guy she needed to talk to right now. Even though he was retired, he still had connections in high places. Maybe he knew something or had heard something—or could at least steer her in the right direction. His house was too far out of the way for a random visit, so the timing of the fire was perfect.

Caitlin thought about Louie as she drove, and her mood began to lighten. She had met him by chance on the Metro less than a year earlier. The wiry, elderly gentleman had graciously offered her a seat on the crowded train, and then chatted casually with her during the ride. When the seat beside her opened up, he'd sat down and they had talked more in depth. Somehow or another the discussion had led to what they did for a living. The former operative offered to help her with background information on a surveillance story, and they had been in occasional contact ever since.

The pressure on the gas pedal increased unintentionally as she glanced down at the map to see her estimated time of arrival at the fire. She was anxious to put the story behind her and move on to her visit with Louie. A smile played on her lips at the thought of seeing his twinkling eyes again.

It's funny how things work. Run into someone on the Metro and they become a source—and a friend.

Caitlin spotted the plume of smoke from the fire long before she made it to the scene. It rose in a high column before being swept up by the breeze and dissipating into wisps that looked like clouds against the blue sky. When still about a mile away, a fire policeman flagged her to a stop. "Sorry ma'am, can't go any farther." He nodded toward the smoke. "There's a fire."

"Actually, that's why I'm here." Caitlin pulled out her press pass.

The man examined it and then handed it back. "You're Caitlin Sparks?"

When she nodded, he put his arms on her rolled down window and leaned in. "You still digging into the story about the dead State Department people?"

Caitlin answered his question with a question. "Why?"

"My wife works there is all. She talks about how you've been causing unnecessary alarm ever since that guy committed suicide. Got everybody on edge."

"Really?" Caitlin forced a smile, but her hands gripped the

wheel a little tighter. "Sorry to hear that. Just trying to do my job."

"So is she. It'd be nice for everybody all around if you dropped it and left it alone." He stepped aside and waved her on.

Caitlin put her foot on the gas and pulled away, a little bit unnerved at the reach of the State Department. Were his words meant as a threat to keep her from pursuing the story? Was that another deliberate attempt to frighten and intimidate her?

Or was she letting her imagination run away?

By the time she reached the site of the fire, she'd convinced herself the man on the road was just a concerned husband voicing his opinion. Nothing more.

Pulling in behind a water tanker, Caitlin peered down at her skirt and shoes and saw she had other things to worry about. *Dammit. Why am I always wearing heels when I'm sent to cover a fire?* She glanced at the back seat to see if her sneakers were still there, but knew she had taken them out the day before to go for a walk after work.

Scanning the scene, she recognized the chief talking on a radio while standing on the running board of one of the pumper trucks. She started toward him, walking on her tiptoes so her heels wouldn't sink into the mud—but water ran in rivulets back and forth across the driveway creating an obstacle course that left her shoes mud-covered and wet.

"Hey, Chief." She flashed her credentials. "Can you give me any information?"

"Barn fire. Two alarms. Under control."

Caitlin relaxed a little, thankful she had run into someone who was helpful even though he was busy. Fire officials often regarded the media as a major annoyance and were not nearly so accommodating. She wanted to make this as short and sweet as she could.

"Any injuries?"

"None."

"Any animals inside?"

"No. Lost some hay and two tractors. Total loss, including the structure, estimated at about $250,000."

"Cause?"

"Too early to tell."

"Suspicious?"

"Called in an investigator since nothing is obvious."

"Okay. I'll check back. Thanks for your time." Caitlin shook his hand. "Oh, is the owner on scene?"

The fireman pointed toward a tall, barrel-chested man in overalls trying to comfort a woman who had two young children holding onto her leg. "John Brunner. Right over there."

When Caitlin got closer, she saw the owner had a tear running down his cheek as he watched the smoke roll from the destroyed structure. It was obvious this was a devastating event for him, making her sorry she had taken it so lightly. After introducing herself, she asked if he had insurance.

"Not enough to cover an entire year's hay crop and rebuild. I don't even have the equipment to bring in another cutting now." His gaze shifted to a field where a herd of cows stood huddled under a tree. "Don't know how I'm even going to feed the cattle."

"Do you have any idea how it started?"

He shook his head. "I was in there an hour ago and everything was fine. Can't imagine how it would go up in flames so fast."

Caitlin stood beside the family, trying to imagine how they were feeling as they watched everything they had worked for literally go up in smoke right before their eyes. "Thank you for your time, Mr. Brunner. I'm really sorry about the fire."

The man nodded, but Caitlin wasn't sure he had even heard her. She turned and made her way over the remaining fire hoses back to her Jeep.

After throwing her notebook on the seat, she sat and watched the family. The man now held one of the little girls and his wife held the other child.

Even though the editor had sent her all of the way out here, she knew the story would only receive a small amount of space in the next day's paper. Just a blip people would read as they drank their morning coffee and forget before their next swallow. Murders, robberies, fires, scandals—they were more like entertainment than news these days. Here today, forgotten tomorrow, because there was always a new calamity to read about.

She put her Jeep in drive and pulled away, hoping something good would somehow come out of the tragedy.

At the moment, she didn't see how.

Chapter 7

Like other old estates in the hills of Loudoun County, the
farmhouse sat back a long dirt road—the kind of potholed and storm-damaged road that jarred the spine and
tested your vehicle's shocks. Caitlin loved it. She'd give anything
to live down a road like this and have a meandering driveway
marked by a big stone entrance gate that displayed the name of
the estate in fancy script.

In this part of Virginia, all of the homes had names. Fair
Winds, Oak Hall, Woodlawn, Heartland, were just a few of the
ones she'd passed along her way. She loved reading the names and
trying to imagine what the houses looked like beyond the gates.
Nestled as they were behind stone walls and down long winding
lanes, it was impossible to tell. But she could envision them with
their wide chimneys and welcoming wooden doors. Most of them
had stood for more than a century, many for more than two—and
some had remained in the same family for countless generations.

As for Caitlin, she lived in a small two-story cottage, commonly known as the overseer's house. Once part of a large, prom-
inent estate, the land had long since been broken up and built
upon so it no longer resembled the elegant property of the past.

It was located in the country and was somewhat secluded, but the dirt road it sat beside was well maintained and well-traveled. Every vehicle that drove by created a dust storm that settled on her furniture and floors. The backyard and woods behind it were her only respite, offering cooling shade and sheltered relief from the noise and commotion of the busy thoroughfare.

Caitlin drove faster than she should have on the rutted road, but she was excited about seeing Louie. She also wanted to waste as little time as possible driving since she needed to get back to work and write up the fire story so no one would be the wiser. If Stan found out she stopped here, there would be hell to pay. He would know, or at least assume, she was working on the Hillside murders.

Turning onto the tree-lined lane that led to the secluded farmhouse, Caitlin had to smile. It had been so long since she'd visited, she wasn't sure she'd remember the way, but Louie's driveway stood out from the others. The sign hanging off a fence post wasn't in fancy script—and it didn't display the name of an estate. It simply read: *Private Drive. Keep Out.*

Rounding a sharp corner and then cresting the last hill, Caitlin saw the large, sprawling home come into view. She squinted when she noticed a black Ford F-350 parked beside Louie's Volvo.

Hmm. Louie hadn't said he would have company. As she pulled in beside the vehicle, she remained in her Jeep and tried to decide what to do. Even though the truck was fairly new, it was muddy and replete with small dings—signs of wear and hard use. Probably belonged to a local farmer. Maybe one of his neighbors had stopped by unannounced.

Electing to make the best of it, Caitlin hopped out, walked up the slate steps to the front door and knocked. She heard Louie's voice inside and then his footsteps as he came to the door. When he opened it, he didn't step aside right away to let her in. "Didn't expect you quite so soon."

"I got what I needed in record time." She paused. "You busy?"

"Oh, no. Just that someone else dropped by too."

"I was just leaving." The voice that spoke from inside sounded strangely familiar, but Caitlin didn't have time to place it.

"Come on in." Louie took a deep breath and stepped aside. "Caitlin Sparks, I'd like you to meet Detective Madison."

Caitlin lifted her gaze slowly, not quite believing what she thought she had heard. The detective was exhaling a cloud of smoke as he strode toward the door.

"We've met." The expression he wore was one of detached disinterest, which quickly changed into hostile impatience, as if she had intentionally ruined his meeting with Louie.

Louie must have seen it too. He cleared his throat. "Since you know each other, you're welcome to stay and chat, Detective."

"I'll pass. I don't socialize with reporters." Madison strode through the doorway at the same time as Caitlin was entering. "Nothing personal, of course."

Caitlin had to practically put her head back against the door jamb to look up at him, and found those steel blue eyes no less unnerving now than they were at the crime scene. Whether it was his impressive height or his commanding attitude she wasn't sure, but he struck her as one of the most formidable and intimidating-looking men she'd ever met.

"Yes, you've made that pretty clear." She couldn't let his comment pass without saying something.

Madison was already out the door and halfway across the porch. "Catch you later, Louie," he said over his shoulder.

"Wait." Caitlin followed him to the edge of the veranda. "Are you still looking into the Hillside murders?"

"No." He didn't even stop walking. "Make that a *hell* no."

"Okay."

Perhaps it was her dismissive tone that caused him to pause on the bottom step and turn. "Why?"

Caitlin stared into his daunting blue eyes, and almost lost her nerve. "I-I talked to someone from the State Department yesterday—"

"And?" Madison cocked his head, looking interested but impatient.

"And..." She bit her lip, not sure what or how much to say.

"*And?*" He asked again, shooting her a gaze so penetrating she decided his eyes should be registered as a deadly weapon.

The air of confidence and authority he exuded caused her to hesitate. She'd dealt with some of the most powerful and influential political leaders in the county—and even the country—but had never met someone as irascible and imposing as this. She let out her breath, not sure what to say. Did he really think they could have this conversation on Louie's front porch? "It's complicated."

"I have to go." The detective glanced at his watch. "I have a meeting I can't miss."

"Well in case you lost my number." She pulled a card out of her pocket. "Here."

He took the card with a scowl at her sarcastic comment. "Okay, Scoop." He turned and waved at Louie. "See ya, Louie."

Caitlin watched until his truck started backing up, then turned toward the house where Louie stood in the doorway with arms open wide.

"How have you been?" He gave her a warm embrace and pulled her into the house. "Come in. Come in." He led the way through the spacious home to the living room, and pointed to a chair. "Did I hear you tell the detective you met with someone from the State Department?"

"Yeah." She shook off her jacket, surprised he'd heard that part of the conversation. "Just a friend of Vince's."

"Tell you anything important?"

Caitlin almost laughed at the question. If anyone else had asked it, she would probably have been offended at his nosiness. But Louie was a retired CIA operative who was accustomed to asking questions and probing for information. That made him seem a little hard around the edges to those unfamiliar with his type of intensity, but he didn't mean any harm.

"Not really." She thought about telling him everything that had been said, but didn't see what good it would do. "Just told me it would be better if I didn't dig into that Hillside story anymore."

"Is that all?"

Caitlin studied him as she sat down, trying to figure out if he was really interested or just trying to make conversation. She decided it was the latter. "Yep. That's all."

Louie walked over to a serving table. "Want a drink?"

"I wish, but I have to go back to work."

He poured some Jack Daniels into a glass and sat down again, but he seemed to be deep in thought. "Why didn't you tell the detective that?"

"Tell him what?"

"That your friend from the State Department told you to stop checking into that story. Why did you tell him, *it's complicated?*"

Caitlin shrugged, wondering why she did it too. "I guess I was hoping *he* knows something I don't know. I'd like to talk to him again."

"I don't think he does. That's why he dropped by. To see if I'd heard anything."

"Have you?"

"Not a thing—other than that the case has been solved."

"You can't believe that."

"Why wouldn't I?" He regarded her with an inscrutable expression before turning his attention to the amber liquid in his glass.

"Because none of it makes any sense."

"Oh, it makes perfect sense." He lifted the glass to his lips and downed half its contents. "Murder-suicide. Happens all the time."

Caitlin's heart sank. Louie wasn't going to be of any help after all. "Why do you think Madison is asking you about it if he isn't on the case anymore?"

"He's nosing around, searching for things that aren't there. I told him as much."

It wasn't hard for Caitlin to imagine how Madison had reacted to that response. No wonder he wasn't in the best of moods when she'd arrived—and she couldn't really blame him. A part of her was glad to know the detective was following up on every lead he could to solve this crime rather than accept what was being fed to him. She brought her mind back to the present. "So why'd you call me anyway?"

"Just haven't talked to you for a while, and decided to give you a ring. When you said you were going to be out this way, I thought it'd be a good time to catch up on what you're working on." He took another slow sip of his drink and stared at her. "I guess you pretty much just told me."

Caitlin leaned back and sighed. "I'm officially off the Hillside murders but, yes, I'm still looking into them."

"Well, I'll have to be on the side of your editor and friend at the State Department on this one. You might as well let it go. The FBI knows what they're doing."

"What if 'what they're doing' is covering something up?"

Louie laughed. "Why would you think that?"

Caitlin shrugged. "Just a gut feeling." She paused and glanced at her watch. "Geez. I have to get going too. They'll kill me if they find out I stopped here."

"I wish you had more time." Louie stood and walked toward the door.

"Me too." She turned around and winked at Louie. "And I wish you could give me some advice on the Hillside murders."

"I gave you the best advice I could, Caitlin."

She cocked her head and looked at him.

"Drop it."

She stopped just as she reached the door. "Really?"

He shrugged. "You asked me for my advice."

"Well, that means something... coming from you."

"Good. I hope you take it to heart." He reached out and shook her hand. "Good to see you again, Caitlin. We need to get together again when you have more time."

"Yeah. I don't get over this way very often. If you ever leave the farm, give me a call."

He laughed. "Will do."

"And if you hear anything through the grapevine, let me know. Okay?"

"I certainly will young lady. I'll keep my ears open."

Caitlin was halfway across the porch before she paused again and turned around. "Do you know Detective Madison very well?"

Louie shrugged from the doorway. "Not real well. Ran into each other on a case or two before I retired. Why?"

"I was wondering if his hostility toward me is because I'm a woman or because I'm a reporter."

Louie didn't crack a smile. "From what I know, you don't want to ask him that question."

"Why not?"

"I don't think he'd be able to pick just one."

Chapter 8

Caitlin sat at her desk staring out the window instead of working. It was hard to concentrate on the uninteresting, low-priority story she'd been assigned when she would be meeting with Detective Madison in a few hours to discuss the Hillside murders.

Apparently her comment about talking to someone from the State Department had piqued his interest. She'd found an email waiting for her one day after their unexpected meeting at Louie's. It was only one line—just what she would expect from Madison—saying, *Interested in your discussion with State Department staffer if you're willing to share.*

Caitlin sighed and turned back to read over her story on a local school budget, but she couldn't push the upcoming meeting out of her mind. It surprised her that Madison was willing to put his personal distaste for reporters aside to discuss the case, leading her to believe his gut feeling was the same as hers—strong. She wondered if he'd connected the Hillside murders with the supposed suicide of her beloved Vince. If nothing else, the two incidents shared a common denominator: the State Department. Since mentioning that agency is what led to the meeting, Caitlin had to assume the detective was thinking along the same lines as she was.

But could she trust him? That was the real question. Caitlin didn't know him very well. For all she knew, he could have ulterior motives for wanting to learn what had been discussed during her short visit with the State Department employee. Maybe he wanted to find out what she knew so he could pass it on to someone else. A lot of cops were on the take for political payoffs, and the State Department wielded a lot of power even outside of D.C.

She'd seen some questionable behavior from the police with her own two eyes the night Vince had died. When she'd arrived at the scene the police had not appeared to be trying very hard to solve a crime, instead treating it immediately as a suicide. Ever since that incident, it had been hard for her to trust anyone who wore the shield.

On the other hand, she couldn't pass up the opportunity to share what she had with someone who had access to information she hadn't seen and would never be able to get her hands on. She had to take the chance. Her hopes even began to rise. This meeting might provide *something*, some little nugget of truth that would confirm her own theories and help prove her case.

The thought of proving Vince had been murdered motivated Caitlin to put aside Madison's profession. She needed an ally, and he was the only other person in the world who noticed things weren't adding up. It didn't hurt that he was also the type of man who would not wither beneath the blowback he might receive.

When Caitlin's work phone rang, she glanced at the clock before picking it up. "Sparks."

"Hey, Scoop." There was a long pause. "Something came up. I can't make our meeting."

Caitlin's heart plunged. *Darn it.* She knew it had been too good to be true. He had changed his mind. He wasn't going to talk because she was a reporter. He was going to make excuses not to meet and there would never be any information shared.

"Sorry to hear that." Caitlin couldn't keep the disappointment out of her voice. "It's not something I'd feel comfortable doing over the phone."

"I know. Me neither. But the nanny's sick so I have the kids."

It took a moment for Caitlin to catch up with what he'd said. *Kids?* Mad Dog Madison? She didn't even know he was married. Then again, how many men in their thirties, that good looking weren't married?

"Unless you want to stop by the house." He continued talking despite her silence. "It's kind of out of the way in Loudoun County, but if you want to get this done tonight then that's the way it's got to be."

Caitlin shifted uneasily in her chair. Yes she wanted to get this done. *But at his house?* She preferred a neutral setting.

"You still there?"

"Yeah, I'm here. But I don't want to intrude."

"Great. I'm just outside Leesburg."

Caitlin didn't know if he hadn't heard her obvious hesitation or was ignoring it. Was he just that confident she wouldn't say *no*? Or did he know she was desperate to talk to him?

"Let's make it nine to nine-thirty. That way the kids will be in bed."

Caitlin nodded, but then realized he couldn't see her. "Okay."

"Do you know where the Gray Ghost Bar and Grill is? Off Route 50?"

"Is it that uppity restaurant that sits back off the road?"

"I guess you could call it that."

"Okay."

"Pull in there and call me at this number. I'll have to direct you."

"I have GPS."

"You'll never find it." He gave her the number. "Call me."

Click.

Caitlin held the phone to her ear as she was driving until she found the last little turn-off.

"You're good to go. Bear right at the stone gate. See you in a few minutes."

Madison hung up and Caitlin continued driving, over a one-lane bridge, around steep-banked corners, and under a canopy of trees. She wished she could see the rolling hills and pastures that likely laid on either side, but it was too dark to see anything outside the beam of the headlights.

At last she came to a stone gate marked PRIVATE DRIVE, with the name of the estate engraved on a plaque on the wall: HAWTHORNE, Est. 1805.

"Oh my goodness," Caitlin said under her breath as she stared at the ornate stone wall on each side. *It's beautiful.*

When the house finally came into view, she noticed there were only a few lights burning, but they looked warm and welcoming. Caitlin continued to a circular driveway and stopped in front of the large front porch beside Madison's truck. Her imagination ran away with her as she stared at the immense stone house. Two wide chimneys on each side stood as bookends to a home that looked like it had been lovingly cared for and maintained despite its age. She envisioned Civil War soldiers milling about the grounds as they would have done one hundred and fifty-some years earlier. The fact that this part of Virginia was known to be the stomping grounds of the legendary Confederate cavalry officer Colonel John Mosby and his band of Rangers made it even more intriguing. She had no doubt their boots had graced these very halls.

After grabbing the folder she'd brought and getting out of her Jeep, Caitlin lifted her head and tilted it further and further back, trying to find the top of the oak tree that disappeared into the darkness above. Its trunk was massive and its limbs created a canopy that covered a sizable portion of the lawn. Oh, the stories it could tell. She closed her eyes and inhaled, feeling like she had stepped back in time. How could a place this close to the turmoil of Washington, DC, be so peaceful and charming?

Remembering where she was, she walked toward the porch. She had just started up the steps when the door opened.

"You found it. Come in."

Caitlin accepted the smile and the strong hand that was offered as Madison pulled her through the doorway. The warmth of his touch and the charming quality of the greeting confused and un-nerved her. He still wore a pair of navy work slacks and collared shirt, but his tie was undone and hanging loosely on his chest.

"Sorry to run you all the way out here."

"That's okay." Once inside, Caitlin stood awkwardly, gazing at the huge beams overhead and the staircase to her right. "I love old houses."

"Me too. Still a lot of work to do."

Just like at a crime scene, Madison didn't seem inclined to use more words than were necessary. Trying to figure out what went on behind those impassive, unreadable eyes of his was impossi-ble. But what did she care? He was a cop, and she was a reporter. He didn't like reporters and she didn't trust cops. So that was that.

The detective led her down a hall and then pointed to the din-ing room off to the left. "Make yourself at home. I kind of have my stuff all over the table."

As he directed her into the room, Caitlin's gaze fell upon his left hand. No wedding ring. She hadn't remembered seeing one—not that she had been looking.

Madison disappeared into the next room, but yelled out to her. "Coffee?"

"Sure. Just cream."

"Coming right up."

Caitlin stood in the dining room and surveyed the large, ornately carved table and twelve matching chairs. A fire glowed in a large-mouthed fireplace that boasted a beautiful cherry-colored mantel. Gracing the walls on the other three sides were foxhunting paintings—typical of dining rooms in this part of Virginia.

"Here you go." The detective set the mug down on the table and took a seat. His sleeves were rolled up now and the tie had disappeared completely. The way his dark hair and complexion stood out against the crisp, white shirt he wore made him look a little more amiable and pleasant than the last time they'd met. But when he leaned forward with his arms on the table, Caitlin could see why he had such a reputation as a menacing interrogator. The look in his eyes turned intense and commanding—the kind of look that both drew her in and made her want to run away. Fast.

"I don't usually do this."

"What's that?"

"Talk to *reporters*." He exaggerated the word to make clear it was a profession extremely distasteful to him.

Caitlin refused to be intimidated or swayed. "Thanks for clearing that up."

"You're welcome," he said, matching her sarcasm with some of his own. "And just to be clear, I'm no longer on the case so I don't have anything to give you."

"Excuse me?" Caitlin's tone revealed her confusion and surprise.

"I told you I'm off the case." He appeared surprised that she was surprised.

"Yes, and I'm off the story. But I thought we were *sharing*."

"Minor correction. *You're* sharing."

Caitlin blinked. And blinked again. She thought he must be joking, but the expression on his face did not suggest that intent. "If you're no longer actively working the case, why am I *sharing* with you?"

He lifted his mug and took a drink of coffee as he pondered the question. "I don't like what I'm being told. I want to see if you have anything to substantiate my gut feeling."

Caitlin stood her ground. "In my world, s*haring* implies that we both give a little." She closed the file and pushed out her chair. "Thanks for the coffee."

"Hold on." He sat back in his chair, crossed his arms, and stared at her a moment.

Caitlin hated the way he was able to combine unnerving intensity with disinterested detachment. She wondered if it was a natural habit of his or if he had been trained by the military to remain remote and aloof even in the most distressing situations. His body language revealed nothing, and his facial expression, as usual, was that of a stone. She didn't like being around people she couldn't read.

"So you came all the way out here, and now you want to negotiate?"

Caitlin was stunned, both by his self-assurance and his assertion. "Negotiate? I didn't realize I was going to have to negotiate. I'm pretty sure the word you used in your email was *share*."

"Okay, maybe negotiate is the wrong word. How about co-op-er-ate?" He drew the word out, pronouncing each syllable.

Caitlin couldn't believe what she was hearing. "So you lured me out here on the pretext of sharing, and then have the gall to think you can bully me into providing information with nothing in return?" She stood. "You can call it negotiation or cooperation or even collaboration for all I care, but you want to know what I call it?"

He didn't answer, but she thought she saw a hint of amusement in his eyes, which infuriated her even more. She was too angry to think of a word to call it, so she pushed in her chair and turned to leave.

"Hold on."

His commanding voice stopped her in mid-stride. It took everything within her to turn around, but what she saw when she did surprised her.

Madison was fingering through a stack of folders in front of him, intent it seemed on locating one in particular. "Have you seen the autopsy report?" His voice was casual, as if the last few minutes had never transpired.

"Of course not."

He lifted his eyes for just a second at the tone of her voice, and then went back to searching through the manila folders. Finding the one he wanted, he pushed it over to where she had been sitting, and then picked up his coffee mug. "Take a look."

Caitlin stared at the file and then back at his stone-cold face. "From the Hillside murders?"

He gave a single nod of affirmation, but he didn't look happy about it.

She slid back into the chair and picked up the report. He gave her about five seconds to run her eyes over the first page.

"My turn. I understand you did some intensive reporting on the Oakside Park suicide."

Caitlin jerked her head up from the page and cast him a look of disbelief, but he didn't seem to notice.

"Do you have a file of interviews you've done?"

"I thought this meeting was about the Hilltop deaths." She put her head back down and concentrated on the report in front of her. She didn't want him to see the relief in her eyes that he was linking the two cases. She still wasn't sure she trusted him.

"It is."

"So you think the two are connected."

"Don't you?"

She reached up and squeezed her temples. His constant sparring was giving her a headache. "I guess so. Just a hunch."

"Me too. What about those interviews?"

"I have a *list* of the interviews." She rummaged through the folder she had brought with her and handed him the paper. "I don't have the actual interviews with me."

"I want to see the complete interviews." He must have realized his tone sounded impatient and harsh, because he softened it. "Whenever you can get them to me."

As he scribbled some notes on the side of his paper, his phone began vibrating on the table. Since it was sitting close to Caitlin, she pushed it toward him, and noticed the name "Mallory."

He scanned the screen and frowned. "I have to take this. Sorry."

"Sure." Caitlin bent over the autopsy report again as he exited the room, thankful she would actually have some time to read it. A few minutes later she heard the door behind her swing open and assumed Madison had returned. But when he didn't say anything, she turned and saw it wasn't Madison at all. It was a young girl of about three holding a well-worn blanket. She appeared to be on the verge of tears.

Caitlin's heart melted at the sight of her. "Aw, honey, did you have a bad dream?"

The child nodded.

"Um, your daddy's on the phone." Caitlin wasn't sure what to do. She didn't know where Madison had gone, and didn't want to walk through the sprawling house to find him.

The toddler didn't seem to care she was a complete stranger. She padded over in her bare feet and raised her hands so Caitlin could lift her into her lap. "It's okay now." Caitlin wrapped her arms around the child and rocked her a minute. "See? All better."

The girl nodded and snuggled into her, seeming to fall almost instantly asleep. Caitlin inhaled the smell of her freshly washed hair and studied the cute, innocent face. *Wish I could fall asleep that easily.*

Since Madison still hadn't returned, she went back to the file she was reading, turning the page with one hand and cradling the toddler with the other. She didn't hear Madison at the doorway until he spoke.

"What the— What are you doing?" He strode into the room and gently removed the sleeping girl from her arms.

"Sorry. I think she had a bad dream or something. I didn't know where you went."

With the child fast asleep in his strong arms, he stared at Caitlin with a look of frustration and appreciation before turning. "I'll be right back."

Chapter 9

When Madison returned, he had a steaming cup of coffee in one hand and the pot in the other. "Need it warmed up?"

Caitlin pushed her mug toward him. "Sure."

"Sorry about that." He sat down and picked up a file again. "She sleepwalks. Probably never even woke up."

"That's okay. She's a cutie."

"Yeah." He sounded serious and grave. "Not looking forward to her teen years."

Caitlin laughed. She could tell the little girl had her dad wrapped around her finger. She pitied the young men in her future. "No, I guess not." She took a sip of coffee and glanced up just as the detective placed both hands on the table.

"Let's get back to work. What did you hear from your contact with the State Department?"

Caitlin was stunned at the instant change of tone and demeanor. He was all business again, his blue eyes probing hers with a look of dangerous intensity. She'd wished she'd thought ahead of time what she was going to tell him, because his expression told her he wasn't going to fall for anything but the truth—*all* of it.

She swallowed hard and tried not to squirm. "My source told me…" She cleared her throat and began again. "Well this person *warned* me I should stop working on the Hillside murder story."

"Why?"

Caitlin couldn't meet his gaze so she concentrated on the antique clock sitting on the mantle. "Because that's what they told this person to tell me."

"Who are *they*?" Madison sounded frustrated.

"Superiors at the State Department. I didn't get any names."

He frowned. "You trust this person?"

Caitlin nodded. "Yes. I have no reason not to."

"What else?"

"You understand this is a private source." Caitlin tapped a finger on the table. "I won't reveal the identity even with a court order or threat of jail time."

"You don't have to." Madison sounded offended that she would infer it would come to that. "You haven't given a name, and I don't want it. I just want to know what was said."

Caitlin sat back and sized him up. Could she trust him? Even without using the name, she wasn't sure she felt comfortable divulging everything that had been told to her confidentially. She had spent more than a dozen years cultivating sources and developing a reputation of trust. She wasn't going to throw that away tonight.

She must have taken too long to answer because Madison leaned forward. "I don't know who it is, and I don't care who it is. I just want to know what was said."

"But it was told to me in confidence." Caitlin didn't budge.

"Your source asked you not to tell *anyone*?"

Caitlin thought back to the conversation. Mary had only asked her not to use her name in a story. "No, not exactly."

"Then what's the problem?"

"The problem is, how do I know I can trust you?"

He smiled, apparently thinking she was joking. "Newsflash. I'm one of the good guys. I find bad guys for a living."

"How do I know I can trust you," Caitlin asked again without batting an eye.

This time Madison's expression lost all suggestion of humor. "Are you kidding me?"

"This isn't how I operate." Caitlin put her head in her hands and tried to figure out what to do. "You're asking a lot."

The room grew quiet except for the crackling of the fire and the ticking of the clock that sat on the mantle, but then Madison spoke again. "Your source came to you to help figure out what is going on, right?"

"Yes."

"Then I guess you need to make up your mind the best way to do that." Instead of continuing to debate the issue, Madison tipped his chair back on two legs, crossed his arms, and stared at her with a contemplative look that suggested he respected her hesitation, but didn't agree with it. He appeared frustrated and pensive, but not mad.

Caitlin found this calm composure more persuasive and co-ercing than if he'd lost his temper. "I can tell you this." She laced her fingers together on the table, and took a deep breath. "I was supposed to warn you."

"Warn me?" His chair hit the floor with a thud. "About what?"

"That you should steer clear of the investigation. You were taken off the case by orders of someone at the State Department, not the FBI."

"When were you going to tell me this?"

Caitlin looked away. "Since you were already taken off the case, I didn't think it was an issue."

"Who ordered it?"

"She didn't know—" Caitlin's eyes darted up to meet his at her slipup of revealing the sex of her contact, but when he showed no reaction, she continued. "My source only heard one side of a phone conversation."

Madison exhaled loudly. "What else?"

Caitlin pushed herself away from the table and paced in front of the fireplace as she justified in her mind the necessity—and the obligation—of telling him what she knew. Even with her back turned, she could feel his eyes following her, scrutinizing her, but she would not allow herself to be influenced by his intimidating reputation. This was her decision to make.

After deciding on her course of action, she sat down and began the conversation again as if it had never ended. "The two who were killed weren't having an affair like has been claimed. My source knew them both."

"Go on."

"The whole storyline is a tactic to divert attention from the real reason they were killed."

"Which is?"

"Didn't say. Probably doesn't know. My source just feels like we do—things aren't adding up." She bent her head back over the autopsy report to signal the end of the conversation.

"And?"

She ignored him. *How in the hell does he know there's more?*

"And?" he repeated.

She looked up and then regretted that she had. *Damn those eyes. He could make a scarecrow talk.* Focusing on the clock again, she revealed the brunt of the conversation. "These two particular employees were in Renoviah during the Kessler Affair."

When her comment was met with silence, Caitlin returned her gaze to him. His jaw was clenched and he had a thousand-yard stare on his face.

"My source said they were going to testify about what happened there. They'd contacted Senator Wiley's office to alert him they wanted to appear before his committee."

"What do you know about the Kessler Affair? Did you cover it for the newspaper?"

His question was so abrupt and blunt it took Caitlin by surprise. "No."

"But you know about it."

"Yes. I know Randy Kessler was a Washington reporter who uncovered a federally-sanctioned gunrunning operation to the Muslim Brotherhood. The weapons were supposed to be used to topple the dictatorship and establish a more democratic government in Renoviah."

Madison nodded. "Go on."

"But then Kessler discovered the insurgency groups being funded and trained by the U.S. government were using the weapons against our troops." Caitlin tried to summarize the endless number of articles she'd read on the subject. "Right after he broke that story, he was captured in Renoviah, thrown in prison, and charged as a spy by the new government."

"Not by accident, some say."

Caitlin's attention jerked over to him. "What does *that* mean?" She thought about it. "Are you saying *our* government worked with *their* government—or some insurgency group—to keep a U.S. journalist quiet?"

Madison shrugged. "What do *you* think?"

"I want to say I think that's crazy."

"What's crazy is that three people died in Renoviah, another was found dead in a suspicious suicide, and now two more people have been killed. All of them had connections to the State Department and therefore the Kessler Affair."

She hated to admit it, but it all made sense. "So you're saying they never intended for Kessler to be freed. They'd planned all along that the release would fail and Kessler would be killed—that way he couldn't reveal any more damaging information. One dead journalist made no difference to them."

"They just didn't take into account the other lives lost in attempting a rescue." Madison lifted his coffee mug. "Or they didn't care."

Caitlin closed her eyes as she thought about the three former Navy SEALs who had responded to the scene while working for a private security firm. Two of them had been killed during a thirteen-hour battle trying to save Kessler. "It would have all ended there if not for Vince Chandler deciding to blow the whistle about what he knew." She opened her eyes, wishing she could take back her last conversation with Vince… when she had urged him to testify. Maybe he would still be alive today if not for her.

"And now we have two more dead State Department employees who just happen to have a tie to the whole Kessler Affair." Madison stood abruptly and walked over to the fireplace, where he stirred the logs and got them blazing again. Then he stared absently at the painting of an aristocratic gentleman from a previous century hanging over the mantel. "See anything interesting in the autopsy report?"

Caitlin was a little surprised at how quickly he could change subjects. She looked down at the papers he had given her. "I'm sure you've analyzed more of these things than I have." She paused as she scanned the report. "But is it normal that ballistics can't confirm the weapon found at the scene is the one that killed the victims?"

Madison's expression revealed he hadn't expected her to pick that up so quickly. "Only one round was recovered, from the female's body—"

"I see that." Caitlin read from the report. "…hit below the right temple, flattened and expanded on impact, penetrating the skull and brain." She looked up at him. "But they can't link it to the gun?"

"The slug was flat as a pancake, with half of it dispersed through the brain tissue. The projectile deformity was too vast to isolate any verifying characteristics."

Caitlin shook her head, not understanding. "And what about the male victim? His body had an exit wound according to this." She read the report silently. *Shot entered a half-inch above the right ear, traversed the entire brain and exited the other side, leaving a large exit wound with considerable bone and tissue damage.* She looked at the detective. "So where's the slug?"

Madison's jaw stiffened. "Not found."

Caitlin scrunched her face in bewilderment. "How could that be?"

"Our team was being meticulous in going over the room for evidence. We just didn't get that far before being kicked out by the feds."

"Did they explain why they were taking over the case?"

"Because high-level federal employees were involved."

"I wonder how they knew so fast. I mean, that they were State Department employees."

Madison shook his head. "Not sure about that either."

"Did you talk to the person who found the bodies?"

"Yes. The guy who owns the rental house where they were

killed lives about a mile away and was walking his dog. He heard
two gunshots and thought it might be deer poachers—common
in that area." Madison paused and put his hand on a pack of cigarettes lying on the table, but apparently thought better of it and
picked up a pen instead. "After he got home though it bothered
him, because he knew the house was rented for the weekend and
the shots sounded close. He got into his car and drove down
there. Since there was a vehicle in the driveway and the lights were
on, he pulled over and called the house number just to make sure
everything was okay with the renters."

"But there was no answer."

"Right. So he went up and knocked on the door."

"And there was no answer."

This time Madison just nodded. "He said he thought he heard
a bang, like a door slamming shut, so he went and looked in the
window."

"And saw the bodies?"

He nodded.

"And you believe him?"

"Yes. He was pretty shaken up."

"What does he think the *bang* was?"

"He doesn't know. He told me maybe he imagined it."

"What do *you* think it was?"

Madison shook his head. "I don't know."

Caitlin returned her attention to the papers. "Do you know
how much time passed between when he heard the shots and
when he discovered the bodies?"

"He thought it was about thirty minutes at the most."

"So if one were to believe in conspiracy theories, one might
think that his car coming down the road could have surprised anyone else in the house and caused them to hightail it out of there."

Madison cocked his head. "Do *you* believe in conspiracy theories?"

Caitlin sat back in her chair, her chin tilted up as she gave his question deep consideration. "I believe in facts." She tapped the coroner's report. "According to this, there is no proof the weapon found by the male victim's body was the one used in the commission of the crime, and according to you it would be a bit of a stretch to conclude without reasonable doubt that the male victim was even killed in that room."

Madison raised his eyebrows. "That pretty much sums it up."

Caitlin flipped through the pages, going back to another question she had. "Another thing. What about the lack of blood and tissue on the male victim's hands?"

A slow smile formed on Madison's face. "You sure you haven't read a lot of autopsy reports before?"

Caitlin ignored him and kept talking. "If he shot the female victim at close range, as is alleged, there would be blood spatter on his hand and the gun. Right?"

"Correct. And then he shot himself. Again at close range."

"So that would leave two possible explanations." Caitlin tapped her pen on the table. "Either it wasn't at close range—"

"Or he wasn't the shooter." Madison finished for her.

Caitlin held his gaze a moment and then flipped the page. "Who would believe this was a suicide?"

He exhaled slowly. "Apparently the State Department."

"And the *Washington Post* and *USA Today*. They both called it a cut-and-dried murder-suicide." She shook her head and bent over the file again. "Even though it doesn't make a bit of sense."

It was just another example of how the media operated these days, accepting all press releases as relevant information and re-gurgitating government officials' statements without any questions or fact-checking. There didn't seem to be any curiosity, let alone healthy cynicism, about whether or not someone was telling the truth.

"You know you can't use anything in that report for a story. Right?"

"What do I have for a story? All I've got are more questions." She lifted her eyes. "These inconsistencies and the apathy of the press don't surprise you?"

He sat back in his chair and threw his pen on the table. "They did a week ago. Nothing about this case surprises me now."

"What if you gave the media something to get them interested in the story?" She looked down at the report. "Like this?"

"I can't."

"Why not?"

"The coroner sent that before she knew I was no longer on the case. They've officially sealed it."

"On what grounds?"

"On the grounds they can, apparently."

"So you're kind of going out on a limb by letting me see this." Caitlin studied him questioningly.

Madison's steel-blue eyes zeroed in on hers. "*Way* out. On a very thin limb."

Caitlin held his gaze for a moment, acknowledging the substantial contribution he had made. Then she scrawled on her notepad in large letters: *File FOIA for autopsy report in morning*, and underlined it three times. She hated that she would have to file a Freedom of Information Act request in order to get material that should be public information. They would no doubt take at least thirty days to get back to her, and then say they needed clarification on her request, which would start the whole process over again. It was a never-ending cycle that usually resulted in reporters

moving on to other stories. But she didn't fall for those tactics—
in fact, they made her angry.

"I have a newsflash for you, Detective Madison. The State
Department and FBI are going to get tired of hearing from me."

"I thought you were off the story."

"I am officially. I'll do it on my own time."

Chapter 10

Caitlin glanced at the clock in her Jeep. It was after five so all of the department heads at the police station should be gone. She liked to stop by every now and then to catch up on the gossip and stay in touch with some of the officers on patrol. Plus, it was Olson's last week. She hoped she'd get to see him one last time.

After parking on the street, she headed around the building to the steps that led to the basement, knowing that door was generally unlocked. Cops on patrol and a few other employees parked in the lot and used this entrance rather than going through the main lobby and down to the basement offices. She hated going through the receptionist and having to get buzzed through the other door. This entrance was much quicker and less formal.

Ignoring the sign that said *Employees Only*, she pushed the door open and stepped inside, swinging her purse onto a nearby chair. Some of the men looked up, but no one said anything. That was unusual. The officers on the evening shift were a little looser than those on the day shift, and she had known most of them for years. They usually joked around and gave her a hard time whenever she stopped to see them.

"Geez, it's like a morgue in here." Caitlin stood in the middle of the room. "You guys get orders from upstairs not to talk to me? Is Mad Dog on a rampage or something?"

All heads in the room noticeably lowered, like the men were suddenly very busy. Caitlin thought she even heard a groan. From out of the corner of her eye she saw a figure who had apparently been kneeling behind a desk going through a file drawer begin to rise.

Caitlin felt the heat of embarrassment rising through her body, and knew her face must be as red as the exit sign behind her.

Detective Madison ignored her as he straightened up, his attention centered on the door. "Why is that door not locked?"

Nobody moved or spoke.

"Make sure it gets locked and stays locked." His tone was not one to be ignored. Caitlin heard a number of 'yes, sirs,' as he put the file under his arm and began to walk toward the door on the other side of the room. "I need to talk to you, Scoop."

Caitlin flinched and looked around the room for help, but everyone's eyes were diverted. She hoped Madison didn't know that was *his* nickname as she picked up her purse and hurried to keep up with his long strides. When he stopped and held the door for her, she mumbled a 'thank you,' but could tell by the expression on his face that it had more to do with habit than approval. At least he hadn't slammed it in her face—which she probably deserved.

"Follow me." He climbed the stairs to the main lobby, then strode down the hall and around a corner to his office. He closed the door with a bang and walked behind his desk as Caitlin waited nervously for him to unleash on her.

"I've been thinking some more about your conspiracy theory."

She looked up in surprise. "And?"

"Let's go out there."

"To the house?"

"Yeah. I need to see it again."

"Not that it's important or anything, but is that legal?"

"The chance of anyone catching us there is slim."

"That didn't exactly answer my question."

"Put it this way—I'll do it in a legal manner. I'm trying to solve a murder case and the feds are lying."

Caitlin snorted. "I'm sure that defense will go over well." She glanced around his office as he pulled out an appointment book. There were three filing cabinets on one wall and three bookcases on the other. He sat behind an L-shaped desk with files and papers covering every inch. It wasn't cluttered exactly, just crammed.

"You game or not?"

His earnest tone jerked her from her reverie, but still she hesitated. "I don't know…"

"I have a trial tomorrow, so might not get paperwork done until after five." He wrote something in the book and underlined it, completely ignoring her reluctance to commit. "I'll grab something to eat and pick you up at the newspaper office around six. We'd better only take one vehicle."

When she remained silent, he looked up with inquisitive eyes.

"I have a function tomorrow night. I'd have to figure out an excuse to get out of it."

"Sounds doable." He put his head back down and made another note, as if she had agreed to go and everything was set.

She let her breath out in a loud exasperated sigh, causing him to raise just his eyes. "Come on, Scoop."

"What do you need *me* to go along for? A lookout?"

"No." He put down the pen and sat back in his chair. "A second pair of eyes to pick up anything I miss."

Caitlin's felt her heart thump with a double-beat. Was he saying he *needed* her? Trusted her to observe the scene and pick up small details? She pulled out her phone to double-check her schedule as she considered his request. *What harm could it do to check it out again? And who knows? Maybe, just maybe, we'll find something.* She made her decision and met his gaze. "I have an interview at three-thirty with a locksmith who's retiring after fifty years. I guess I could write that story and hang around until six."

"Perfect. Maybe he can give you some tips."

She didn't have time to figure out if he was joking. He stood and opened the door, letting her know the meeting was over.

In the short time she had known Detective Madison, Caitlin had learned he always made decisions quickly and decisively, giving her no time to argue or even contemplate her options. She liked decisive men, but he brought the word to a whole new level.

Madison was just pulling in when Caitlin walked out the back door of the newspaper building to the parking lot. Giving a quick glance toward the dark sky, she pulled her coat tighter, glad she'd taken the time to change into jeans and her fur-lined boots. She hadn't listened to the weather report, but it would take at least forty-five minutes to get to the scene at this time of day. Who knew what it would be like outside by the time they left?

She climbed into the high cab of the truck and threw her purse on the seat beside her.

Madison turned down the radio. "Ready to do a break-in?"

Caitlin shook her head. "I tried to get some tools of the trade from the locksmith, but he wouldn't give them up."

"That's okay. I've got that department covered."

"So you've done this before?"

Madison shot her a cockeyed grin. "Not at this job. I picked a few locks in my last job." He shifted gears and headed out of the parking lot. "When explosives weren't the way to go."

Caitlin was aware the detective had served in the military, but wasn't sure which branch sanctioned the use of explosives for breaking and entering. She was just about to ask him when he spoke again.

"Anyway, we don't need to break in." He held out his hand and showed her a key. "It's all legal. I sweet talked the real estate agent who handles the rentals."

"You mean you were *nice* to her?"

Madison's eyes narrowed. "What's that supposed to mean?"

Caitlin held up her hands innocently. "Just asking. I mean I've never exactly seen your charming, I-need-something-from-you side."

"Very funny."

"So there's no one in the house?"

"No. The final cleaning crew just cleared out last night. She wants to rent it, but with the recent events she's not sure how much luck she'll have." He jingled the key again. "She was more than happy to give me the key—for one night's rental."

"Then it's all on the up and up."

"That's how I like to do things."

It had started to sleet by the time Madison maneuvered the truck up the bumpy dirt road that Caitlin had only seen in the dark and rain. It wasn't nearly as narrow or potholed as she remembered, so she was surprised when he slowed down and turned into a driveway.

There it was, looming in front of her like a bad dream. They both sat there and stared at it in silence. "It's kind of creepy," Caitlin finally said.

"That's a fact." Madison opened his door. "Let's go."

Once they exited the truck, the detective slowly scanned the area.

"What are you looking for?"

"It would be pretty easy to approach the house unseen," he said, nodding toward the raised first floor. Because the house sat on a hill, the front of the house was on stilts, and the back was level with the ground. The large wrap-around deck made it hard to see anything happening down in the driveway from the front windows.

"If there were any signs of another vehicle, they would be long gone with all of the police tramping around here that night."

"Exactly." Madison started walking toward the house. "That's why we'd better find something inside."

After climbing the stairs to the deck, and seeing nothing out of place, Madison pulled the key out of his pocket. "Here we go." He turned the knob, causing the door to creak and whine like a warning.

As they stepped into the dimly lit interior, the detective turned toward the window Caitlin had looked through the night of the murders. "Kind of strange that all of the blinds are pulled except the one."

"I noticed that." Caitlin hit the light switch. "I mean, there's nothing surrounding this place but trees. Why do you need the blinds down? And if you're renting a house in the country, wouldn't you like to see the view?"

As the lights illuminated the space, they both silently examined the scene. The room was immense, with large plush rugs covering a polished hardwood floor. A poker table and a couple of different sitting areas were clustered throughout, and a wide-mouthed stone fireplace encompassed the entire far wall. The kitchen was off to the right.

Madison walked in and shined a powerful flashlight on the floor and the walls, but didn't' say anything.

"Can I look around?"

He nodded, so Caitlin strode through the main room and entered a hallway. Passing the first door, she pushed the second door she came to open, and found herself in what she surmised was the master bedroom. A sliding door on the far side exited to the wrap-around deck in the back.

"Why'd you come in here?"

Caitlin glanced over her shoulder. She hadn't even heard Madison enter the room just behind her.

"I don't know." She continued staring around the room and felt a chill go up her spine. She could almost feel the terror that must have rippled through the house that night.

"You think something happened in here?"

Caitlin continued to stand quietly and concentrate on her breathing. She could feel her heart racing, could feel it almost like she was in some kind of danger herself. She put her hand on the wall to steady herself. "I feel a lot of energy in here. I'm not a psychic, but something happened in here."

She turned to the detective. "You guys go over it?"

Madison shook his head. "Didn't have time. The bodies were both found out there, so that's where we started. By the time we were starting to move to a new grid, the Feds arrived."

Caitlin turned on her flashlight and concentrated the beam on the latch of the sliding glass door. "Doesn't look like you needed your key."

Madison exhaled loudly beside her and walked to the door. After giving it a tug and watching it slide noiselessly in its track, he bent down and took a closer look. "Appears to have been tampered with at some point. Question is, was it before or after the murders?"

"Or during."

He nodded. "Or during."

Caitlin followed him outside to the deck where they surveyed the rear area of the house. The back continued to slope upward and consisted mainly of trees and shrubs, but there was a level, bare spot about thirty yards away with a small gazebo perched in its center.

"I want to check out that gazebo." Madison walked to a set of stairs that led over a retaining wall, and then turned around. "Watch your step."

The sleet had turned to tiny ice pellets that pinged and bounced on the deck, but it was also starting to accumulate in places. Caitlin tagged along behind, trying to keep up as he strode along the stone-lined path, yet trying to be careful not to stumble on the slippery surface. She saw him lift his foot quickly as he sunk down in a spongy area just before they reached the structure. "The ground is really soft here." They both stopped and stared down at their feet. It was obvious they weren't the first to slosh through this area. There were no discernible footprints after all the rain they'd had, but the grass was gone, like it had seen a good bit of foot traffic.

"Maybe the Feds were up here."

"Maybe." Madison's tone did not convey much confidence that the federal agents had taken the time to walk up the path, causing them both to turn and survey the house again. From the gazebo, there was a clear line of sight into the master bedroom.

"Interesting," Madison said as he reflexively pulled a pack of cigarettes out of his pocket. Before he could get one out, he swore under his breath and put them back.

"Trying to quit?" Caitlin actually felt sorry for him. She had never smoked, but knew it was a hard habit to break.

"Yeah." He started walking back to the house, not waiting to see if she followed.

"So that's why you're always so irritable and snippy." Caitlin said the words under her breath, but he apparently heard them nonetheless.

He stopped abruptly and turned around. "What did you say?"

"I said, it's sure getting slippery." She put her hand out and grabbed a handful of his coat for balance, and to reinforce her statement.

He looked at her with an expression of perplexed irritation, but didn't say anything. When they got to the door, he stopped and let her go through first in his typical gentlemanly fashion.

As Caitlin walked across the threshold, something in the far upper corner of the room caught her attention. Her breath caught in her throat and she froze, causing Madison to run into the back of her.

His gaze followed hers to the corner where the wall met the ceiling. Without saying a word, he pulled a UV flashlight out of his pocket and scanned the walls and ceilings.

"I thought the bodies were found in the front room."

"They were." Madison's voice was low and solemn.

The two continued to gape at the dark spots caught in the beam of the light that could only mean organic matter—like blood spatter. Caitlin's eyes had been drawn to a rust-colored splotch on the wall that had apparently been missed by the cleaning crew. The UV light revealed lots of other droplets that were invisible to the naked eye.

"So someone watched what was going on, then made their way down here when one of the two State Department employees was in this bedroom."

Caitlin stood quietly, frozen by the thought that her instincts had been correct. Someone had lost their life in this room. "Whoever did this wasn't too concerned about cleaning up. They must have known their tracks would be covered."

"Or they were rushed out before the job was completely done."

Or both. Caitlin didn't say it out loud. She just stared at the small stain, wishing it could provide more answers to the questions she had.

"Political power makes people do crazy things." Madison seemed to be reading her mind. "Makes them think they are invincible."

"They kind of are." Caitlin shook her head. "Here we are with another funny coincidence—two more deaths connected to the State Department—and there's not a darn thing we can do about it."

"Except it's not very funny." The detective stood with his hands on his hips surveying the scene, his lips pursed in deep thought. "I know some people at the State Department, but no one who is capable of doing this."

"You do? Have you talked to them? Are you sure they don't know anything?"

"No." He started speaking before she had even finished her questions. "No one I know at State was in Renoviah or would know anything about this."

Caitlin examined the blotch on the wall. "I think I remember reading there wasn't very much blood spatter found near the male victim's body."

"I wrote that in my report. Makes sense now." Madison nodded. "The male victim also had questionable blood tracking patterns on his cheek. Like his head had rested in different positions."

"Someone is going through a lot of trouble to keep something secret."

"And I think we both know what that *something* is."

Caitlin locked eyes with Madison. "The Kessler Affair."

"You got it."

Caitlin pulled a camera out of her purse and began to take photos of the room, the door and the view to the gazebo so they wouldn't have to rely on their memories later.

"If we had the time, I bet we could find that other slug."

"Or at least the hole where the slug had been."

Madison looked down at her. "You're probably right."

They stood silently for another minute and then he looked at his watch. "Can't believe we've been here more than an hour and a half. You ready to go?"

"I'm right behind you."

As they walked back outside, Madison looked up and held out the palm of his hand. "Wow. It's sleeting hard now."

Caitlin listened to the sound of the icy mixture hitting the porch and the trees in a cacophony of sound. Holding onto the railing, she slid her foot on the wooden boards to test the footing. "Yeah. And it's really slippery."

Taking small steps and holding onto whatever was near, they made their way to the truck. After starting the engine and turning the defroster on high, Madison pulled out his phone and read a message.

Caitlin thought she heard him swear under his breath.

"Mind if I run by my house and take the nanny home before I take you back?"

"No problem."

He put the truck in reverse and began to back out. "She takes care of her mother down the road and she's panicking about not being able to get home."

"Understandable. It looks pretty bad out here."

"We can make a pot of coffee while we're there." He shifted gears. "Get warmed up, and then I'll take you back."

"Sounds good." Caitlin stared out the window as they inched their way down the hill, her mind turning over what she had just seen.

"What are you thinking?"

She looked over at Madison and sighed. "That we discovered something new, and yet all it did was produce more questions."

"Well, I think we answered one question—it doesn't look like it was a murder-suicide."

"Now all we have to do is figure out who did it and why—and then prove it."

"You don't sound very optimistic."

She turned her head and studied the icy pellets tapping against the window. "With the people we're working against, I'm afraid I'm not."

Chapter 11

The weather grew worse by the minute as the sleet turned everything it touched, including the windshield, into an ice-glazed mess. Even with the defroster and wipers on high, it was hard for Madison to see where he was going. Branches encased in a shimmering shell of ice hung low over the road, and every few feet one would fall and splinter into dozens of tiny pieces in front of them.

"Damn, my truck's getting beat to hell," Madison said as another limb crashed onto the cab roof above them.

"At least it's not a whole tree." Caitlin leaned forward and squinted through the icy windshield, sure they were going to have to stop any moment for a large limb blocking the road—or have one crash down on top of them. "Yet."

Madison didn't respond. He was busy trying to maneuver the truck up the last hill before his house. Even in four-wheel drive the back end kept slipping, making it hard to apply enough power to carry them up the incline. They both breathed a sigh of relief when they crested the slope.

After pulling up to the porch, Caitlin was surprised when Madison was at her door before she even got it open. "Here, give me your hand."

She didn't want his help, but her feet almost slid out from under her the minute they made contact with the ground. They had to shuffle and use each other for balance in order to make it to the door.

The nanny, a matronly middle-aged woman, was standing right inside wringing her hands. "Sorry to make you take me home Mr. Madison, but I can't drive in this weather."

"It's no problem, Maggie. I wouldn't want you to try."

The woman seemed relieved. "I wasn't sure how soon you'd be here, so I put the kids to bed. I was hoping we wouldn't have to get them up."

They both looked at Caitlin.

"Do you mind staying here?" Madison walked over to a closet and pulled out a pair of gloves. "I shouldn't be long."

"Sure. Be careful."

"There's a pot of coffee on in the kitchen." The nanny pulled on her coat and tied a scarf around her head before heading out the door with Madison right behind her. Once it slammed shut and the truck pulled way, the house fell eerily silent.

Caitlin was almost afraid to move. She felt strange being in someone else's house when they weren't there. But when a chill worked its way up her spine, she made her way to the kitchen, found a mug on the counter, and poured some coffee.

Checking the time, she went back to the dining room, the only room she felt comfortable in. How long would it take him to drive there and back? At what point should she get worried that his truck had been crushed by a tree or had crashed at the bottom of a hill? What if one of the kids woke up? How in the hell did she get into this situation?

Caitlin sat down and tried to add up the minutes in her mind.

It had taken them more than thirty minutes to drive five miles. He said the nanny only lived a few miles away. Two? That would mean four miles there and back. And the roads had gotten worse. *What if he doesn't make it back?*

Standing back up, she walked around the table, gazing at the painting of the man that hung over the fireplace—an ancestor of Madison's maybe? She studied his face and nodded as she noticed definite similarities. Broad shoulders. Strong jawline. Mesmerizing blue eyes. Perfect lips. She turned her head away. *Geez, Caitlin. He's a married man for goodness sake.*

Or at least she thought he was. But where was the wedding band? And where was his wife for that matter? Maybe she just worked long hours and he didn't like wearing a ring—lots of men didn't.

What if his wife shows up unexpectedly and finds me in the dining room? Caitlin took a deep breath and shook her head. Was this really what she wanted to be thinking about?

When she had drained the last of her coffee, she went back into the kitchen to pour another one.

"Hope you saved some for me."

Caitlin jumped so high she almost spilled the entire cup. "Geezuz! Did you have to sneak up on me?"

"Sorry." Madison laughed. "Funny how this old stone house keeps you from hearing anything outside." He walked to the cabinet and pulled out a mug. "I hope you're not in a hurry to go anywhere. It's bad."

"Is it supposed to warm up?"

"Not sure. The forecast wasn't calling for it to be this cold to begin with. I know that much."

Caitlin walked to the window and gazed out at the darkness, starting to worry now. Madison flipped a switch and illuminated an ice-covered tree right outside. "It's beautiful," she couldn't help saying under her breath.

Madison stood beside her. "Yes. If you don't have to drive in it." He pulled out his phone and looked up the weather. "Temperature isn't moving. Sorry." He put his phone back in his pocket. "I'll be right back. I want to bring some wood in while I still can. Probably need to chisel it out piece by piece as it is.

"Need help?"

"No, I got it."

Caitlin could hear activity in another part of the house, but decided to stick to the dining room. The house was massive; she didn't want to get lost somewhere. About twenty minutes later she heard his voice just before he strode back into the dining room with a phone held to his ear. His hair was matted with ice and his cheeks were red. "Thanks for the info, buddy."

Caitlin looked up at him.

"Route 50 is closed."

"Really?"

"Yeah. That was the dispatcher. There are apparently so many fender benders and stuck cars it's impassible." He paused a moment. "So, I hope you don't mind spending the night."

Caitlin felt a squeezing sensation in her throat. It had never occurred to her she wouldn't be able to make it home—that she would end up staying here. "I don't want to put you out."

"It's no problem... You can have my room." He turned toward the hallway. "Follow me."

"No. Absolutely not." The squeezing sensation in Caitlin's throat dropped to her stomach. She wasn't sure if her distress was caused by his gentlemanly act of offering her his room or the uncomfortable thought of sleeping in his bed.

"The only other option is a couch." Madison stopped with his hands on his hips and frowned. "Three spare bedrooms, but not a stick of furniture in them."

When Caitlin eyed him questioningly, he said, "Divorce."

"The couch is fine."

"You sure? I don't mind—"

"I'm positive." Caitlin didn't give him time to continue. "Lead the way."

He studied her a moment, then turned and gestured for her to follow. "It's pretty comfortable." His glanced back over his shoulder. "The couch I mean. Let me give you a quick tour."

Caitlin followed him to the foyer where he turned left and opened another door. "This is part of the original structure."

Caitlin followed him into the room. "Built in 1805, right?"

Madison turned his head, his eyebrows arched in surprise, but then he seemed to remember the date on the sign at the end of the lane. "Yeah. That's why I keep the door closed. There are a lot of drafty rooms we don't use much."

He flipped on the lights, causing Caitlin to come to an abrupt halt after she closed the door behind her. An electric chandelier made to look like flickering candles illuminated the room, casting a soft glow on ceiling-to-floor bookshelves.

A yawning fireplace with a decorative marble mantle graced the far wall, and a rose-colored couch with two matching chairs sat in an inviting arrangement in front of it. She scanned the shelves filled with leather-bound tomes and took in the beauty of the ornately carved legs and backs of the furniture. It was the most beautiful room she had ever seen. It almost brought her to tears.

Madison turned around when he didn't hear her following him. "Can't say I've read too much of what's in here. Always thought I would someday."

"So this is a family home?" Caitlin still didn't move. She stood soaking in the room's magnificence, trying to imagine what it would be like to grow up in a house where you could grab a book on a rainy day and curl up on this couch in front of a blazing fire.

"I'm the sixth generation. Can barely afford the taxes, but I couldn't stand to let it go."

Caitlin remained spellbound as her gaze continued to sweep the room. Some of the furniture appeared to be original, causing her to envision the former generations who had read and talked and gossiped in this cozy space. She didn't realize Madison had started walking again until she glanced over her shoulder and saw he had already opened the door to the next room, and was waiting for her to follow.

"Oh, sorry." Caitlin hurried to catch up and noticed he had a pleased look on his face, as if he appreciated her interest in the historic value of the house.

"This is a newer addition," he said as they entered a huge, modern room with a vaulted ceiling and gaping stone fireplace that contained a few glowing logs. She noticed a definite trace of disapproval in his tone. "Doesn't fit with the decorum of the house, but I lost that argument."

Caitlin nodded. She assumed he meant his ex-wife had been the one to insist on adding the addition.

"It's for *entertaining.*"

Hearing the contempt in his tone confirmed her belief, but Caitlin didn't respond. She surveyed the huge room with a sense of awe. Entertaining indeed. Three couches in the one corner formed a little seating arrangement around a gigantic television hanging on the wall. A bar with four stools sat in another corner and a large pool table loomed off to the side. The toys that were scattered here and there indicated the children probably used the room more than anyone right now.

"This one's the most comfortable." Madison pointed to the middle couch.

Caitlin thought it revealing that a strong, good-looking man like Madison would know which couch was the most comfortable to sleep on—and admit it to her—but she didn't know him well enough to comment on it. He impressed her with his candidness.

"It's perfect. Sorry you have to go to all this trouble."

"No trouble." He sounded sincere. "The bathroom's right here." He flipped on the light. "You want a tee shirt or something to sleep in?"

Caitlin felt her face turning red, but glanced down at the itchy turtleneck sweater she had worn for its warmth on their little outing—certainly not its comfort. She had no desire to sleep in it. "That would be nice."

"Coming right up."

He returned a few minutes later with a blue tee shirt that said NAVY, as well as a pillow, sheets and a blanket.

"How do you work this thing?" Caitlin had picked up the television control that appeared to be something from outer space. "It looks like I might need an engineering degree or something."

Madison laughed and gave her a quick lesson on turning it on and off and changing the channel.

"If you'd rather sit in the library or find a book and read in there, help yourself." He gestured toward the next room. "The light switch is on the right."

Caitlin felt a gush of warmth and delight surge through her—like he had just handed her a magic wand or given her a free ticket to the best show in town. She inclined her head so he wouldn't see the pure delight reflected in her eyes. For some reason she didn't want him to know how much she preferred the feel of a quiet room and a good book over watching television or socializing.

"It might be a little chilly in there though." He interrupted her thoughts. "I didn't build a fire, and it's been closed off."

"That's okay." Caitlin shot him an appreciative glance, but didn't bother to explain that the exuberance of standing in a room where countless generations had stood and read and re-laxed would be enough to keep her warm. Good grief, if he knew how she was feeling right now he would probably think she was off her rocker.

Madison snapped his fingers as if remembering something and walked over to the bar area. "One more thing." After digging around in a drawer, he strode back. "Here's a flashlight in case the electricity goes off."

"Oh, good thinking. Thanks." Caitlin accepted the flashlight, her hand touching his for the slightest moment—long enough for their eyes to meet, and long enough for Caitlin to realize how vulnerable she was. After all, she barely knew the man in whose house she was spending the night. Yet, incredibly, she had never felt more safe and secure in her life.

Trying to act unaffected by his deep blue eyes, she put the flashlight down on a side table and turned on the lamp beside the couch. "Is this place haunted?"

"Not on this side so much." A glint of humor softened his usu-ally granite-like face. "Lots of bumps in the night on the old side."

"Oh." Caitlin was torn between being disappointed and re-lieved.

Madison flipped off the overhead light, and turned back to her. "You hungry or anything?"

Caitlin looked up from preparing her makeshift bed. "No, I

ate right before you picked me up. Thanks though."

"Okay. I'm going to be in the dining room finishing up some paperwork for a little bit yet." He paused and seemed to be lost in thought. "If you think of anything you need, let me know."

"Thanks."

Walking over to the fireplace, he stirred the embers before picking up two large pieces of wood. "This should be fine until morning."

"Thanks." Caitlin pretended to be busy straightening the blanket on the couch, but was captivated with how easily he gripped the logs, one in each large hand, before skillfully placing them onto the bed of coals. "It feels wonderful in here."

After giving the fire one last poke, he headed to the door. "Night, Scoop."

"Good night, Detective Madison."

Madison sat straight up in bed from a dead sleep, his heart pounding, his hair wet with sweat. Gazing wildly around the room he saw only smoke and fire and a scene of destruction at first. But slowly, just like every other night, the images of enemy soldiers and the sound of gunfire and mortars faded as his eyes grew accustomed to the shadows and the surroundings. He was home. Safe.

Lying back down, he breathed slowly and deeply to catch his breath, then opened one eye and turned his head toward the window. A soft glimmer of light was forming a layer of pink on the horizon. Good. It was morning. Almost anyway. It had been the kind of night that seemed much too long, while providing way too little rest. He was glad it was over.

Still groggy, he rolled over onto his side and tried to think what may have caused his mind to be so active. As his brain began to function, he remembered the houseguest he'd left down-stairs on the couch. His subconscious mind had apparently been busy fretting all night about the intrusion into his home life, even though his conscious mind knew he hadn't had much choice in the matter.

Truth be told, there were probably a lot of men who would envy his situation. Caitlin Sparks wasn't hard to look at. Try as he did not to notice, those deep brown eyes sometimes glimmered in such a way that could pull a man in. And her hair, usually held back in a professional-looking braid, had the power to captivate—or at least fascinate—because one had to wonder what it would look like loose and wild.

He rolled onto his back again to change the direction of his wandering thoughts, and stared at the ceiling in the dim morning light. Despite her assets in the looks department, Sparks wasn't the type of woman who tried to use them to her advantage. Intel-ligent and curious, she had no qualms about going head-to-head with those who held power and influence—and wasn't the type to back down from a fight.

She had proven that to him while sitting at his dining room table. She hadn't given in. Had refused to provide information un-less he gave something back. He chuckled to himself. He thought he would have the upper hand that night by inviting her to his home. He'd hoped to throw her off balance by not meeting in neutral territory, but she had turned the tables on him. He found that impressive.

Madison put his hands over his head and stretched. He had never met anyone quite like her, that's for sure. Maybe it was her position as a reporter that made her so fiercely skeptical and cau-tious. Even last night she'd kept her guard up—not acting out-right suspicious of him, but uncertain, leery. He had read in her expression a kind of discretionary distance, like she didn't completely trust him.

Throwing off the covers, he got out of bed and pushed aside the curtains so he could see more clearly. The sight that greeted him was simply breathtaking. Every tree branch, shrub and surface glistened with a sparkling layer of ice in the early glow of the rising sun. Even from inside with the windows closed, he could hear the popping and snapping of branches as they gave way beneath the weight they could no longer sustain. He glanced back at the clock on his nightstand, relieved to see it was still lit. They hadn't lost power, but there would be lots of cleanup—lots of firewood.

Thinking of firewood, he went in search of a pair of jeans and shirt. He'd better get up and throw some wood on the fire, then start a pot of coffee so it would be ready when Caitlin woke up. Tiptoeing past the kids' rooms so he wouldn't wake them, he walked noiselessly down the stairs and opened the door to the entertainment room. He was surprised when he saw the fire was already stoked and blazing with fresh logs.

His attention drifted over to the couch, where Caitlin was sitting Indian-style on the floor with her back against the sofa. His son, Drew, sat beside her in the same position. Both were staring at the television screen, concentrating on a video game. His daughter, Whitney, was on the couch with Caitlin's long hair on her lap, brushing it while babbling to herself. Both of the kids were still in their pajamas.

"Guys, I thought I told you not to wake up houseguests." He ran a hand through his hair suddenly aware of his own disheveled appearance.

"She told us it was okay, Daddy." Whitney paused to pick up a different brush from the array of tools she had laid out in a row beside her, and then continued to concentrate on her task.

As for Caitlin, she never turned around. "You should have told your son it's not polite to beat houseguests at video games."

"I'm killing her, Dad," Drew said gleefully.

Madison shrugged and headed toward the kitchen. "Want some coffee?"

"I made a pot, but I could use a refill."

He stopped at the kitchen door and eyed the pot, glad he didn't have to wait for it to brew. He needed some caffeine badly. After pouring himself a cup, he took the remainder to the living room and splashed some into Caitlin's mug.

"I hope they didn't get you up too early." He sat down on another sofa and took a swallow of coffee, thankful she'd made it strong. "Sorry if they did."

"No." She didn't look at him, but continued to concentrate on the game even though she was losing by a few hundred points.

Her distraction gave him a moment to study her unnoticed, and what he saw made him smile. Her hair was down and loose, but not quite like he envisioned—it was a disaster. He couldn't tell if Whitney was combing it or teasing it as tangled as it appeared. Yet even in this current unrefined state with no makeup and hair a mess, he could hardly tear his gaze away. She was alluring in a natural, unpretentious kind of way. Attractive without trying—and seemingly without knowing.

He shook his head in amusement. There was definitely no charade of social pretense with her. Even the night of the murders, with raindrops dripping off her lashes, she'd been occupied with getting the story—not worried about her looks. Not many women could look as good in a conservative business suit as they did in a pair of faded jeans. Three-inch heels or a pair of boots— she seemed as comfortable in one as the other.

"You're never going to get those knots out," he comment-ed, taking another slug of coffee and turning his attention to the game they were playing.

For a second he didn't think Caitlin had heard him, but then she absently reached up and tried to run her hand through her hair. "Guh. You're probably right."

"I'm *fixing* it," Whitney insisted, as she diligently messed it up some more.

"Yes. I can see that." Madison stood. "Who wants pancakes for breakfast?"

"Me-e-e." Whitney put the brush down. "I'll help, Daddy."

"Great." He turned to Caitlin. "You in a hurry to get out of here?"

"No, I'm okay. It's Saturday." She still didn't take her eyes off the game. "Need help in the kitchen?"

"No, I got it. You keep getting whipped by a six-year-old."

That made her look back at him. "Thanks for rubbing it in."

At that moment the sun shot its rays through the window, causing Drew to shift his attention to the view. "Whoa." He put down the video control. "Look at the ice."

Caitlin stopped too, and stood. "Wow. It's beautiful. Let's go outside."

"Don't go off the porch. There are trees and branches falling all over the place." Madison herded the kids out of the room. "Let's get your coats and boots on."

Caitlin picked up the brush and began to get her hair in order. "Be right there."

Madison glanced back when she spoke, and then did a double take. After bending over and bushing her hair from the nape of her neck toward the floor, she stood up quickly, flinging the long locks back in one big wave. She stood there absently brushing the tangles out to one side, completely unaware he remained in the room. Still dressed in his tee shirt, which hung halfway to her knees, she had a slight smile on her face, as if she were perfectly comfortable and content in her surroundings.

He found that unsettling.

Mostly because it was a feeling he shared.

Chapter 12

The traveling was still slow when Madison took Caitlin back to the newspaper office and dropped her off. He'd waited until almost noon after hearing about the condition of the roads. Even though they were no longer icy, many were partially blocked—and others completely impassable due to downed tree limbs and wires.

When they finally arrived at the newspaper parking lot, Caitlin saw there were only a few cars. For a Saturday morning the crew was sparse, made up of those who lived close enough to walk, and those who had stayed all night because they couldn't get home.

Instead of going straight to her Jeep, Caitlin decided to check in with the newsroom and see what was happening in the aftermath of the surprise storm. She especially wanted to make sure she still had power at her house—there would be no sense heading home if she didn't.

The clock in the newsroom showed it was a little past noon when she sat down. She'd hoped to be back on her way in about an hour, but the phone wouldn't stop ringing so she stuck around to help answer it. In between phone calls, she checked emails and put together the file of interviews Madison had requested about Vince's supposed suicide.

By the time she called it quits, the afternoon shift was starting to arrive. Long shadows crisscrossed the road as she headed back to Madison's house to drop off the memory stick. Even though the ice that had held her captive here had vanished, reminders of the storm were evident everywhere. Shattered and scattered branches on the road and the edges of the fields beyond made the landscape look like a hurricane had blown through. Caitlin regretted having taken no pictures in the morning when the world had glittered and shimmered. It had seemed almost magical, and was now just a memory.

After maneuvering around a rather large limb, Caitlin rounded the last turn before the house. Her heart dropped when she saw a second vehicle sitting beside Madison's truck. She didn't want to interrupt if he had company, but he *had* called her at work and reminded her to drop off the interviews. Actually it had been more like a "strong request" than a "reminder." It had slipped her mind that he wanted the files, and now it had apparently turned into an urgent matter. He wanted to spend time looking at them over the weekend.

Pulling in behind a gold-colored Mercedes, Caitlin put her Jeep in park and tried to decide what to do. The shiny Mercedes looked out of place sitting in stark contrast to Madison's banged up truck. As Caitlin contemplated her options, she couldn't help but notice the distinct difference between the flashy vehicle and the house as well. Even though the home was elegant and massive, it was not ostentatious or pretentious in the least.

Oh well. I drove all the way out here. I may as well drop it off.

Walking up the steps of the porch, Caitlin lifted the big brass knocker, let it fall twice, and then waited. It sounded awfully quiet inside until at last the hurried tap of high heels hitting the wooden floor reached her ears. The door opened to reveal a woman in a short black skirt and black pumps, wearing an expensive-looking blue silk shirt. Her head tilted to the side as she stuck a diamond-studded earring through her lobe and secured it.

"Can I help you?" The woman's tone was that of forced friendliness, and the fake smile planted on bright red lips made it clear she was not familiar with the need for being pleasant.

Caitlin tried to ignore the sudden buzzing in her ears and concentrate instead on the woman's face, but that only served to make her more breathless—because it was one she recognized. She felt her face blossoming with heat. "Um, no... I mean, yes." She made a tight fist around the memory stick she was planning to give Madison and concealed her hand in her coat pocket. "Is Detective Madison in?"

The woman eyed her curiously, and none to warmly. "He's in the shower. Can I help you? If you're dropping something off, I can take it." She held out her hand.

"Um, no. I just stopped by." Caitlin started backing up. "To say hi."

"Are you sure? You ran out all this way for *that*?"

Caitlin took another step back, wondering if the woman had known she was coming. "I'm sure."

"Have it your way." The door slammed shut, but the suffocating and sickening smell of perfume lingered. Caitlin stood there with her eyes closed even after she heard the door latch click inside. She couldn't move. Could barely breathe. It seemed like she was in the middle of a bad dream.

Finally pulling herself together, Caitlin walked to her Jeep and climbed inside. She made her way back out the lane, past the fallen limbs to the main road, and then pulled into the first empty parking lot she found and turned off the engine. Clutching the steering wheel with both hands, she sat sucking in deep breaths of air, creating puffs of steam in the cold air as she tried to wrap her mind around what she had just seen.

At last, with shaking hands, she pulled out her cell phone and inhaled deeply before opening her photo file. Paging through the pictures until she found the right one, she double-tapped and studied the mystery woman in the photo. It wasn't like she needed to have it in front of her. She'd long ago committed every feature to memory, having gazed at this picture at least a thousand times.

She let her phone drop into her lap.

She wanted to cry. She wanted to die. The one person she thought she could trust was probably sleeping with the one person she knew was connected to Vince's death. *Probably* sleeping with him? Seriously, could it have been any more obvious? Her standing there, putting on an earring. Him in the shower?

Caitlin's phone began ringing. *Madison.*

She threw it into her purse and ignored it, but a few minutes later she heard it ding with a text message. Still sitting in her freezing-cold car, she pulled out the phone and read the message: *Sorry I missed you. Call me.*

"Yeah, right." Caitlin started her Jeep and headed home.

Monday morning Caitlin leaned closer to her computer screen, concentrating on cutting a few inches off a story, when she noticed movement out of the corner of her eye. She glanced up, and then did a double take.

With one arm resting on a bookcase, Detective Madison stood watching her work, relaxed and casual as if he owned the place. She had no idea how long he had been there, but instinctively leaned sideways to look around him, checking for the receptionist. Helen excelled at bossing people around, and was both feared and respected for keeping intruders out of the newsroom unannounced—especially during deadline.

"How'd you get in here?"

Madison moved his tweed blazer out of the way to reveal his weapon, then flashed his badge and a half a smile before turning grim-faced again. His massive, self-confident presence was infuriating.

Caitlin gave him a disbelieving look. "You pretended it was official business?"

"It *is* official business. You didn't return my call. I gave you the courtesy of two days."

Caitlin bent back over her computer. "I can't talk right now. I'm on deadline."

"I know. That's how I knew you'd be here." Madison sat down in a chair beside her desk and crossed his arms. "I'll wait."

Caitlin's head jerked back up. "No you won't. I have to finish this story in twenty minutes and I can't write with someone staring at me."

Madison turned his head. "I'll stare this way then."

Caitlin stood. "I'm serious. Do I need to call security?"

He looked over his shoulder and kind of grinned. "That would be interesting." Then he stood and rested his hands on the desk, his head level with hers. "Okay, Scoop. Tell you what. I'm going to walk across the street and grab a cup of coffee. If you're not here when I get back, I'll put out a warrant for your arrest."

Caitlin sucked in her breath. "You can't do that."

He just stared at her with a penetrating gaze, authoritative and in control, seeming to say *try me*, without the use of words.

Caitlin lifted her chin before sitting back down. "I'll be here." Trying to appear calm, she spoke as she stared at her computer screen. "I can't leave until the paper comes off the press anyway."

Thirty minutes later, Caitlin walked back into the newsroom after making sure everything had gone through pre-press smoothly. She found a steaming cup of coffee beside her keyboard and Detective Madison sitting by her desk again, looking at his watch.

"Is this some kind of bribe?" She took the cup and sat down.

"You should know the answer to that. You've used the technique before, I believe."

Caitlin felt her cheeks start to blush. She had walked right into that one.

Madison didn't seem to notice. "I shouldn't need a bribe. I thought we were working together."

Me too.

"Weren't you going to drop off a memory stick with your interview files on it last week?"

Caitlin hadn't expected to see him again and didn't know what to say. She forced a smile. "I did stop out, but you weren't around."

"But you didn't return my text."

She turned in her chair so she wasn't facing him directly and pretended to be interested in something on her computer screen. "Oh, well… I figured you were busy. I mean, it did *seem* like you were busy. I didn't want to interrupt anything."

"Does this have something to do with my ex-wife being at the house?"

Caitlin spilled coffee down the front of her shirt, revealing the shock of her surprise as she turned to face him. "Your ex-wife?" Her mind began buzzing a million miles a minute. If he was married to her when Vince had been killed, then surely he knew more than what he was letting on. She was glad she had been cautious and not revealed all of the information she had. She suddenly could not meet his gaze. She did not trust him.

He continued the conversation, not seeming to notice her uneasiness. "She showed up earlier than expected to pick up the kids. We have shared custody."

Caitlin nodded while gazing at the clock over his shoulder again. She was thinking, *dressed like that?* But all she said was, "Um hmm."

"Get your coat."

Caitlin's eyes darted back to his. "What for?"

"It's chilly outside."

"You're probably right." Caitlin turned to the window. "But I'm inside."

"Not for long. We're going for a ride."

"That's a really nice *invitation.*" Caitlin did not even attempt to keep the sarcasm from her tone. "But I have work to do."

He stopped and regarded her with a look of disbelief. "This is important." His tone insinuated nothing she had to work on was as significant as talking to him, yet his expression had softened, making it more persuasive.

Caitlin stared at the pile of files on her desk.

"Please."

The word wasn't said in a questioning or pleading manner, but rather implied a demand, indicating that things would go easier for her if she went voluntarily. Raising her eyes to meet his, she saw a don't-mess-with-me look on his face that matched his tone.

For a brief moment Caitlin envisioned him forcefully removing her, kicking and screaming, from the newsroom—yet still she resisted. He had fooled her into thinking he was on her side. Fooled her completely. What other tricks did he have hiding up his sleeve?

"I would." She tried to sound as pleasant and agreeable as possible. "But I know your time is precious. And I don't want you to *waste* it."

She turned back to her work, hoping to end the conversation, but he was suddenly right beside her, leaning down to within inches of her face. "Thanks for the concern." He grabbed the coat hanging on the back of her chair, and placed it on her lap. "But I'll be the judge of that."

Caitlin didn't move. Yet even with her eyes locked blankly on the computer screen, she could feel the intensity of his impatience beside her—almost like a physical heat.

Her mind raced as she weighed the pros and cons of capitulating to his demand. If she didn't go, he might continue to show up in the newsroom every morning on deadline to harass her. If she did go, he would have the opportunity to have his say—and she would have hers.

With her mind made up, she bent down and unlocked the bottom drawer of her desk. Reaching into the back, she pulled out a well-worn brown envelope, which she stuck in her purse. "I have to be back by noon."

Madison didn't answer. He was already heading out the door.

Chapter 13

Caitlin struggled to keep up with the detective's long strides as he headed for his truck. Once they reached it, she was a little embarrassed when he stopped and opened the passenger side door for her. Tossing her large purse onto the seat, she put her foot up on the high running board and climbed in. She stared out the window as the diesel engine churned to life, wondering if she had made a bad decision by agreeing to this. "Where are we going?"

He didn't answer for a minute as he backed out of the parking space. "You'll see."

Caitlin's nerves were so tightly strung at his sullen tone that she winced when the door locks snapped into position. The fact that he didn't turn the radio down or initiate a conversation didn't help relieve her concerns, so she kept her mind occupied by trying to convince herself he meant her no harm. She'd spent the night with him for heaven's sake, and he'd been a perfect gentleman.

But as the truck sped out of town and then turned right onto a secondary road, her heart began to hammer, and warning spasms of alarm erupted within her. She turned her head toward Madison, trying to form words, but the seatbelt restricted her from taking the deep breath she needed to clear the whirring in her ears. "Why here?" she asked, recognizing in an instant where he was taking her.

"So we can talk. It's quiet."

Caitlin swallowed hard, mostly as a way to keep things moving in that direction. They were heading toward the park—a place she hadn't been since the day Vince had been found dead in his car. She curled her hands into fists to keep them from trembling and shifted her position in the seat. Air seemed suddenly hard to find, so she concentrated on breathing slowly and deeply with her eyes closed.

Relief surged through her when the detective ignored the first parking lot where the supposed suicide had taken place, and instead pulled into the next one a hundred yards away.

Caitlin chewed on her cheek and concentrated on remaining calm as the truck came to a stop. Could she trust him? Did she *want* to trust him? He seemed so sincere, yet secretive. Impossible to read. Was he on her side? Or was he a part of the web of deceit she had been dealing with for the past eight months?

She took a quick glance at him as he turned off the truck, trying to read his expression. It was a waste of time. His eyes never revealed anything he didn't want them to.

Studying her surroundings, Caitlin was surprised to find the parking lot completely empty. The air was chilly, but the sun was shining brightly, making it a beautiful day for a walk. Maybe everyone out enjoying the weather had parked at the other lot. Her mind kicked into high gear. Maybe Madison hadn't driven past it to protect her raw emotions, but because it had been crowded with potential witnesses. Maybe he *wanted* a place that was desolate and remote.

Before she had time to question him, Madison got out of the

truck and headed toward a picnic table, apparently too preoccupied with his own thoughts to remember the courtesy of opening her door.

He rested against the table with his arms and legs crossed as Caitlin approached. "So what's the problem?" His badge, which was clipped to his belt, reminded her he was a cop, sworn to serve and protect. But that didn't make her feel any better.

"Why do you think there is a problem?" Without realizing it, her gaze shifted to his broad shoulders and powerful physique, and then to the holstered gun that stuck out from beneath his jacket. She was beginning to think coming to this isolated park *was* a mistake. How hard would it be for a homicide detective to kill her and cover it up? She put both hands on her purse and pulled it closer. She felt awkward taking it out of the truck with her, but the handgun inside provided some measure of comfort in this remote setting.

Madison nodded toward her purse. "I hope you're not thinking about using that."

"What do you mean?" Caitlin cocked her head and frowned. "You're afraid I'm going to hit you with my purse?"

"No. The Glock. Not the purse."

"Are you *serious*?" Caitlin took a step back in surprise and stared at him accusingly. "You ran a background check on me?"

He stuck his hands in his pockets in a nonchalant manner and shrugged. "I noticed you had a concealed carry permit."

"You *noticed*?" Her voice hit a tone that was shrill even to her, but she was too angry to care. "Like when you were running a check on me?"

"You don't think I would allow someone into my home without running a background check on them, do you?" He seemed almost amused at her reaction.

Caitlin didn't reply, but neither did she remove her angry eyes from him.

"Don't worry, I didn't find anything out of the ordinary. You're thirty-five. Served in the Army as a public affairs specialist. You were honorably discharged and got a job as a reporter for *The Independent Post*, where you've been causing problems for federal, state, and local politicians for the past twelve years."

Caitlin continued glaring at him, wishing her eyes carried the power that his did so he could see—or maybe feel—the ammunition of her stare.

"Don't tell me you didn't search for everything you could find on me."

"That's different."

"No, it isn't. I just have a few more resources than you do."

Caitlin sat down on the bench, hard, feeling like she'd just had the wind knocked out of her. "Just because I looked doesn't mean I found anything." She paused a moment. "Which, by the way, I find odd."

He studied her closely. "Maybe there's nothing to find. Did you ever think of that?"

"No. Actually, being a reporter makes me think just the opposite."

"You're too cynical. You need to relax."

Caitlin turned her head away and stared out over the trees. She did in fact find it very peculiar that there was not much to uncover about Madison's background—other than that he had served in the Navy. His record in the police department was fairly extensive and complimentary, but his early life and military career were a complete mystery. *Why would that be?*

"What's your problem, Scoop?"

His voice shook Caitlin from her thoughts. "Why don't *you* tell *me?* I didn't know I had one." She knew she sounded childish, but she didn't know what else to say. This man had a way of pushing her buttons and making her lose her self-control.

He straightened and put his hands on his hips. "If you don't have one, why didn't you return my call? What happened between the last time we talked and now?"

Caitlin clutched her purse even closer, thinking about the folder she had placed inside, and the woman it pertained to. She wanted to trust him, but the nagging in the back of her mind refused to be stilled.

"It has something to do with Mallory, doesn't it?"

Her eyes darted back to his. He seemed to be reading her mind. That scared her.

"Like I told you, she came by early to get the kids. I'm sorry I missed you. I just ran down to the barn."

Caitlin looked up at him, her mind whirring. *I don't remember seeing a barn.* "That's funny. She told me you were in the shower."

"She did?" Madison appeared genuinely confused. "I wonder why she would say that?"

Yeah, me too. Caitlin had a sudden surge of fear. One of them was lying—Madison or his ex. She didn't have any desire to find out which one. "Um, I have to get back to work." She stood, and even though she had the urge to run to the truck, she forced herself to walk slowly.

"Hold on." His voice was low and authoritative.

Caitlin stopped walking, but didn't turn around. If he was going to shoot her, he would have to do it in the back. She held her breath and closed her eyes, waiting for the shot, but without warning he appeared in front of her.

"What in the hell is wrong with you?"

She jerked her head back and looked up into eyes that were

deeper and more intense than she had ever seen them.

"What's wrong with you?" he repeated as if she hadn't heard the first time.

"I need to get back to work." She looked away. She had to.

He took her arm and guided her back to the table. "Tell me what's going on first."

Caitlin sat down on the bench with her back to the table, breathing hard, as if she'd just run a race.

"Start at the beginning."

For some reason, his calm, composed, commanding voice turned her fear into anger.

She stood and stabbed her finger into his chest, causing him to take a step back in surprise at her intensity. "Explain to me why I should tell *you* anything."

His brow was creased in bewilderment. "I thought we were working together."

She rolled her eyes. "So did I."

"For the love of Pete, will you tell me what is going on?"

Caitlin sat back down. "Ask your wife."

"Ex-wife, you mean? Is that what this is about?"

"Pretty much."

"What does *she* have to do with anything?"

Caitlin turned her head toward him and scrutinized his face. He appeared genuinely confused, but maybe he was just a good actor.

"Tell me." He walked over to her and squatted down so she could look him directly in the eyes. He seemed to want her to read the sincerity there. "Please."

"It's a long story."

"I have time."

She continued to weigh the consequences. What if he already

knew everything and just wanted to see what she knew? That's how the political hacks in Washington operated.

"*Damn.*" He stood and rubbed his forehead as he walked a few steps away. "What is wrong with you?"

"I'm just trying to be careful."

He turned around. "You don't trust me?"

"Not really."

"But I'm a cop."

"Maybe that's why I don't trust you."

"What in the hell is that supposed to mean?"

Caitlin stood and started pacing, trying to decide how much to say. "Vince Chandler called me the morning he died," she blurted out.

"What? I never saw that in any reports." He took a step toward her looking stunned, his brow creased with incredulity. "Did you tell the police that?" Caitlin shook her head. "No."

"Why not?"

"Because he told me not to trust the police."

Madison sat down on the top of the picnic table and squeezed the bridge of his nose, as if that would help him think more clearly. "But I'm sure they would have checked his phone. There would have been a record."

Caitlin shook her head. "He used a pre-paid phone when he called me. He probably ditched it later that morning."

"Why you?" Madison studied her with a thoughtful, questioning look. "Why did he call you? Because you're a reporter?"

Despite every effort to stay strong, Caitlin felt tears welling. She didn't speak. She didn't want her voice to crack. Anyway, she didn't know what to say. She stared out over his shoulder and bit her lip, concentrating on not letting her emotions show, but her resolve weakened as the memories washed over her, making her want to drop to her knees and sob. She had never mourned Vince's death the way she should have—and she didn't want to. She had no desire to move on and let him go until his killers were found.

When a loud sigh escaped from Madison, she knew he had put two and two together.

"You were a couple?"

She lifted her glistening eyes to meet his and cleared her throat, but when no words would come, she lowered her head and nodded.

"That explains a lot." The frustration in his voice was evident as he rubbed the back of his neck. "Except maybe why you didn't tell me your relationship to the victim before *now*."

"I didn't think it was any of your business." Caitlin hurriedly brushed a tear from her cheek as he pulled a cigarette out of his coat pocket.

"Really? None of my business to know that the person I'm working with is set on vengeance instead of the truth?"

Caitlin hit the table with her hand. "The only thing I'm set on is justice." Her voice cracked, so she made a noticeable attempt to lower it. "And the facts."

"Okay. Calm down." He held a lighter up to the cigarette and talked out of the side of his mouth. "What did he say?"

Her chin trembled as she remembered the conversation. "He said he'd contacted Senator Wiley about testifying, and that he needed to tell me something important in case anything happened." She paused and tried to ignore the surge of emotions washing over her. "And that in the meantime I shouldn't trust anyone. Especially anybody in the State Department. Or the police."

She glanced at him to read his reaction. He appeared to be

deep in thought, as if running across the events of that day in his head and trying to piece things together.

"That still doesn't explain why you suddenly won't talk to me."

Caitlin let out her breath in exasperation. "Okay. Maybe this will."

She put her purse on the picnic table and reached in to pull out the envelope, but with a move she didn't even see coming, Madison grabbed her wrist with compelling force and said, "Whoa. What are you doing?"

Caitlin realized he thought she was going for her pistol. "Calm down, Detective," she said, using the same words he had used on her. "Just want to show you something."

He slowly released his grip, and nodded. "Okay."

She pulled out the brown envelope, and removed a file from it. "I was right down the road when I heard the call come over the scanner about a shooting at the park." She tried to keep her hand from shaking as she placed the file on the table.

"But you didn't know it was Vince." Madison's voice sounded gentle and kind.

Caitlin shook her head as the day came back to her in vivid clarity. "No."

When he remained silent, waiting for her to continue, she took a deep breath. "Even though the chatter on the scanner quickly changed to calling it a suicide, I could tell from the number of vehicles responding that something wasn't right."

Caitlin ignored the way Madison was studying her, as if he were trying to figure out what made her tick. "I knew it would be close to impossible to get through the roadblock, so I turned around and parked on the other side." She nodded toward the small creek that ran through the park.

Madison turned around and looked. "There's a footbridge?"

"Right off that upper lot. There was an officer posted there, but I knew him so he let me through." She thought of Olson and the chance he had taken by letting her across that night. "I crossed over and took some pictures before I was spotted and they kicked me out."

For the first time, Madison's gaze went down to the folder. His hand moved slowly to open it as if sensing it contained something he wouldn't want to see.

"It appeared to me they were more intent on wiping the scene clean than investigating." Caitlin waited until his attention had settled on the first photo. "That woman was orchestrating the whole thing."

Madison's jaw tensed when he saw the photo of a woman—his ex-wife—talking on the phone while appearing to point and direct police officers around a parked car. He moved to the next photo and the next.

"You never showed these to the police?" His voice was raw. His expression was like someone who had been struck in the face.

"To the people who were covering up my boyfriend's murder by calling it suicide?" Caitlin's voice cracked, but then she gained control and shook her head. "No. I wanted to find out who that woman was on my own first."

Madison closed the file. "What does it mean?"

"I would think you're in a better position to answer that than I am." Caitlin took the pictures from his hand and put them back in the folder. "I just found out who she was two days ago."

"And so now you think I'm involved." His angular jaw was set in a determined way and his blue eyes portrayed deep concentration.

"It's a little suspicious, don't you think?"

When he didn't answer, Caitlin noticed the cigarette, still

smoking, in his hand. "I thought you were quitting."

Again, he didn't answer. She wasn't sure he had even heard. He turned around, put the cigarette in his mouth, and started pacing as a smoky haze rose and circled around his head. Caitlin waited for him to say something, waited for the inevitable moment when he would defend his ex-wife's character or deny that she could possibly be involved. But his words, when he did finally speak, took her completely by surprise.

"She has partial custody of my kids." She thought she heard a slight tremor in his voice. "I can't do anything else until I make sure they're safe."

He crushed out the cigarette and headed back to his truck with long, purposeful strides, as if there wasn't anything more to discuss.

Chapter 14

Caitlin sat back in her chair and picked up her steaming mug of coffee. Deadline was over, but she had finally gotten a Congressional aide to provide a copy of some testimony on the Kessler Affair. She glanced at the time. She had a fifteen-minute break coming—she would read while she wasn't on the clock.

Opening the file, she flipped through the pages until she found what she was seeking—a timeline of what had transpired during the rescue attempt. Some of the testimony was redacted on the operation, but there was enough there to give her some idea of what had occurred.

On the night of August 11, hostage Randy Kessler, a journalist, was taken to a location close to the American embassy in Renoviah for a supposed exchange. The ambassador rode in an armored car along with two native bodyguards, and was followed by two more vehicles of armed security personnel hired from the local population and five employees of the State Department, who were on their way back to the compound near the exchange site.

Immediately upon arriving at the designated location, gunfire broke out and the vehicles fled to the American compound, about two blocks away. A crowd of rioters followed, setting off rockets and general gunfire, but it was thought that all had made it safely into the compound.

The head of security called the embassy, which forwarded a request for immediate help to the State Department as the event continued to escalate. The request was not acted upon.

In the meantime, special operations units were alerted about Americans under attack, but were never given orders to respond. A group of three former Navy SEALS working for a private security firm in a neighboring city, heard about the situation and deployed to the scene without orders. Under severe and heavy fire, they were able to get the ambassador and the state department workers into an armored vehicle with a security detail to escort them to the airport.

The three then began to search for Kessler, who was unaccounted for, and continued to defend the compound with whatever firepower they could find to keep attention off the fleeing vehicles. Throughout the night they phoned in coordinates and updates, and asked for aerial support or additional firepower. These requests were never acted upon.

Caitlin looked up and then back down at the paper, reading the line again. She wondered why they kept saying the requests were "never acted upon." It sounded to her like they were "outright denied." She closed her eyes, thinking about what she had read. *How could our own government just leave these guys out there to die?*

The gun battle continued for thirteen long hours, until a mortar landed on top of the building where the SEALs were positioned. Caitlin scanned down to the testimony of Captain Ralph Minter, U.S. Army, upon his arrival at the site eighteen hours later.

Captain Minter: There was debris everywhere, things burning, dead bod-

ies on the street. It looked like a bomb had gone off.

Congressman Gunter: Did you find any survivors?

Captain Minter: After making our way to the compound, we found only one.

Congressman Gunter: And who was that?

Captain Minter: Retired Navy SEAL [name redacted]

Congressman Gunter: Where did you find him?

Captain Minter: He was in a room, a large closet really, in the basement of the building. He was severely injured but had managed to drag two others in there as well.

Congressman Gunter: But they were deceased.

Captain Minter: Yes, sir. By the time we got there.

Congressman Gunter: And what kind of wounds did the surviving operator have?

Captain Minter: I believed at the time they were mortal. I don't know how he got the other two down there, but—

The phone rang, interrupting Caitlin's heavy thoughts. She picked it up reluctantly. "Sparks."

"Caitlin Sparks?"

"Yes." She rolled her eyes when she recognized the voice and closed the file, as if she were afraid he would see what she was reading.

"This is Josh Kernst from the State Department."

"What can I do for you today, Josh?" She pretended she didn't know, but the current administration was so predictable it wasn't hard to guess. Josh had worked at the State Department as low level support staff under Vince, so she was well aware of his character and reputation. Unfortunately his job was no longer low level and neither was the sparking point of his out-of-control temper.

"I think you know what I want to talk about." His voice quivered with anger.

"You're right. I do. So do you mind if I record this?" She smiled and sat back, waiting for the fireworks.

"No, you can't record this!" Caitlin pulled the phone away to save her ear from his usual screaming tirade.

"Hey, Josh. Calm down." She tried to sound as casual as possible, because she knew that would get under his skin even more than arguing. "I don't actually need your permission to record this conversation. I just asked to be nice."

"You don't know what you're talking about—"

"Actually I do know what I'm talking about." She didn't give him time to respond. "As I'm sure you know, both Virginia and D.C. are one-party consent jurisdictions. That means a party, meaning *me*, has a right to record their own conversations or phone calls without the knowledge or consent of the other party, meaning *you*.

"Don't you dare—"

Again she cut him off. "You can look it up if you want." She leaned forward and squinted at the piece of paper she had taped to the wall for just such an occasion. "It's nineteen point two through sixty-two of the Virginia Wiretapping Statute. Basically since I've given my consent to have this conversation recorded, I don't need yours." She paused when she heard nothing but heavy breathing. "I'd be glad to read the whole thing to you if you're not familiar."

Caitlin laid the phone down a minute because the sound on the other end of the line had reached a decibel probably not good for her ear. When he stopped yelling she picked it up again. "I'm sorry. Could you repeat that in your quiet, grown-up voice?"

"No, I'm not going to repeat that. And you'd better not be recording this." His voice shook again even though he was obviously trying to pretend calmness. "You know damn well what I'm calling about."

"Yes, I think I have a pretty good idea." Caitlin turned her chair toward the window as she talked, a habit of hers when in the midst of an unpleasant conversation. "But seriously, don't you think the public would be interested in knowing what you say to reporters who are doing everything they can to uncover the truth?"

"The truth?" His voice cracked. "The truth is there are more than two dozen FOIA requests sitting over here from you, and another dozen at the FBI. Do you think we come to work every day just to serve you?"

"I think you get *paid* by me, and every other taxpayer. If you would stop covering up scandals, you wouldn't have so many FOIA requests." Caitlin took a drink of coffee. "Why don't you come clean and respond instead of stalling on them—which, by the way, Josh, *is* illegal."

"If you're recording this conversation, I'll have you thrown in jail so fast your head will spin."

When he went off on another tirade, she put the phone down again. Hard. So he could hear it. Which caused him to scream loud enough for her to hear. "Pick up the phone. I'm talking to you!"

"No, actually you're yelling," she said, placing the phone to her ear. "If you have anything of value to say, say it. I have actual *work* to do."

"What I have to say is that your contempt for authority will no longer be tolerated."

"What's that supposed to mean?"

"It means you are no longer invited to or permitted into State Department briefings."

Caitlin laughed. "Thanks for the update. Writing it down now. *Not allowed to listen to any more propaganda bullshit from the State Department in person.* Got it. Thanks for the call. Have a nice day, Josh." She started to hang up, but heard him yelling again.

"You'll be sorry. This is your last warning."

She quickly put the phone back to her ear. "Was that a *threat?*"

Click.

Dammit. The call and its abrupt ending shook her a bit. She hated it when people hung up on her.

After staring at her blank computer screen and wondering how she could have handled that better, Caitlin went back to her "to do" list for the day, and tried to forget it. But trying to get her mind off the phone call was easier said than done. Josh's words kept replaying in her mind.

Should she take his last words as an actual threat? Or was it just a State Department mouthpiece trying to scare her to keep her in line?

What did it matter? Caitlin knew the newspaper executives wouldn't take her side if she bothered to complain about it, so she'd have to be content with the fact that the FOIA's were getting under their skin.

She became lost in her thoughts as she stared absently out the window, pondering what was going on at the State Department. *What are they trying to hide? What are they hiding?*

"Stan wants to see you."

Caitlin turned to find Fred standing by her desk with his hands on his hips. She didn't try to pretend the interruption didn't irritate her. "What does he want?"

"I guess you'll find out when you get there."

She picked up her coffee and walked to Stan's office, but was confused when Fred followed her in and closed the door. When she glanced at him questioningly over her shoulder, he wore a smug, mocking expression, which made her a tad bit apprehensive. Fred was Stan's go-to guy when he needed someone to witness a firing.

"Hey, Stan. What's up?" Caitlin pretended a composure she did not feel, forcing herself to walk with an air of confidence to his desk.

Stan responded by frowning, as if just having her in his office was a source of unpleasantness.

"I'm going to take a wild guess this meeting isn't about me getting a raise." She smiled at her own joke but Stan didn't react, nor did he explain why he had called her to his office. He just stared at her with an annoyed expression on his face.

Caitlin stared right back, unblinking and undeterred.

He finally nodded toward the chair beside Fred. "Have a seat."

"I'll stand. Thanks."

Stan threw the pencil he was holding onto the desk and leaned back in his chair. "I just got off the phone with the State Department."

"What a coincidence. So did I." Caitlin put her fingers under her chin and pretended to be thinking. "Let me guess. They're whining about the FOIAs."

Stan shot her a piercing glare. "I don't think whining is quite the right word. It's more like they are *understandably* upset by the time suck of all your requests."

"Really? You fell for the time-suck line?" Caitlin was dumbfounded.

"It would take a team of three people more than a week of work to fulfill your requests. That is not a wise use of taxpayer money. I have the breakdown of man-hours right here." He held up a piece of paper where he had diligently written down the numbers given to him by Josh, and repeated most of what Josh had told her word for word as if he'd taken the time to memorize it.

"If they would do what they are getting paid to do and release public information, there would be no FOIA requests—and therefore no so-called time suck." Caitlin shook her head, not understanding how a supposedly educated man would fall for the agency's bogus reasoning. "The State Department employees do realize they are public *servants*, right? Paid by the taxpayers to do their jobs?"

"My point exactly. They can't do their jobs if they are working on FOIA requests."

"My requests are for legally public in-for-ma-tion." Caitlin spoke slowly so that maybe her words would sink in. "Our readers deserve to know the answers to those questions and it is our duty to find out what they are covering up."

Stan threw his hands in the air. "See, there you go again. Pretending there is some big conspiracy out there. Some big cover-up or evil plot."

Caitlin remained unbendable. "If they have nothing to hide, why do they continue to stall me on the answers I'm seeking? Aren't you the least bit curious?"

"What I'm curious about is what we are going to do with you."

"What's that supposed to mean?"

"I mean you were taken off the political investigative reporting beat a few months ago because you pissed off every politician in town—"

"You mean, because I asked questions and didn't write what they told me to write." Caitlin stated it matter-of-factly to show she was merely correcting his version. "And when they called and complained, you pretty much caved. Instead of putting up a fight, standing up for the First Amendment, and protecting our readers, you put your hands up and surrendered to the pressure."

Stan pursed his lips, trying to control his anger. "I can't afford to lose my job. Unlike you, I have responsibilities and a family to feed."

Caitlin raised her brows, wondering if he was making a point about her status as an employee or the fact she was still single in her mid-thirties. He didn't give her time to ponder the question.

"That's why you're now being taken off the government and crime beats. If you want to keep your job…" He paused, as if wanting to see if she would take the bait and quit, but her expression apparently made the answer clear. "The only other reporting position we have open is G.A."

Caitlin's jaw dropped. "General Assignment? That's an *entry-level* position."

He threw his hands up again. "What do you want me to do?"

She looked away so he would not see what she was thinking. *I want you to be a man with some semblance of a backbone and stand up to these bastards.*

She turned back just in time to see him exchange a hopeful, if not jubilant, glance with Fred, and understood exactly what was going on. They didn't have the authority to fire her—or they feared what she would do if they did—so they were going to make her life miserable until she quit. She decided it was time to play it smart, say nothing to anyone in the newsroom, and listen carefully to everything going on around her.

She nodded. "Okay. Is that all you wanted to tell me?"

Stan's and Fred's faces both dropped with surprise—and disappointment—at her reaction. Stan nodded and she turned toward the door with her lips still curled into a smile, albeit a forced one. She knew that trying to do her job would be pure torture, but she wasn't going to let it get to her. All of this was happening for a reason.

"Is everything I said clear?" Stan's voice had a tinge of anger in it.

Caitlin paused with her hand on the doorknob, then turned around with a big grin planted on her face. "Crystal." She opened the door and let herself out, walking with a straight back and head held high. She was getting to them.

And she had no intention of stopping now.

Chapter 15

Caitlin went back to her desk and began doodling absent-mindedly to take her mind off what had just transpired. She could tell her blood pressure was outrageously high because she could feel her pulse pounding in her temples. When the phone rang, she picked it up before it had even completed a whole ring. "Sparks."

"Hey, Scoop."

Caitlin pressed the phone closer and put her hand over her other ear to muffle the sound of the newsroom. It had been weeks since she'd heard that voice. "Hey. What's up?"

"Can you meet me at Mickey's Pub?"

"You mean that dive in McLean?"

"That's the one. Don't wear reporter clothes."

"What's that supposed to mean?"

"Wear something that will make you fit in—or at least not stand out."

Caitlin's head began spinning. "*Now?*"

"How about three-thirty?"

Caitlin glanced at the clock. "Wow, thanks. It'll be rush hour. I have to figure out an excuse to get out of here and run home to change clothes."

"Sounds good," he said without pausing. "Get there as soon as you can. I'll be at a table in the back room."

Caitlin was just about to ask what exactly the "back room" was, but heard a *click* as Madison hung up.

Caitlin put the phone down and contemplated the strange turn of events. A few months ago Madison was a cop she'd never met who was legendary among journalists for his intimidating demeanor and outright hostility. And now, out of the blue, he was calling and telling her to meet him at a smoky bar in a different town.

She put her head in her hands and rolled it back and forth. And yesterday she was a government beat reporter with a lot of clout. She could have just told Stan she was going to follow up on a tip and walked out the door. But after the meeting she'd just had she was more like a "gofer," expected to sit at her desk and wait to be sent to a ribbon cutting or some other equally boring and agonizing non-story.

She decided there was only one way for her to leave early, so she walked to Stan's office, knocked on the door frame, and leaned in. "I don't feel good. I'm taking the rest of the day off." She made sure to word it so he knew she wasn't asking for permission. She was stating a fact.

Stan regarded her with a hostile look in his eyes, as if he were trying to figure out a way to say 'no.' She met his hostility with an air of confidence, knowing he had no authority to stop her. She had never taken a sick day or personal leave in the entire twelve years she worked for the paper.

Finally he nodded. "Okay."

But his words when she turned to leave sent a shiver down her spine. "Be careful, Caitlin." His tone didn't convey any concern. In fact, it almost sounded like a threat.

Caitlin pulled into the parking lot a little after three-thirty but remained in her Jeep. Although she had passed this bar a million times, she'd never had the nerve to walk into the place. All of the locals swore it had the best fried chicken for miles, but it looked downright scary from the outside. This was as near as she had ever been to it, and her opinion was not improving by seeing it up close.

The plain cement structure was protected from the elements by a rusty metal roof that didn't look capable of withstanding a half decent thunderstorm. Tall weeds grew in abundance all along the front of the building and some sort of vine had taken over the west side. If not for the parking lot full of vehicles, one would think the building was abandoned—or condemned.

Caitlin's gaze shifted to the side and settled on Madison's black truck. Covered in mud, it looked right at home among the other pickups and older model cars parked haphazardly here and there in the unmarked gravel lot.

Taking a deep breath, Caitlin reached into her purse and touched the comforting steel within before getting out of her vehicle and heading inside.

The door squeaked loudly when she opened it, but no one within the dimly lit barroom seemed to take notice. They appeared busy playing darts, shooting pool, or knocking down shots.

Not wanting to call attention to herself by asking for directions to the *back room*, she walked hesitantly toward another doorway on the other side of the bar. The short walk seemed to take an eternity, as the sounds in the barroom seemed to diminish into a sort of hushed buzz.

Pretending a confidence she did not feel, Caitlin crossed the threshold of the doorway and took a squeaky step down to another room that was even darker than the one she'd just left.

She breathed a sigh of relief when she saw Madison sitting alone in a corner. It was obvious why he had chosen this place. They had the room to themselves and could speak freely.

He nodded when he saw her, and never removed his eyes as she walked across the room. "Nice job. You fit right in."

Caitlin slung her purse onto the back of a chair. She was afraid she'd gone overboard with her ripped jeans, barn boots and ball cap, but it appeared he approved. She didn't bother to mention it, but he didn't look too bad himself. His jeans were faded and worn, and the sleeves of his flannel shirt were rolled to his elbows. The business attire he usually wore made him look smooth and refined, but she kind of liked this casual, gritty look.

"The only problem is, you probably had every man in the front room watching you walk in."

"I don't think so." Caitlin pulled out the chair and sat. "No one seemed to notice."

Madison shot her what appeared to be a look of approval before turning to wave at a waitress walking through the room. "Oh, they noticed. Believe me."

Caitlin's heart skipped a beat at his open appraisal of her, but she didn't have time to ponder it.

A waitress wearing tight pants and a tank top appeared at the table, smiling broadly. "Hey, Blake. What can I get you?"

Caitlin tried to process that the man in front of her actually had a first name. Of course she knew that. She'd seen it in paperwork. But she'd never heard anyone call him *Blake*. It sounded so personal and intimate.

"Hey, Roxie. I'll take the usual."

"And your friend?"

Caitlin jerked from her thoughts. "I'll take a gin and tonic on the rocks—make it a double."

"Two double gin and tonics on the rocks, coming right up." The waitress nodded and walked away.

Caitlin met Madison's look of surprise and humor. He reclined back in his chair and seemed amused. "Nice call. You have a hard day at work or something?"

Caitlin sighed and nodded her head. "Now that you mention it. Yes."

"Thought so. I never took you for a drinking girl."

"Really? Why?"

"I don't know. You're a journalist... they sip wine or fancy non-alcoholic beverages or something."

Caitlin laughed out loud. "Yeah, well, it hurts when you put me in that general category so I'm glad I disproved your theory."

The detective's mouth turned upward in a grin, but he quickly became all business again.

"Everything's worked out with the kids. Preliminary paperwork anyway... for full custody."

"Wow. That's nice. I thought it would take longer than that."

"Usually does, but no one anywhere near Washington wants to make waves in an election year." He crossed his arms on the table. "Let's just say strings were pulled."

Caitlin didn't know what that meant and didn't ask. "Anything new on the Hilltop case?"

"No. I've been asking around, but the Feds are stalling."

"On purpose?"

His jaw tightened noticeably, even though his attention was focused on the doorway. "If you're asking my opinion, yes."

"Hate to say it, but I'm not surprised."

"Why not?"

Caitlin crossed her arms on the table. "After what happened to me this morning, nothing surprises me anymore."

"What happened?"

He leaned forward, a penetrating look in his eyes, causing Caitlin to lose her train of thought. Those eyes, even in the dark bar, had a reach that Caitlin found captivating—or maybe the term was intoxicating. She tore her gaze away. "The State Department called to complain about the FOIA requests I've submitted—and I got demoted."

"Can they do that?" He sounded concerned.

"This has been going on awhile." She took a deep breath. "They seem to be getting a little more desperate now."

"What do you mean?"

"Back when I started digging around about Vince's death, the State Department pulled this same type of stunt. They called the newsroom and screamed a little. Told me to back off."

"So?"

"I pretty much laughed it off, which really pissed them off."

"I bet."

"Then they called my editor and threatened *him*. Even told him to pull one of my stories—said it was inaccurate and that if I did any future stories all access to high-level officials would be denied."

"How'd he take that?"

"He had my back."

"Well, that's good."

"Yes. Except a month later he was fired."

Madison shot her an incredulous look. "You think it had something to do with this?"

"Absolutely. And that was just the beginning. The State Department started spreading rumors and innuendos about me, trying to make it as hard as possible for me to do my job."

"Sounds like they were using Saul Alinsky's theory. *Ridicule is man's most potent weapon."*

"Pretty much straight from the book *Rules for Radicals.*" She tried to sound cheerful, as if she hadn't been shaken by their efforts to demoralize her. "Isolate the target—me— from sympathy and any support network."

"Surrounded by enemies and suspected by friends." He shook his head. "Somehow I have a feeling that didn't stop you."

"I wanted the truth. That's all." She paused a moment as she thought back over all that had transpired in the last few months. "The worst part is they got to someone at the newspaper... The board of trustees or the publisher, I don't know who. But now we have an editor completely intimidated and browbeaten by this administration. When the State Department or whoever calls and says 'don't do a story,' we don't do a story."

"The newspaper heads don't realize you're doing the readership a favor by exposing this stuff? I would think that would help their circulation."

"Whether they do or don't, I don't know. I only know they cave to the pressure."

"So what now?"

"I have a contract, so there's no way they can terminate me—but after this morning's meeting it's clear they're going to make my life a living hell until I quit."

Madison talked in a low, serious tone. "I have a feeling this is bigger than either one of us figured. It's dangerous."

He moved his arm from the table as the waitress brought their drinks and lingered. "Anything else I can get for you guys?"

Caitlin shook her head and studied Madison. He was a complex man, not easy to get close to. Yet she got the feeling these two knew each other very well.

"No. Thanks, Rox." Madison smiled at the waitress and she

smiled back in a wordless exchange before turning to leave.

"It's dangerous," he said again after she'd left.

Caitlin nodded. "That's what Vince told me right before he died."

"You can stop anytime you want."

In response, Caitlin picked up her drink and held it up for a toast. "To justice."

The detective nodded and tapped his glass to hers. "To justice," he repeated before taking a big swallow and sitting the glass down with a firm hand. "Let's get down to business."

Chapter 16

Caitlin absently stirred her drink with her straw. "So you agree with me that the Kessler Affair is somehow tied to Vince's death?" She wanted to make sure they were on the same page.

"Maybe. But we still haven't connected the dots."

"Yes, we have." Caitlin paused to collect her thoughts. "Vince worked at the State Department and was getting ready to testify about the Kessler Affair. Two other employees who happened to be present in Renoviah *during* the Kessler Affair are also dead, along with the journalist who broke the gunrunning story and two special ops guys who tried to save people's lives. They all have a connection—the State Department."

"Or it's all a bunch of very unfortunate coincidences."

When Caitlin frowned and shook her head, he spoke again.

"Just trying to play devil's advocate here. You know we need more than that."

"I know." She nodded. "Gut feelings don't hold up in court very well, do they?"

"Not in this town."

Both were silent as Caitlin tried to figure out how to proceed.

She decided to just come right out and ask. "What exactly does your ex do at the State Department?"

"She was recently promoted to head counsel, but she's been an advisor of sorts for years."

"Funny, I never heard Vince talk about her."

"She stayed out of the spotlight for the most part. Did a lot of behind-the-scenes consultations."

"Behind-the-scenes... like orchestrating the cover-up for the Kessler Affair?"

Madison's brow tightened and his gaze grew distant. "If it was a question of protecting the integrity of the Secretary of State, then yes, I think she was capable of doing that."

"Three men died in Renoviah as a direct result." Caitlin tried to keep her voice as even and businesslike as his, but it rose noticeably. "There's no integrity in that."

Madison brought his attention back to her. "You don't need to lecture *me* about it. Two of them were my buddies." He looked away and took a deep breath to regain his composure.

Caitlin had never seen so much emotion on his face. "Sorry about that."

Now her mind was racing. The man sitting across from her lost two military brothers because they'd responded to help a fellow American in need. And the person who had concocted an elaborate cover-up to hide the details of the deaths was most likely his wife? Okay, ex-wife.

It was like pulling the layers off an onion, but she was finally beginning to see why he was so interested in this case. He was in as deeply as she was.

"Before I forget." Madison reached into his coat pocket and laid a phone on the table.

"What's that?"

"It's a phone."

"I can see it's a phone. What's it for?"

"It's for you." Madison pushed it toward her. "I'm taking a page out of Vince's playbook. When you need to call me from now on, use that."

"Good idea." She stuck the phone in her pocket, then stared at her drink. *Was he thinking that Mallory had tapped his phone? That his ex-wife knew the two of them were collaborating and wanted to try to stop it? If that is the case, it almost worked.* She didn't lift her gaze. "You think someone's monitoring our calls?"

"I don't know. But if anything happens, they'll definitely be checking. It's better if we don't have a lot of calls from each other on our regular phones."

"You have one of these too?" Caitlin looked up at him.

"Yep. The number is already programmed into that one."

Caitlin pulled the phone back out and went to the contacts. There was just one. It said Mad Dog.

She shot him a grin. "Good one, Detective."

"You know, you can just call me Blake." He took a sip of his drink. "I mean when we're not at work."

"And Mad Dog when we are?"

"Apparently you do that anyway."

Caitlin stared into his depthless eyes, and then shifted her attention to her drink, hoping her cheeks weren't too red. She hurriedly changed the subject. "You're kind of in a unique position to know what Mallory was doing those days. Did she seem different? Distant?"

He laughed, but with a look that showed no hint of amusement. "Funny wording. She had been different and distant for quite some time, actually."

Caitlin felt her cheeks turn red for sure this time. "Sorry. I don't mean to pry."

"It was an honest question." Blake picked up his glass and swiveled the ice cubes around, immersed in thought. "I deployed within six months of getting married, and between training and other deployments was home fewer than two months a year for ten years."

"You were in the Navy, right?"

He lifted his gaze for just a moment and then lowered it again, as if trying to gauge how much she knew about his background. "Yeah."

"Not the best way to lay a foundation for a marriage."

"We pretty much grew into two different people." He focused on the distant wall. "I didn't know her and she didn't know me."

"It's easy to grow apart when you're not together." For some reason Caitlin felt the need to console him.

"There was more to it than that. Mallory didn't come from money and didn't marry into it, but she wanted it. Especially after working in the State Department and having to keep up socially with the political elite." He focused his attention on Caitlin again. "So to answer your question, at the time of the Kessler Affair we were living together but barely speaking."

Caitlin felt a physical twinge in her heart at the look of pain on his face. Funny how she had judged him as this cold-hearted, distant alpha male, when in reality he was a loving father who had tried to be a good husband. Maybe his gruffness was just armor, an outer core of defense he used to hide and conceal an easily wounded heart. He was more kindhearted than he wanted anyone to know.

"She did spend quite a few nights in DC though during that time. I do remember that."

"Was that unusual?"

He took another swallow of his drink and nodded. "I was working long hours, and Whitney was so young, it didn't seem right to leave the kids with a nanny. Now that you mention it, I think that was pretty much the last straw."

Caitlin nodded. She never dreamed this investigation would take such a personal turn. It was awkward… painful. But it had to be done. They could leave no stone unturned.

She noticed Blake's tanned hands resting against the white tablecloth. They looked strong and lethal, the hands of a man who worked hard. Yet everything he had told her today indicated he possessed a soft touch.

"So how did Vince get involved in all of this?"

Caitlin knew it was her turn to lay bare her soul. She thought about it for a moment. "He was in charge of communications for the department. He was seeing and hearing one thing behind the scenes, and then being told to spin it differently for the media."

"That's a pretty important position—lots of responsibility."

"He was really honored and proud to get that job. And he was perfect for it." Caitlin tied the straw from her drink into little knots. "Except for one thing, I guess."

"What was that?"

"He wasn't morally corrupt like the rest of them."

There was a long pause as Blake took in what she'd said. "What do you mean?"

"That position requires some twisting of the truth, embellishment, things left out. That's the way the political game works and Vince understood that. But he didn't like outright lying. He didn't have the stomach for it."

"He was told to lie?"

"The way he put it… it was getting hard to keep all of their lies straight and everyone on the same page." Caitlin shook her head.

"He didn't go into detail, and I assumed he was talking about little, insignificant things. But it became clear there was something much bigger going on."

She tore her eyes away from Blake's sympathetic expression and cast them on the wall as she felt tears begin to well. She hated showing weakness, getting emotional. "Sorry." She took a deep breath and tried to think about something else. "Emotions get to me at the strangest times. I'll be fine and then, *boom*, it all comes rushing back."

Blake moved his hand over to hers. "That's the way grief works. I understand."

Caitlin felt his touch all the way through her. It wasn't like a lightning bolt or a surge of electricity, but more like a warm, comforting blanket across her shoulders. It surprised and terrified her.

Blake cleared his throat and removed his hand. "So how did you two meet?"

Caitlin thought back to carefree days when the world didn't seem so complicated and confusing. "I covered the State Department for the newspaper—way before he was promoted—so we ran into each other off and on."

"Strictly business though."

"Definitely. At first, anyway." She felt a smile twitch at the corner of her lips at the memories evoked. "I have a strict rule about not mixing business with pleasure, but after a particularly long and grueling day he asked me out for a drink as I was leaving."

"Ah, caught you at a weak moment."

"Yeah. I guess you guys all think alike." She shot a contemplative look toward Blake. He looked so different when he grinned like that. "Anyway, I thought it was completely spontaneous, but he told me later he'd been waiting for just the right moment for months."

Blake nodded knowingly but didn't say anything.

"We agreed to not talk about our jobs when together, and we kept our relationship completely secret. But when he became head of communications I requested to be reassigned to another beat. I didn't want to ruin my credibility as a journalist—or his new position, with a conflict of interest if anyone found out."

"How in the world did you keep your relationship a secret?"

"Not that hard really." Her smile grew wistful. "Our schedules were so busy, we only saw each other a couple weekends a month. When we had free time during the week we'd chat on the pre-paid phones. No one knew about it as far as I know."

"He must have been dedicated to work that hard."

She nodded absently. "Vince loved that job… before the Kessler Affair anyway."

"What did he tell you about that whole incident?"

"Well, I already knew about Randy Kessler's work on the gun-running operation because I'd been reading his articles. The only thing Vince told me after Kessler was taken prisoner in Renoviah is that it didn't seem like the State Department had much interest in securing his release."

"Why did he think that?"

"They just didn't seem to be moving on it I guess. He got the feeling they were almost content with having him out of the way in prison."

"But they did eventually arrange the release."

She nodded. "Yes, they helped arrange the release. Partly because the president needed to look decisive on something, but mostly because of the public outcry over an American left behind in a foreign country."

"Did Vince ever mention Mallory?"

"Not by name. But when I think back on our conversations, it

was clear he was always implying a woman was calling the shots—
and that most of the people in the office feared for their jobs."

"Was he in a position to work with her directly?"

Caitlin nodded. "Yes. If Mallory was as important a player
as you say, they would have been present for the same briefings."

"So, do you think Vince had uncovered something specific, or
someone was just worried about him testifying in general?"

"For all I know, they killed him because they knew he contacted me." She paused, her brow wrinkling at the memory. "They
may have thought he was getting ready to spill his guts for a story."

Blake put his drink down with a thump. "You can't possibly
think they killed him because of contact with you."

Caitlin chewed on her cheek. "Just so happens, he called me
from his office phone two days before he was killed because the
throw-away cell he had wasn't charged." She toyed with her glass
as she recalled the events of that day. "It was a quick call to set
up a dinner date—we hadn't had time to see each other for days."
She picked up her drink and tried to keep her hand from shaking. "Just a coincidence, right? He calls a reporter from his office
phone and ends up dead two days later, a few hours before the
dinner date."

A long pause ensued. "I hope you don't blame yourself."

Caitlin stared at the wall and tried to keep the tears at bay.

Blake reached over the table and touched her arm. "I hope
you don't blame yourself." His voice was gentle and intimate.
"There's no way his death is your fault."

"Really?" She shot him a distressed look. "Because if I wasn't
a reporter, I bet you a million bucks he'd still be alive." She turned
away so he wouldn't see her tears.

"Dammit. It's not your fault, Cait."

Caitlin tilted her head at the sound of her name. It was the first time she remembered him calling her anything other than *Scoop*.

"There's no way you can shoulder the blame for that. I don't know what happened—or why—but you were only searching for the truth. There's no fault in that."

The certainty and reassurance in his voice soothed her, but the memories would not let go. Her sorrow and sense of guilt were tied together like a huge, painful knot. "Maybe not in the search—only in getting the man I loved killed." Caitlin could feel her lips start to tremble, a precursor to tears, which she despised. "I'm sorry to be so weak." She took a shaky breath and tried to speak again, but failed.

Blake nodded. "Don't let them wear you down. We have to stick together." He waited a moment to give her time to collect herself, and then patted her hand. "You okay to talk about this?"

Caitlin nodded, swiping at a tear before it ran down her cheek. The concern in his voice and the calm, reassuring look left her feeling frazzled inside. More than anything she wanted to put her face in her hands and have a good cry, but she just turned her head slightly away as another tear let loose, and hoped he wouldn't notice. "Yeah. I'm fine."

"Let's go over the basics." Blake's voice was businesslike again, yet strangely soothing. It was comforting to have someone take control. "Is your theory on his death based on fact or speculation? Do you have anything concrete?"

"It's speculation based on fact." Caitlin took a deep breath and lifted her head, trying to keep her expression under stern restraint. "I mean, they pretty much cleaned everything up to make sure there were no forensics, but lots of things still don't add up."

"Like what?"

"Well, like from day one they used threats and intimidation to make their facts mesh with the State Department spin. Everyone seemed to buy it."

"Such as?"

Caitlin spoke softly even though they were alone. "The National Park Service Police were the first ones on the scene when Vince was found. Normal procedure in the case of a violent death is to treat it as a homicide until all doubts are resolved. Right?"

Blake nodded.

"But before I even arrived they were calling it a suicide."

"And a homicide investigation was never launched." Blake didn't ask a question. He stated what he knew to be true.

"No homicide investigation, and the first park police officer on the scene turned all of Vince's effects over to the State Department—who later said his briefcase was empty."

"I saw that on the police report. Thought it was pretty strange. Same with the results for gunpowder residue. No stippling or burns. No internal muzzle staining or traces of powder in the wound track. It's all pretty suspicious." Blake tapped his fingers on the table and shifted in his chair. By the way he was fidgeting, he could tell he was going to ask something uncomfortable.

"I hate to ask this, but what about the reports that Vince was depressed?"

Even though Caitlin was surprised he knew that much detail about the case, she was eager to answer. "Yes, the State Department spent a considerable amount of time in their press conference saying he was being treated for depression, but no drugs were found in his system. They also trotted out some employees who said he'd seemed stressed and lost weight." She paused for effect. "He had his annual physical about three weeks before he died—he'd gained six pounds."

Blake cleared his throat nervously. "But wasn't there a suicide note?"

Caitlin took a deep breath. "Oh yes, the note. Everything was based on the note that was supposedly found three days later."

"Was it written by Vince or forged?"

"Actually, it *was* written by Vince, but they only released one line: *I can't take it anymore.* Caitlin absently tore her napkin into little pieces as she talked. "Those are the exact words he used the morning he called me, except he said: *I'm going to testify. I can't take it anymore.*

Blake let his breath out slowly. "So they only released the part of the note that fit their narrative."

Caitlin nodded. "When I came forward and asked to see the entire note, they changed their story. Originally they said they had an entire suicide note, but then they revised that statement, saying Vince had ripped it up and tossed it in the trash and they had only found that one line."

"I don't remember any of the news media picking up on that."

She raised her eyes to meet his and then looked back down. "I guess it didn't fit *their* narrative either."

They remained quiet a moment, but then Blake seemed to sense she had something more to say. "Anything else you can think of?"

"I'm not sure…" She paused, uncertain if she should continue. Maybe things weren't adding up because of her close relationship with the victim. Maybe all of these inconsistencies were just the product of a wild imagination. After being told so many times she was a crazy conspiracy theorist, she was beginning to question her own judgment.

"Go ahead."

"I went to the impound lot and sat in Vince's car once it was processed and towed there. The seat was adjusted to someone very short—shorter than me."

Blake cocked his head, appearing to ponder why that was of any importance.

"Vince was your height. Why would the seat be forward?"

"You think someone other than Vince drove the car to the park? That he was already dead?"

"What do you think? When the body and car were found, there were no keys in the ignition. The body was supposedly searched at the scene. Again, no keys. Then two State Department aides showed up at the morgue and, presto, car keys show up in Vince's pants pocket."

Blake lifted his ball cap off his head and put it back down. "Whoa." He pondered what she'd said a minute. "If he was killed somewhere else, why do you suppose they picked that park to deposit the body?"

"Believe it or not, I have a theory on that."

"I thought maybe you would."

"The deputy medical examiner who did the autopsy has been under suspicion for labeling two obvious homicides as suicides. That park is his jurisdiction. A very convenient coincidence for the State Department."

He sighed and shook his head.

"You ever see so many inconsistencies in a case?"

"Not until the Hilltop deaths." He squeezed his temples as if agitated there weren't more answers. "There sure are a lot of convenient coincidences, I'll give you that."

"Too many convenient coincidences, if you ask me. They all add up to one big lie."

"Well, it seems we've narrowed it down to a connection with the State Department. Now all we have to figure out is who… and why."

"I feel like we've hit a stone wall."

"There's always a way around it."

"Glad you're so optimistic." Caitlin shook her head and looked at him. She pretended to be exasperated, but she really did admire that about him. He was not the kind of man to let anyone keep him from reaching an objective—no matter what the cost. He was fearless and tenacious and direct, making her glad that a delicate thread of friendship had begun to form between them. Their shared pain of loss because of seemingly senseless acts had united them to achieve a common goal: find out who killed the people they loved. Nothing else mattered. "I guess it's good we ran into each other at Louie's."

Blake smiled out of the corner of his mouth. "Two heads are generally better than one. And we bring two different perspectives. With your sources and my contacts—"

"You two ready for a refill?" The waitress suddenly appeared beside them.

"No, I'm good." Blake pulled out his wallet and handed the waitress a bill. "Keep the change, Rox."

The way he said the words made Caitlin look up just in time to see him wink at the blushing waitress. Caitlin cleared her throat. "Thanks for the drink."

"My pleasure." He waited for the waitress to leave again. "You let me know if you think of anything else... another angle we can attack this from." He pushed his chair out and stood. "I'll walk you out."

Caitlin headed toward the door to the main barroom. Again, much of the chattering seemed to stop in the smoke-filled room, but this time she assumed it was because of the man beside her. He possessed a commanding presence and a kind of magnetic force that attracted attention from both men and women.

When Blake opened the door and she stepped outside, Caitlin

reflexively lifted a hand to her eyes to shield them from the bright light of the setting sun. Neither spoke until she stopped in front of her Jeep. "Thanks again for the drink." She fumbled through her purse for the keys and unlocked the door.

"You're welcome, Scoop. Stay out of trouble."

Blake didn't glance at her again. Just hopped into his truck, turned over the engine, and pulled away before she even had time to wave goodbye.

Chapter 17

Caitlin was talking to another reporter about a comprehensive story they were working on when she thought she heard her phone ring. Hurrying toward her cubicle, she hurled herself onto the desk to reach it in time, but when she picked it up no one was there.

"Hello?" she said one more time for good measure before hanging up. *Oh, well. They'll call back if it's important.*

Going back to work on the story she hadn't finished, she was interrupted a short time later by the tones of a fire call coming across the scanner. She listened for a minute and then looked around the newsroom to see if any of the so-called "police" reporters were taking notice. It did not appear they were. Some of them were bent over their phones, others were merely staring at their computer screens. Either they didn't know the particular tones coming over the scanner were local ones, or they had tuned it out and didn't even hear it—not really a good habit for someone who is supposed to report the news.

Caitlin shook her head and listened as the dispatcher announced a pedestrian had been struck about four blocks away. There was still no reaction from any reporters, even though from

Caitlin's point of view more than a few of them could use the exercise, and almost all of them could use some time in the sun. She shook her head and went back to work, trying to ignore the sounds just like everyone else. Even when the fire trucks, ambulance and police cars went screaming past the building a few minutes later no one made a move—except one reporter, who turned toward the window with an irritated scowl at the interruption. "What is going on out there?"

Caitlin pursed her lips. *That's what our readers will want to know too, don't ya think?*

Not until the dispatcher announced a Class Four victim and called for the coroner did Caitlin decide to check it out. She grabbed her notebook and headed toward the door, but didn't bother to move with any sense of urgency. It would take at least thirty minutes for the coroner to arrive. She had plenty of time.

When still a block away, Caitlin noticed a crowd had gathered and were quietly watching the proceedings. Yellow police tape kept them back from the scene, but they were standing three or four deep along the sidewalk staring at the street. Peering around them, she saw Detective Madison standing over a sheet-covered body talking in a low voice to a uniformed police officer who seemed to be in charge.

So this is a crime scene, not an accident? Interesting.

"Anyone see what happened?" Caitlin turned toward the people in the crowd.

"I heard it was a hit and run." An older woman with gray hair kept staring toward the body as she spoke. "That poor girl."

Caitlin got out her notepad. "It was a female then? Are you sure?"

The woman nodded. "I saw her before they put the sheet over her. A young woman. About your age."

A slow shiver of dread began working its way up Caitlin's spine, but she ignored it. "And no one stopped?" She examined the scene again, but saw no car, damaged or otherwise, near the body. "In broad daylight?" She looked around at the crowd, but they all were shaking their heads. No one had seen anything.

Caitlin stayed back and allowed the police on the scene to do their job until the coroner arrived. When it appeared they were making preparations to remove the body, she slipped under the police tape and walked toward the coroner for a statement.

But as she drew to within a few yards of the group surrounding the sheet-covered corpse, something caused Blake to glance over his shoulder. He quickly turned to her and sidestepped at the same time, placing himself between her and the body. "Don't go any closer." She had never heard him speak in that tone before. Not angry exactly, but very commanding—demanding.

The seriousness of his voice and the urgency of his order made Caitlin curious, so she instinctively looked around him as they began lifting the figure for transport. As they raised the gurney to push it to the waiting ambulance, the sheet got caught and slipped off the victim's head, revealing a young woman with bright red hair. Mary Barto.

Caitlin's hand shot to her mouth and her eyes darted up to meet Blake's. The expression on his face confirmed her suspicion that this was a State Department employee and made her take a step backward. She felt like she was going to faint. His strong hand reached out and grabbed her arm. "Don't make a scene."

His tone sounded calm and reassuring, even though it was accompanied by a powerful grip on her shoulder as he escorted her back across the police line. "No press." The words were spoken loudly for the benefit of those around her, but they barely registered over the roar in her ears.

"There'll be a statement later."

In the flurry of motion that followed, which was all a big blur, Caitlin saw a black SUV pull up and men wearing FBI shirts get out.

This can't be happening. She looked over her shoulder and saw Blake heading toward the newly arrived investigators. *Please God. Not again.*

Blake felt uncomfortable driving to Caitlin's house, but he didn't want to talk over the phone. He'd driven around aimlessly for the past thirty minutes to make sure he wasn't being followed, and was now getting close to her address according to the GPS.

Straining to see in the darkness, he distinguished an opening for a driveway, and then saw her black Jeep. After a quick survey of the layout of the property, he pulled his truck in behind a shed and a hedgerow of trees so it couldn't be seen from the road.

The building appeared to be a small tenant house, probably predating the Civil War, but it was in pristine condition and neatly kept. He walked up three steps to the porch and tapped twice on the door.

After just a few moments, he heard the doorknob turning. It concerned him that the door had apparently been unlocked— and that she didn't check to see who was there before swinging it open.

Caitlin stood in the threshold bathed in the warm light of the house, gazing straight ahead with the dull stare of someone who has been through too much. She didn't seem surprised to see him, but then again she made no effort to greet him or ask him in. Blake stood there trying to think of something to say when she stepped into his arms, sobbing.

Gently nudging her into the house, Blake closed the door behind them. Again, he didn't know what to say or how to console her, causing him to wonder if he should have come at all. He didn't have much experience with crying women, and wasn't all that interested in gaining that expertise. This type of situation made him uncomfortable.

"I'm like poison," she said in between sobs. "Killing everyone around me."

"It's not your fault, Cait."

With her arms wrapped around him tightly and her cheek pressed against his chest, he could feel her entire body trembling with emotion. Except for the few tears he had seen one time in the bar, she had always appeared strong and in control. It was alarming to find her so distraught and emotional.

"Why don't you sit down?" He helped her over to the kitchen table and pulled out a chair.

Caitlin lowered herself into the seat and put her head in her arms on the table. "What happened?" she murmured in a low, tormented voice.

Blake eased into a chair beside her and let out his breath. "Officially? Hit and run." He saw her head start moving back and forth as a low moan escaped her. "They're searching for vehicles with damage." He waited, but she made no effort to speak. "One person thought they saw a black SUV-type vehicle leaving at a high rate of speed."

"Did you know? Who she was?" Her voice was whispered and distraught.

"She was wearing a State Department ID. From the look on your face, I figured it was someone you knew."

She didn't move or reply, so Blake reached out and gave her arm a gentle squeeze. "You okay? You know this could just be another terrible coincidence."

"She called me," she mumbled in a barely audible voice.

"Excuse me?" He leaned forward.

She raised her head slowly. "She called me."

He gazed into eyes that were swollen and red and full of pain. "When?"

"About an hour before…" She gulped in some air. "I mean, my phone rang, and when I picked it up no one was there." She put her hands up and ran them through her hair, as if just realizing it was not pulled back in a braid. "I didn't think anything of it and went back to work, but when I…" She took a deep sobbing breath. "When I found out who had been killed, I checked the number on the call log." She looked down at her hands, now resting on the table. "It was her."

Blake took a deep breath, and let it out slowly. "You didn't tell anyone, right?"

She moved her head back and forth while staring straight ahead.

"They didn't find a phone on her."

"Of course not." She turned her head toward him with a glazed look of despair. "But they know she called me."

Both of them were silent as the kitchen clocked ticked in the background. Finally Caitlin spoke. "She was only four blocks away. She must have been coming to see me in person."

The investigative instinct in Blake kicked in as he mulled over what she'd said. That made sense. Whoever had hit her had probably been told to stop her. There had been no planning beforehand. It was pure desperation.

"You need to keep your door locked." His voice was firm. "And you need to see who's on the other side before opening it. You understand?"

She didn't say anything, but nodded in response.

Blake walked toward the door and opened it, running his hands along the frame. Then he closed and locked it, and tested the knob.

"What are you doing?"

"You need a better lock than that." He looked around the room. "Is there another door in the back?"

"No. It's an old house."

Blake stood in the middle of the room with his hands on his hips. "I'll send someone over to put a deadbolt lock on there."

Caitlin sighed heavily and shook her head, her hair hanging in wild disarray around her face. "I'm not worried about me."

"I *am.*"

Her tear-filled eyes lifted to meet his, solemn and surprised. "I wish you weren't involved in this," she finally said in a shaky voice. "If they find out you came…"

"They won't find out I came. I know how to watch my own back."

Caitlin stood and nodded, still staring into space as if under a spell that left her only partially aware of her surroundings.

Blake walked over to her, and put his hands on her shoulders. "You okay, Scoop?"

"I'm fine," she said, but her voice wavered in such a way that he knew she wasn't.

"Do you want me to stay?" He wasn't sure why, but his own voice trembled now.

"No, I'm good." She shook her head. "Thanks for coming."

He studied her a moment—the disheveled, tousled hair, the heartrending, sad expression—and resisted the temptation to sweep her into his arms and comfort her. He knew she prided herself on being strong and independent. "There'll be someone here tomorrow afternoon to fix that door. Okay? I'll have them call first."

Again she nodded, but he wasn't completely sure she heard him. Giving her shoulders a final squeeze, he turned to leave.

"Blake?"

He stopped with his hand on the doorknob. "Yeah?"

She looked like she wanted to break down and have a good cry, but instead she just gripped the chair that seemed to be holding her up and shook her head. "Nothing. Thanks for stopping and checking on me."

He watched her a moment, wondering if she was really okay, unsure whether he should go or stay. "Do you need something?"

She nodded. "I need you…" She cleared her throat. "I mean, I need you to be careful."

"I will, Cait. You do the same." When she didn't say anything else, he turned to leave. "Call if you need me." He turned the knob and stepped outside. "And lock the door behind me."

He waited on the porch until he heard the door lock click, then headed with reluctance to his truck. For reasons unknown, he didn't pull away until long after all the lights went out in her house. When he finally headed home, he was exhausted by the lateness of the hour and confused by the powerful tug of protectiveness that had forced him to remain until he knew she was safe in bed.

Chapter 18

Caitlin paced back and forth in her living room, biting her fingernails. It was Saturday. She hated to bother Blake at home, but she had run across something interesting and wanted to see what he thought.

She hesitatingly picked up the phone and tried to convince herself it was okay to call him. Although she had been too emotional to recall much about his visit the night Mary had been killed, she remembered he'd called the next morning to remind her someone was coming to install a deadlock. He'd also told her he had back-to-back trials, and would probably be out of the office most of the week.

Caitlin still felt stunned and dazed by the latest turn of events. She'd made it through the past few days, but she wasn't sure how. The grief, remorse, and sense of guilt over Mary Barto's death had overwhelmed her, but those emotions were slowly being replaced with a fresh determination to find out who was responsible.

What had Mary wanted to tell her? Had she known who was behind the murders?

She looked down at the phone and pushed the send button for Mad Dog before she could talk herself out of it again.

"What's up, Scoop? You okay?"

Caitlin smiled. She had almost forgotten she was the only person who called him at this number, and realized for the first time that she was probably listed in his phone under that name. "I'm fine. I ran across something last night. Might not be anything, but I wanted to run it by you."

"That's funny. I ran across something interesting yesterday myself."

There was a long pause, and his breathing increased as if he were talking and walking at the same time. "I'm home if you want to stop by. I'll probably be in the barn."

"In the barn?" Caitlin remembered him saying he had been in the barn the day she'd run into Mallory at his house, but didn't remember ever seeing one.

"It's in the back and down the hill. Just follow the driveway around. You'll see it."

She heard a noise, like he was sliding a large barn door open. "And, Cait?"

"Yeah?"

"Make sure you're not being followed."

Caitlin did as Blake instructed, running some errands and trying to appear inconspicuous, all the while checking her mirrors to make sure no one was following her. She even pulled over once along the side of the road to see if any suspicious-looking cars were behind her, but all appeared to be clear.

As she proceeded up the dirt lane that led to Blake's house, she discovered it did indeed continue around the back to a large old barn. When she pulled to a stop, Drew and Whitney waved from where they were sitting on the fence, and came running. As soon as she got out, Whitney grabbed her leg on one side and

Drew grabbed her jacket on the other.

"Caitlin!" Whitney held on tight. "Did you come to play?"

"No, she didn't come to play."

Blake strode out of the barn, a bale of hay in each hand. Caitlin had always taken him for a man who enjoyed the outdoors, but now she knew how his time was occupied. Wearing a canvas barn jacket, a pair of faded jeans and work boots, he looked like he had just stepped off the page of an LL Bean catalog.

"Hey," she said, as she felt her heart do a double-tap in her chest.

Blake gave her a sideways glance and kept walking, but she thought she saw a smile breaking on his face. "Yes, it's hay."

Oh my gosh, he has a sense of humor. Caitlin tried to hide her surprise. "Need a hand?"

"No, it's just going right here." He walked briskly, yet his movements were spare and efficient like an athlete. The strength he displayed in the careless way he carried the bales made Caitlin turn her attention back to the kids. She took each by a hand and started walking to the barn. "I didn't know you had horses."

"Two. Hard to believe there was a day when I actually had time for them."

"Well, since I'm here, let me give you a hand." Caitlin strode confidently into the barn. "What do you need done?"

"I was just going to get the horses out of the back paddock and turn them out up here. Kids, go sit in the tack room while Luke and Lucy walk through."

Caitlin noticed a lead shank hanging on a hook and grabbed it as she kept walking toward the back of the barn where he'd pointed. When she slid open the huge barn door, she saw two horses standing in a paddock with their heads hanging over the fence staring in her direction. They both nickered and swung their heads up and down as if telling her to hurry. Without hesitation, Caitlin walked up to the one impatiently stamping the ground, and opened the gate.

"You in a hurry there, big daddy?" Putting a firm hand on his halter as he danced around, she clipped on the shank and led him through the gate. He was a massive horse, the top of his back being a few inches taller than the top of her head, so closing the gate behind her proved a little more difficult as he pranced and pulled against her.

"Slow down, dude." Once the gate was latched, Caitlin wrapped her fingers around his halter, gave it a jerk to let him know she was there, and then continued into the barn. Just as she reached the doorway, her cell phone vibrated. Without missing a step, she retrieved the phone from her back pocket and read the text message with one hand, while the rambunctious horse tugged and pulled on the other.

When she glanced up, Blake was propped against one of the stalls with crossed arms watching her with an amused smile. "You know that horse weighs more than fifteen hundred pounds, right?"

Caitlin pulled the horse to a stop by leaning back and using all of her one hundred and twenty pounds of body weight. "If you say so."

He remained quiet, studying her. "I was going to warn you he's a little strong for a woman, but I can see you've been around horses before."

The look of approval he shot her was not without effect. Caitlin felt her cheeks turning red. "Oh, I've been around a few."

"So I take it you ride?"

"Used to. All the time."

"Can we go riding, daddy?"

"Not today, honey." Blake headed out to get the other horse, and then stopped in mid-stride. After gazing up at the sun shining brilliantly overhead, and then at his daughter holding tightly onto his jeans, he turned his head to Caitlin. "Unless you're game."

Caitlin tried not to hide her delight. "Say no to a horseback ride? Are you kidding me?"

Blake still hesitated. "They haven't been ridden for a while. As you can see, Luke there is a bit on the hot side."

"Sounds good to me."

"Somehow I knew you would say that. I'll grab Lucy. Just hook Luke up to the cross ties.

Once Blake had retrieved the other horse, he unlatched a door and flipped on a light. "Tack's in here. Let me guess. You ride English."

"I used to foxhunt a little and show hunters."

"Living in this part of Virginia will do that to you." Blake picked out bridles, saddles and saddle pads. "Here, this should fit Luke."

"What are these guys anyway? They look Thoroughbred-ish, but they're awfully big boned."

"That's exactly what they are—big-boned Thoroughbreds." Blake carried another saddle out of the tack room. "Too big to be fast. They were going to slaughter, believe it or not."

Caitlin tilted her head. "And you saved them?"

He stopped what he was doing and turned toward her. "Is that so hard to believe?"

"No. I guess having a soft spot for animals is not that hard to believe." She paused a moment for effect. "It's just humans you have trouble with."

He laughed. "I won't even bother to deny that."

Caitlin slid the bit into the horse's mouth and pulled the bridle up over his ears. "So were these two together when you got them?"

"Yep. Skinny. Lame. All beat up. I was working undercover at a horse auction and had no intention of going home with two hay burners, but I just couldn't let them go."

"It's nice that you kept them together."

"Thanks. I thought Mallory would get interested in riding, but..." He threw a saddle on Lucy's back and never finished.

Caitlin glanced at him from around Luke's head but went back to adjusting the straps on the bridle.

"I wonder if I should have you lounge him a few minutes." Blake spoke after a brief pause. "He can be a real handful."

"I don't mind if he's a little hot. It'll be fun."

"I usually ride him and let other people ride Lucy, but I'll have the kids."

Caitlin scrutinized the other horse for the first time. The mare was just as big as Luke, but stood with drooping head and half-closed eyes, as if trying to catch a quick nap before anyone climbed onto her back.

"She looks like a good babysitter—not really my type. I'll be fine."

When the horses had been tacked up and were ready to go, they walked out into the sunshine, the kids skipping along beside.

Blake glanced over at Caitlin. "There's nothing like the outside of a horse for the inside of a man."

"I was just going to say that." Caitlin laughed. She didn't express it out loud, but it appeared to her that horses were good for the *outside* of a man too. Blake had taken off his jacket and was down to a blue denim shirt with the sleeves rolled up, revealing a completely different appearance to the man she usually saw wearing a tie. Although still mysterious and mystifying, Detective

Blake Madison had this other comfortable, protective, caring side that Caitlin found somewhat endearing.

"Here, I'll give you a leg up." Blake's deep voice came from right behind her.

"No, I can—"

Before she could get the words out of her mouth, he had grabbed her left leg just below the knee. She bent it automatically and was lifted with a strong arm into the saddle. With his free hand, Blake grabbed the reins to quiet Luke while she adjusted her stirrups. "Okay. All set."

Blake nodded toward a small fenced ring. "You can take him in there and trot around a few minutes while we mount. Get the steam off."

As Luke sidestepped and swung his head, Caitlin nodded and turned him toward the ring. After a few trips around at a fast, but comfortable, trot, she watched Blake swing into the saddle and maneuver Lucy up to a fence. Drew hopped on behind him, and once horse and riders were settled, a giggling Whitney was hoisted up to sit in front of the saddle.

"Hold on," he instructed Drew, as he put a protective arm around Whitney. "All ready?" He turned toward Caitlin.

"I think so. He's a little high strung, but we'll be okay."

"Just keep a tight hold on him. He's not crazy, just full of energy."

"I noticed that." Caitlin tried to loosen the reins rather than keep pulling on Luke's mouth through the bit, but as soon as she gave him an inch he took it as a sign to go faster.

"Was he originally from the track?"

"Yeah. He's got a lip tattoo." Blake talked while guiding his horse toward a trail into the woods. "He's strong, but not very fast by racing standards, I guess."

Luke automatically followed his stablemate, but now the going was single file so Caitlin didn't have to work so hard to keep him under control. She inhaled the cool, fresh air as the horses plodded along the pine needle-covered path. Every now and then one of their hoofs would strike a rock, causing a loud clank that caused the kids to giggle. It became a game, with the kids remaining perfectly quiet until they heard the *clank* again. Then they would erupt in laughter, causing Luke to shy sideways so Caitlin would have to regain control. She enjoyed every minute of it.

"You all right?" Blake turned his head back and glanced at her when he heard the rustling behind him as Luke sideswiped some heavy foliage. "Sounds like a rodeo going on back there."

"Oh, we're fine." Caitlin laughed as she reined him back in. "He hasn't bucked me off yet anyway."

Once she got him quieted down again Caitlin's attention turned to the beautiful vista around her, and then to Blake's strong, erect back as he guided Lucy down the path. He had one hand on the reins and the other securely wrapped around his little girl, while Drew clung to his waist from behind. She would never have believed the detached, reserved detective was really a warm, loving, family man.

Caitlin was smiling broadly when Blake looked over his shoulder again. "We're coming up on an open field so you better tighten up on him."

She nodded, thankful for the warning.

"Unless you're up for a run." Blake pulled Lucy to a stop and twisted around in the saddle. "He needs to get a little exercise."

"Sure. Why not."

"We'll stay here. Just trot him to the first corner to make sure you have control, then let him canter to the next two corners, and pull him back down to a trot at the last corner."

Caitlin nodded as she tightened her hands on the reins. Her heart thundered wildly, but it was more from excitement than fear. She hadn't ridden for more than a year, and was getting ready to gallop a large Thoroughbred around a field.

Luke, seeming to anticipate the run, pulled hard on the reins as she let him trot. When they got to the first corner of the rectangular field Caitlin gave him a little more rein, which he accepted by breaking into an immediate gallop. Blake had said "canter" him, but at least they were not in a flat-out run.

When they got to the last corner, she see-sawed the reins and shifted her weight behind his center of balance to get him to slow down, bubbling with laughter when it took practically the whole length of the field to accomplish the feat. It was hard work—and it was exhilarating. Before she knew it, she was approaching the trail where Blake and the kids sat watching.

"Let's do that too, Daddy." Drew urged Blake to take Lucy around the field, as Caitlin brought Luke to a sudden halt, showering them with clods of dirt.

"Lucy's tired from carrying all this weight," Blake said, winking at Caitlin. "Time to head back."

Chapter 19

"Thank you, Blake."

"For what?" He slid the saddle off the horse's back, and then tilted his head questioningly.

"Letting me do that. It was a blast."

"Oh that." He took the saddle into the tack room. "Glad you had a good time."

"Look, Daddy." Whitney pointed toward the house. "Nana's here."

Blake stuck his head out and watched the car park beside his truck. "She'll probably wonder where we are." He turned toward Caitlin. "I'd better get them up to the house. I'll be right back."

Caitlin was already leading Luke into the wash stall. "No problem. I'll rinse them both to get the saddle stains off." She paused and watched Blake walk away holding Whitney in one strong arm and clasping Drew's hand with the other. Whitney's head relaxed against his shoulder, and the way it swayed with each step, it appeared she had already fallen asleep.

After hosing both horses down, Caitlin put them into stalls and began sweeping the barn floor. The scent of hay, horses, and leather, flooded her mind with memories of earlier years and brought a reflective smile to her face. Her job on a horse farm when she'd been in her teens had been hard, dirty, and exhausting—but she'd loved every minute of it.

"You're hired."

She turned at the sound of Blake's voice right behind her. Her gaze went from his laughing blue eyes to the two frosty-looking bottles of beer he carried in one hand.

"Thought you might like a cold one."

Caitlin's eyes grew wide. "Wow. You read my mind. Nothing like a cold beer after a ride."

"I thought you were a gin drinker." He twisted off one of the caps and handed her the beer.

"Gin after work. A beer after a ride." Caitlin held up her bottle and tapped it against his. "Here's to…"

"A productive day," he finished for her.

Caitlin lifted the beer to her lips and was instantly reminded of the enjoyment a cold beer brings after working hard on a hot summer day. "I don't know how productive it's been," she said, turning her attention back to Blake.

"Have a seat." He pointed toward a bale of hay sitting against the stall door as he grabbed a big bucket, turned it over, and sat down. "I'm hoping it's going to be. You said you thought of something."

"Oh, right." Caitlin reached into her coat pocket and pulled out a folded piece of paper. "Sorry it's a little wrinkly."

"What's this?" Blake squinted at the blurry copy of a man sitting at a desk signing something while a number of other people stood behind him.

"It's a copy of a copy, so I know it's not real clear." Caitlin pointed to the man at the desk. "That's Jay Brown."

Blake jerked his gaze up to meet hers. "The guy killed at the

Hilltop house?"

Caitlin nodded. "See what he's doing?"

He brought the paper closer and squinted. "Just looks like he's signing something."

Caitlin remained silent as he continued to study the paper. Then his eyes slowly lifted. "With his left hand."

"Yep. I called someone and confirmed he was left-handed."

Blake put the paper down and let out a deep sigh. "Why would a left-handed person shoot himself on the right side of the head?"

"I was hoping you could explain that one to me."

He rested his elbows on his knees. "As much as we have, we're still missing something."

Caitlin pursed her lips together, deep in thought. "You know who might be the key to all this?"

Blake shook his head. "No. Who?"

"Senator Wiley."

He turned his head and spit out the beer that her comment had made him choke on. "Why do you say that?"

She studied him curiously, wondering what had caused that reaction. "Well, he's chairman of the foreign relations committee, right?"

"Yes. With aspirations of becoming president."

"Maybe he wasn't directly involved, but he has to know something. He had to have been briefed on Renoviah."

Blake frowned and reached for the folder he'd brought back from the house with him. "Just so happens, I ran across some information that kind of coincides with that line of thought."

"Really?" Caitlin inclined forward to take the folder from him. Her gaze lifted when she opened it and saw what it contained. "Phone records?"

"I had a friend of mine do some checking on Mallory. Nothing stood out to me before, but I ran across it last night and took another look."

Caitlin scanned the handwritten notes that showed to whom the numbers belonged. "Seems like she had Senator Wiley on speed dial."

"It didn't hit me at first. I just figured it was business. But if you look closely, you'll see how it spikes right around Vince's death."

Caitlin closed her eyes and tried to concentrate. Something was bothering her. Something bubbling right under the surface she couldn't quite bring into focus.

"What's wrong?"

She shook her head, still thinking. "Nothing… just that I heard Wiley's name not very long ago and I'm trying to figure out where."

"Was it at a meeting?"

"No. I think it was in conversation." She shrugged. "Oh well, it will come to me. In any event, I'm going to get a meeting with Senator Wiley."

"Really? I don't think that will be as easy as you think." He took a swig of his beer. "He's a candidate for president. You're not going to be able to waltz right into his office and ask him."

"I know. Believe it or not, I have a better plan than that." Caitlin remained quiet as she pondered her idea. "It relies on a little strategic planning, and a lot of luck." Glancing at her phone, she read the email again. "You know there's a big shindig at the Capitol building tomorrow night, right?"

Blake had gone back to looking at the picture she'd given him. He shrugged. "I think I saw something about it in the paper."

"It's kind of an open house with the legislators. You oughta go. Just to see what's up."

"Maybe. I'm not much into black tie affairs." He changed the subject. "So if you get this meeting, what are you going to ask him?"

"I'll set it up under the pretense of doing a nice profile story. I'll keep it light, just feel him out for now." She paused and raised her eyes to meet his. "Sure would be nice to bug his office while I'm there though." She raised her brows hopefully, knowing that whatever strings Blake had pulled to get phone records he could probably pull to get his hands on a simple bugging device.

"It would take a miracle to get a judge to sign something like that for a sitting senator."

Caitlin shrugged. "I wasn't really thinking about going through a judge."

"That would be illegal." Blake took a sip of beer, disregarding the idea as if it were completely out of the question.

"So is covering up a murder," Caitlin quipped.

Blake paused and looked at her over his bottle. "We don't know that for a fact."

"Maybe *you* don't."

"No, Cait. Absolutely not."

Caitlin could tell from his tone it was useless to continue and tried to hide her disappointment. If she did succeed in setting up a meeting with the senator and he divulged anything of interest, it would be her word against his—or more accurately, the senator's word against a supposed rogue reporter with no backing from her employer. Her mind started wandering again.

"You need to be more cautious." Blake's voice brought her back from her reverie.

"About what?"

"Everything." He lifted the bottle to his lips, but never took his eyes off her.

"What's *that* supposed to mean?"

He leaned forward with his elbows on his knees. "This isn't a game, Cait. They're serious and getting desperate."

"I'm not afraid. Are you?" She smiled, trying to lighten his mood. "You don't strike me as a man afraid of anything."

He stared at her with a look so intense it both thrilled and terrified her. "Just one thing scares the shit out of me."

Caitlin tilted her head and eyed him inquisitively, fully expecting him to make a joke.

"*You* getting hurt."

The smile disappeared from Caitlin's face, and she almost blushed at the sincere concern radiating from his eyes. "I appreciate the worry, but—"

"I know. I know," he interrupted her. "You're a big girl."

"Yeah. Something like that." She wanted to change the subject, but he spoke again before she could think of anything to say.

"Don't blow it off, Cait," he said with quiet emphasis. "I'm serious."

The intensity of his voice now matched the look in his eyes, causing Caitlin's heart to twinge—or more accurately, buck. His strong, serious expression, mixed with the forcefulness of his words, held a certain sensuality that threw her off guard. It took all of her willpower, and then some, to resist placing her hand across her chest to calm her throbbing pulse.

Who was this man? A few months ago he was the notoriously elusive Detective Madison. Now he was just Blake, and she was sitting across from him discussing her personal wellbeing.

"I'll be careful." She forced a smile and tried to appear unaffected. "It's nice to know someone has my back."

He stared at her a moment longer and then stood, stretching

his legs. "I'm getting too old for this riding thing."

She stood as well, testing her legs to see if they hurt. "I'm sure I'll feel it tomorrow."

They both sat back down and she handed the folder of phone records to him. "Thanks for the information. I appreciate you sharing it."

"No problem."

"I guess it turned into a pretty productive day after all." Caitlin leaned back against the wall. "And I like your office."

"Me too. Wish I could spend more time here." Blake drained his beer. "I like doing business like this."

Caitlin laughed. "Sitting on a bucket?"

He grinned and nodded. "Sitting on a bucket, drinking a cold beer with good company. Not a bad gig."

Chapter 20

Blake stood in the middle of the cavernous marble-floored room staring at the extravagant gowns and abundant cleavage spilling from them. Pulling at his collar and shifting his weight in discomfort, he lifted a glass of champagne from a tray as a waiter walked by. It was his second glass since arriving at the legislative open house forty-five minutes ago— and he hated champagne. At least the appetizers were better than anything he had ever tasted. That helped prevent the afternoon from being a complete waste.

Sticking a finger in the collar of his shirt again, he tugged at the black bow-tie. *Where is Cait? Wasn't this shindig her idea?* He hated being around politicians and the type of people they attracted more than he hated being around hardened criminals. On second thought, there wasn't a whole lot of difference.

He took a gulp of champagne and looked around the room. He could pick out a member of the political social elite class from a mile away. A big fake smile and a 'trust me' glint in the eye were dead giveaways for someone adept at lying right through their teeth.

Trying to keep from checking his watch again, Blake almost dropped his drink when Caitlin walked through the door on the arm of Harvey Roberts, a well-known Washington lobbyist. He finally remembered to swallow the champagne he had in his mouth as he stared at the couple, then took another sip to cover his surprise.

Sitting his empty glass on the tray of a waiter passing by, he grabbed another drink and wondered why he was so surprised. Caitlin was a good-looking woman. Why had he thought she would arrive alone?

But Harvey Roberts? Really?

He tried to look away, but failed to prevent his gaze from drifting down to the three-inch heels she wore. His eyes narrowed and flickered as he took in the slim ankle, exposed by a slit that ran up the side of her dress, and then the perfectly formed leg that disappeared into the black fabric way too soon.

Blake let out the breath he didn't realize he'd been holding, turned his head, and scanned the room. The gown Caitlin wore was plain and very conservative in comparison to most others in the room. No sequins. No plunging neckline. No bows or ruffles or frills. But even with very little exposed skin, the dress left little to the imagination. It was tight, accentuating every inch of her fit body. And as far as Blake could tell, there wasn't a man in the room who hadn't noticed it.

He inhaled deeply and contemplated her again. She had apparently spared no effort to fit in with this crowd. Her luxurious, blond hair was twisted and curled on top of her head—except for a few curled tendrils hanging loose by her smiling face. As for makeup, she looked like she had just left a cover shoot for Vogue.

Blake found it hard to believe this was the same woman who had relaxed on a bale of hay in his barn drinking a beer yesterday. Today she was pure elegance—a striking contradiction of style and steel. The way she casually mingled and shook hands with members of this pretentious crowd made her appear like an honored member of D.C. aristocracy.

As Caitlin accepted a glass of champagne from a waiter, her gaze lifted and met Blake's from across the room. She turned and said a few words to Harvey before making her way through the crowd toward him. Maybe he imagined that her eyes lit up at the sight of him—or maybe he just hoped they had.

"Glad I found you near the food." Caitlin sidled up to the table and reached for a plate. "I'm starving."

She seemed so distracted by the wide array of hors devours in front of her that Blake was surprised when she spoke again while loading her plate. "By the way, you clean up nice." She shot him a sideways glance full of admiration and approval.

Blake didn't answer at first. He could never quite tell when she was joking. "Thanks. I think."

She looked up into his eyes. Hers appeared to be sparkling. "Seriously? You haven't noticed all the women staring at you?"

He scanned the room and shrugged. "No. I've been staring at the door, waiting for the minute when I can walk back through it." He cleared his throat. "You don't look too bad yourself."

Seeming to be preoccupied with the food, Caitlin ignored the compliment and turned back to the table. "You come alone?"

This time he felt sure she was trying to make a joke so he didn't answer at first. She stopped what she was doing and asked again in a louder voice, as if he hadn't heard. "You have a date?"

"Yeah, she's in the restroom." He didn't mean it as a lie— more like a joke. But her face fell in apparent disappointment.

"Oh. Because I thought I might be able to catch a ride."

"I thought you came with Harvey."

"I did." She jerked her head toward the corner of the room where her supposed date was stroking the arm of a woman in a sleeveless dress. "We're old friends. He called me and asked if I was planning to attend, then suggested we ride together."

Blake examined the man with a look of aversion. "I heard he's quite the womanizer."

"That's putting it mildly." Caitlin popped a stuffed mushroom into her mouth. "I wasn't sure my credentials would get me through the door, so I agreed."

"You don't think he'll take you home?" Blake watched Caitlin shrug.

"Pretty sure he only mentioned riding together *to* the event."

She said the words matter-of-factly, as if it was her fault she hadn't questioned Harvey about whether or not he intended to take her home. "That's his old fling." She continued talking while searching the table of food for anything she'd missed. "I'm beginning to think he just wanted to make her jealous."

Blake shifted his attention to the woman who was laughing and holding onto Harvey's arm, and then returned his attention to Caitlin. "Looks like it worked."

She just raised her eyebrows, kind of frowned, and nodded, while Blake stood there wondering what kind of guy would take someone like Caitlin Sparks to a party with no plans to take her home.

Then again, it shouldn't surprise him when it came to Cait. He'd heard her name mentioned plenty of times at the precinct, even before he had met her. The officers on the evening shift pretty much accepted—and treated her—as "one of the guys," giving and taking jibes and insults. She was good-looking and intelligent, but she was also unassuming and easygoing, treating everyone like a friend—until they gave her a reason to treat them otherwise.

That was Caitlin. Sophisticated. Unpretentious. Tenacious. Audacious.

But as for being one of the guys... He ran his eyes over her quickly and then looked away. *Sorry. With a body like that—no way.*

Caitlin handed her plate to Blake and hurriedly smoothed her dress. "There's the senator. Do I look okay?" She stared up at him with an earnest expression, her eyes so deep and dark they appeared almost black. "I only have one shot at this."

Blake's gaze moved from her eyes to her shiny red lips where it lingered for a moment. He swallowed hard and nodded. "Yeah. You look okay."

Instead of accepting that answer, Caitlin took a step closer, tilted her head back, and stood on her tiptoes, holding onto his arm for balance. "Are you sure? No mascara smeared or anything?"

Between the heels and her tiptoes, she was now almost Blake's height. He looked into her eyes, just inches away from his, and saw why they appeared so dark. They were expertly outlined with brown liner, and her lashes were long and full. She stood there gazing at him with her glossy lips slightly parted as she waited impatiently for an answer.

"You're good to go," is all he said.

"Then it's show time." Caitlin turned and walked toward the politician without a backward glance, a look of determination on her face so steadfast, she seemed completely indifferent to everything going on around her. To Blake, she looked like a racehorse under tight restraint. Yet to an outside observer she probably appeared casual and relaxed.

"Blake Madison?"

Blake turned at the mention of his name and put down the plate Caitlin had handed him.

"Chief, is that you?"

Blake broke into a huge grin and shook the man's hand. "Hey,

Podge, how've you been?"

"Never expected to see *you* at a place like this. You into politics all of a sudden?"

"Something like that." Blake's attention shifted back to Caitlin. In the few seconds that his attention had been drawn away she had somehow made it through the throngs of people surrounding the Senator and already introduced herself.

Seemingly enraptured by whatever she was saying, Wiley placed his hand on her shoulder and then they both laughed as if she had told him a good joke. A moment later, he pulled out a silver holder and took out a card. Blake could not hear the man's voice over the general din of noise, but saw that someone produced a pen. Wiley scribbled something on the card and handed it to Caitlin.

Podge gave Blake a nudge. "Hey, you still with me?"

"Yeah, man. I'm still here."

"You got something going on with that blonde?"

Blake jerked his attention back to Podge. "No. Just trying to make sure she doesn't get in over her head."

"She looks like she's holding her own to me." He laughed. "You her bodyguard or something?"

Blake frowned. "Yeah, right."

"Well, she's a hottie, that's for sure. How well do you know her?"

Well enough to know she's probably doing something she shouldn't be doing. "Pretty well," was all he said.

"Want to introduce me to her?"

Blake stopped with his glass near his lips and cocked his head. Podge was a tall athletically built man with wavy blonde hair who looked like he'd just walked off the beach in Malibu. "I don't think she's your type."

"What's that supposed to mean? I'm human aren't I?"

"You're a dog from what I remember."

A woman came up from behind Podge and grabbed his arm. "Sorry to make you wait, honey. The restroom was full."

"We were just talking about you, weren't we Blake?"

"Yep." Blake knew Podge well enough not to miss a beat. "He was just talking about the most beautiful woman here."

The look of thanks and surprised amusement Podge shot him did not go unnoticed. It wasn't the first time Blake had saved his former teammate's hide, but he'd accomplished it without telling a lie.

The woman smiled and held out her hand, waiting for an introduction.

"Blake, I'd like you to meet by fiancée, Vicki. Vicki, this is an old buddy of mine from the Navy, Blake Madison."

Blake tried to hide the amusement from his own eyes as he heard the introduction. "You haven't changed a bit," he said to Podge as he shook Vicki's hand.

"What do you mean?" Vicki peered up at Podge with a look of confusion, and then at Blake.

"I mean, he's always been good at picking out the good-looking women." Blake tried to cover his mistake. "What have you been up to anyway, brother?"

Podge drew a little closer so no one could overhear. "Just started a new company actually."

"What kind of company?"

"Communications," his fiancée answered for him.

Blake glanced at Podge and he winked. "You got a card? You never know when you're going to need a *communications* service."

Podge reached into his back pocket for a wallet. "Of course." He pulled out a card and handed it to Blake. "It's a highly specialized type of service if you know what I mean."

"I think I know exactly what you mean." Blake nodded. "And it may be just what I'm looking for." He stuck the card in his wallet. "You just made coming to this affair worth my while, brother."

"Glad I could be of help."

"Colt and I have been toying with the idea of starting a side business too."

"Oh, yeah? What kind?"

"Private security." Blake winked. "Highly specialized if you know what I mean."

"Sounds like our businesses might align perfectly." Podge had a beaming smile on his face. "Keep me in mind for sub-contracting work."

"You'll be at the top of the list."

"How's Colt doing anyway? Lost track of him after the hoopla he created by saving Calloway."

Nick "Colt" Colton was a former Navy SEAL they'd both served with—and Blake's best friend. While working for a private security firm overseas, Colt had saved a young senator's life. That man, Jason Calloway, was now running for president.

"He's good. Looking for something gritty to sink his teeth into."

"Yeah. Colt's a hard man to keep down." Podge walked over to the food table and began filling his plate. "So last time I heard anything about you, you were in the cop business."

"Still there." Blake's attention went back to Caitlin, who was now talking to a congressional aide. "Detective work."

"That's a little tame compared to what you're used to, isn't it?"

"In some ways." Blake didn't remove his gaze from Cait. "It's a heck of a lot easier on the body for sure."

"Anytime you're not taking enemy fire it's easier on the body."

"You two aren't going to start telling war stories are you?" Podge's fiancée studied her nails like she'd rather be getting a manicure than hear anything relating to war.

"Honey, you're standing in the presence of one of the bravest freaking fighting SOBs in the history of the military."

It took a while for Blake to catch up to what Podge had said since he was concentrating on trying to overhear the conversation Caitlin was in. "Don't let him pull your leg," Blake said before turning his attention back to Caitlin.

"I'm not pulling your leg, Vicki. This guy right here single-handedly rescued more than a dozen—"

"Not singlehandedly. And not everybody," Blake interrupted, his tone frosty.

"You're not still beating yourself up about that, are you?"

Blake didn't answer, hoping that would bring the conversation to an end.

"Man, you did everything you could. The number of bullet holes you came home with should say something about how hard you tried."

"You got shot?" Vicki now sounded interested, as her attention became drawn to his military background.

"Like I said, honey, this man here is the bravest, most fearless fighting machine you're ever going to meet. And he has seven bullet holes to prove—" Podge's attention drifted to just over Blake's shoulder. "Well, hello. I don't think we've met."

Caitlin stepped forward and held out her hand as Blake cleared his throat, surprised by her sudden appearance. "Caitlin Sparks, this is an old friend of mine, Jimmy Podge, and his fiancée, Vicki."

"Nice to meet you." Caitlin nodded at each. "Just caught the tail end of your conversation." She turned to Blake and shot him an inquiring look.

"Oh, just talking about the old days." Podge laughed. "I'm sure you know all about this guy's record. He's pretty much a legend."

Caitlin barely had time to tilt her head in surprise before Blake grabbed her arm and led her closer to the food table. "Here's your plate. You said you were hungry, right?" He glanced over at Podge. "Great seeing you again, buddy. Keep in touch."

Podge took the hint. "Make sure you keep me in mind if you need anything in communications." He took Vicki's arm and started leading her away.

"Communications?" Caitlin took a step toward Podge. "You're in communications?"

Podge's eyes flitted over to Blake and then went back to Caitlin. "Yes. Just started my own company."

Caitlin began digging through her purse. "Well, I'm a reporter. Do you mind if I give you a call if I ever have a question about the new technology that's available?" She handed him her card.

"No. Not at all." He dug another one of his cards out of his wallet. "Call anytime."

Vicki took Podge's arm and started to lead him away. "Come on, honey."

"Nice to meet you, Caitlin." Podge winked as they turned and walked away.

Caitlin turned back to Blake. "Where's your date? Still in the restroom?"

Blake gave her his best downcast look. "I told her you needed a ride home and she dumped me."

"Oh. Sorry about that. You ready to leave?"

He couldn't tell by her tone if she believed him or not, but she appeared apologetic.

"Ready?" Blake took her by the arm and started guiding her

toward the door. "I was ready an hour and a half ago."

"You probably just got here an hour and a half ago."

"Like I said, I was ready an hour and a half ago."

Blake strode across the lobby, pausing only long enough to hold the door, and then headed for the parking lot. He was a little amazed at how well Caitlin kept up with him in her heels—he could hear her clicking only about two steps behind. When he got to his truck, he unlocked the passenger side door, opened it for her, and waited to help her in.

Caitlin hesitated when the door opened, staring at the distance from the ground to the running board. There was no way she could take that high of a step. "Close your eyes," she finally said.

Blake leaned closer and tilted his head. "Excuse me?"

"Be a gentleman and close your eyes." Caitlin didn't wait to see if he did or not. She wiggled and hoisted her tight dress over her hips so she could take the large step.

"Okay," she said once she was inside and had readjusted her dress. "You can open them now."

Blake shook his head and closed the door behind her. As soon as he was in his own seat and had started the engine, he turned to her. "You know, if you hadn't worn such a tight dress you wouldn't have to do that."

"If I hadn't worn such a tight dress, I wouldn't be having a private lunch with Senator Wiley in his office on Tuesday." She waved the senator's business card under Blake's nose. "I'd be eating alone, like you will be."

"Good one." He glanced over at her before returning his attention to the road. "With your bulldog reputation among politicians, I'm a little surprised he fell for the dress."

"Are you kidding me?" Caitlin put her head back against the

headrest. "His ego is bigger than his brain."

"What do you mean?"

"He thinks he's smarter than I am." She turned her head toward him. "He thinks I'm just a dumb blonde who's captivated and infatuated by his wealth and power."

"He's a senator," Blake said, sounding a bit surprised. "He didn't get there by being stupid."

"I didn't say he was stupid. I said he's so powerful, he's not afraid of anything or anybody. And I plan to use that to my advantage."

"Did you ever think maybe he's acting that way so you'll think he's easily manipulated?"

"So you think *he's* manipulating *me?*" She shook her head and laughed. "No way."

Blake frowned as he shifted gears. "I hope you know what you're doing."

"Don't worry about me. I'm a big girl. Remember?"

"Yeah, yeah. But I told you before, that doesn't stop me from worrying about you."

He didn't give Caitlin time to say anything. "I need to stop at the precinct to pick up a file. It'll only take a minute. You mind?"

Caitlin shook her head. "No. That works. I'll go down and check in with the guys. Do you know if they've arrested anyone in that string of robberies in Glenville?"

"Not my case."

"I know it's not your case." She glanced at him sideways. "My question was, do you know if they've arrested anyone?"

Blake maneuvered the truck into his parking space. "N-o-o." He drew the word out. "Because it's not my case."

Caitlin shook her head and turned her attention to her seatbelt. By the time it unclicked, Blake had opened her door. "You need a hand getting out?" He eyed her skeptically.

"No, I can manage." Caitlin turned so her legs were out of the truck, then rested her feet on the running board. She stood, took a deep breath and jumped, landing expertly on her heels. Straightening back up like an Olympic gymnast, she threw her hands in the air and shot Blake a triumphant smile.

"I'll give you a nine on the landing," he said sarcastically.

"A nine? That was a solid ten, dude."

Blake was already walking toward the building's main door.

"I'll be down chatting with the guys." Caitlin gave him a wave as she headed toward the steps to the basement. Blake paused like he was going to say something as he strode toward the lobby entrance with his keys in his hand, but then just shrugged and kept walking.

Caitlin hurried down the steps, knowing she didn't have much time. Expecting to be able to push through the door, she ran straight into it with a loud *thunk* when it didn't open. It was locked.

"Damn you, Mad Dog," she muttered under her breath as she banged her fist on the door.

Two officers having a conversation nearby stopped talking, and one of them opened the door slightly. "Sorry, ma'am, you have to enter through the main lobby."

Caitlin heard someone else whistle softly under his breath from further away in the room.

"Whoa, guys. It's just Caitlin."

A patrolman with a cup of coffee in his hand walked toward her once they opened the door. "Cait-lin. What the hell happened to you?"

She plopped down in her usual chair. "I'm working undercover today."

"What—as a lady?"

The whole room exploded in laughter.

"I think she had a hot date and got dumped."

"Ha. Ha. Very funny, Sully." Caitlin sat back in the chair. "I just stopped by to see if you guys have anything on the robberies in Glenville yet." She fished around in her purse. "I got... let me see here. I got a pair of Twinkies to the guy who can give me something on the record." She had learned long ago that men were more willing to talk when they had food in their stomachs.

She held the trophy up in the air as one of the men grabbed for it. "Not so fast. Spill it first."

"Scoop!"

Caitlin's head jerked around to the other door, where Detective Madison was standing—as did all of the others in the room.

"You ready?" The sleeves of Blake's crisp white shirt were now rolled up, and he was holding the black tux carelessly by his side. The bow tie hung loose and the top button on his collar was undone.

"Oh, yeah. Sure. If you are." Caitlin slowly lowered her hand as if he wouldn't notice the package she was holding over her head. "I'll meet you at the truck."

Blake closed the door without saying another word.

Damn, Blake. Couldn't you just have called me or blown the horn?

Caitlin stood and smoothed down her dress, pretending nothing was out of the ordinary. She put the Twinkies down on the nearest desk, knowing there would be a free-for-all when she left that might take the attention away from the gossip that was sure to follow. She'd call later about the robberies.

As she headed for the door, she paused and turned back around, shaking her finger at all of them. "I don't want to hear any wisecracks. It's not what you think."

Everyone in the room heard the diesel engine crank to life in the parking lot.

Somebody whispered something under his breath she couldn't quite make out.

"Give me a break, guys." Caitlin opened the door and talked over her shoulder as she was going out the door. "He just gave me a ride."

Somebody snickered. "Or was it the other way around?"

Just then Blake gave the horn two quick blasts. Caitlin bolted through the door, hopped up the basement steps as best she could, and ran across the parking lot to find him in his truck shaking his head. When she reached her side, he got out, opened her door, and obediently turned his back as she lifted her dress and climbed in.

She glanced over at him when he'd settled back into the driver's seat, and saw he was actually smiling.

"What's so freaking funny?"

"You run faster in heels than any chick I've ever seen."

"You did that for kicks, didn't you?"

Blake's smile disappeared, but she could tell it was only because he was making an effort to look serious. "I would never do that."

She shook her head, deciding then and there to give up trying to understand this unpredictable, disconcerting, impenetrable man.

Chapter 21

Caitlin reached for her coffee and took two big swallows, savoring its strength and flavor. The chaos of deadline was long over, and there were only a few things on her schedule for the day. She had a few minutes to enjoy some downtime and glance at today's paper before getting started.

Just as she reached over to pick up the copy that had been tossed by the librarian onto her desk, the phone rang. She almost hoped it would be something that would get her out of the office. After two days of rain, the sun was shining and there didn't appear to be a cloud in the sky. It was too nice outside to spend the day sitting behind a desk.

"I warned you not to burn me."

She recognized Blake's voice, but she didn't have any idea what the words meant or where the anger in them was coming from.

"Burned you? What are you talking about?"

"Don't play dumb with me!"

Caitlin had to move the phone away from her ear, so loudly were the words spoken. Two reporters walking by her desk started laughing, proving they had heard it too. She turned her chair around and talked quietly into the phone.

"You'll have to explain what you're talking about."

"Page five," came the immediate response. "Don't even try to pretend you didn't write it."

Caitlin turned back around, spread the paper on her desk, and flipped to page five. The instant she saw the headline, her heart felt like it had ruptured, then dissolved, in her chest.

Single dad: Police detective gains full custody of children from State Department official.

"I wouldn't write anything like that." Caitlin's voice was almost a whisper as she read the story, detailing the ages of his children and the approximate address of his residence. It was all public record, but not something that had any place in a newspaper, especially considering the dangerous nature of his work.

Her eyes went back up to the byline that read "Staff Report." Turning to her computer, Caitlin started punching in searches frantically. The software the newsroom used tracked every person who made changes to a story and where it originated. But there was no record of the story anywhere.

"I-I-I didn't write it," Caitlin stuttered.

"And I suppose you didn't give that blonde chick from Channel 2 my direct office line either?"

"No. I would never—" Caitlin stopped herself. The fact that he didn't trust her—even more so than the accusation itself—left her speechless. She didn't have the will or the strength to defend herself. "I don't know what else to say."

"Neither do I."

Click.

Caitlin's hands trembled as she closed the paper.

"Something wrong?" Stan stood beside her desk, staring at her with a look of curiosity mixed with smug satisfaction.

Caitlin focused her gaze on him. "Who wrote the Madison story? And why?"

"Why?" He shrugged. "Because we can."

"That doesn't answer my other question." Caitlin could feel her heart start to pound again as she watched the editor's face. He knew something. And he was enjoying not telling her what it was.

He bent over her desk and stabbed his finger at the byline. "See that? It says s-t-a-f-f report."

"What staff? There's no record of it in the system."

"Oh? You checked the system?" Stan smirked. "Darn it, I just did a purge of the system this morning."

Caitlin no longer looked him in the eye. She was staring into space, trying to figure out how deeply all this ran. Who was on her side? Anyone? Or was the whole world part of an effort to stop her? "Today is Tuesday." Her voice was low, but still it shook. "You only purge on Fridays."

"Well, I felt like purging the system today. It gets cluttered up with stories that are better left *alone*."

Caitlin's eyes darted back to his.

"You know what I mean?"

She nodded, her mind numb.

Stan bent down and put both hands, palms down, on her desk. "I don't like the things that are going on around here any-more than you do, but I'm responsible for a wife and three kids." His voice was no longer menacing. He sounded somewhat con-trite. "We need to play along and put this behind us."

He straightened up and took a step back. "You don't look very good. Maybe you should take the rest of the day off. Think about things." He didn't wait for her to answer. "See ya tomorrow."

Caitlin picked up her jacket and her purse and walked me-chanically through the pressroom to exit through the back door.

She had no idea where she was going or what she was going to do. The only person in the world she trusted in this town was now an enemy who would not talk to her. Hell, he'd probably arrest her if he had the chance.

Well, I got my wish. She peered up at the brilliant blue sky and the warm sun shining down. *A day out of the office.* The thought reminded her of something her grandmother used to tell her: "Be careful what you wish for. Sometimes the best outcome comes with the worst consequences."

When the door behind her clicked shut with thundering finality, she paused and watched people driving by, talking on their phones, and going about their business as if it were just another day. Didn't they know her world had just collapsed around her and she had nowhere to turn?

Caitlin walked around the block aimlessly, trying to figure out what to do, and then climbed into her Jeep. She drove with no destination in mind, but somehow ended up pulling into the parking lot where Vince had been found. Turning off the engine, she stared straight ahead with both of her hands gripping the wheel.

Despite the birds singing in the trees above her and the sunlight streaming through the tree branches, Caitlin saw only darkness and the stabbing blindness caused by the flashing lights of police cars. She blinked, trying to clear her mind of the visions, and then realized what had brought her here.

This is where it had all began. This is where her world had begun to unravel and had never been the same. The life she had imagined was never going to be, and the man she had intended to marry was never coming back. A choking sob shook her body as she realized she was no closer to discovering the truth than she had been six months ago—she actually felt even further away, with even more questions and fewer answers than before.

Would she ever know what happened and why? She put her forehead down on the steering wheel, a feeling of despair and guilt sweeping over her. Not only did she feel responsible for Vince's death, she had been unable to avenge it by finding his killers. And now her chances of doing so had been reduced even more. Without Blake as an ally, she had no place to turn. The whole world had turned against her.

Despite her mournful thoughts, Caitlin shed no tears. Maybe she was too angry to have any. Maybe too hurt. Or maybe she didn't have any left. She was too numb to think. Too numb to care.

Caitlin didn't know how long she sat there, but the shadows had lengthened considerably by the time her stomach started growling, reminding her she hadn't eaten all day. She gave one last look around at a scene she never wanted to see again, started the engine, and pulled out of the parking lot.

Now where? She didn't want to go anywhere she might be recognized. She didn't want to talk to anybody, but she didn't want to go home. After driving around for another hour, she noticed a small bar along the side of the road and pulled in. It was not the kind of bar she would normally consider, let alone enter. Rough and rickety, it appeared to have a large clientele of Harley riders, judging by the number of shiny motorcycles parked in a tight line out front.

Maybe not what I would consider a perfect place, but just what I need.

Without hesitation, Caitlin walked up the steps, opened the door, and entered the smoky interior. She paused to get her eyes accustomed to the dim light, then zigzagged through the tables in the dining room to the bar. After ordering a double gin and tonic from the tattooed bartender, she took the drink to a small table in the corner. The first swallow made her grimace. Perfect. Just the way she liked it.

But how pathetic was this? She was once an up-and-coming reporter, well respected and admired in her community. Now she was sitting in a dive, drowning her sorrows in a drink. This was so unlike her—or at least so unlike the person she used to be. Nothing in her life was the same anymore.

After a few more sips to calm her nerves, Caitlin sat back and surveyed her surroundings. The bar smelled mostly of sweat and smoke, with a little grease and grime mixed in. And despite the low level of light, all four were clearly visible on the surface of the floor and walls. The other occupants of the bar didn't seem to notice—or at least didn't seem to care. There were a dozen or so bikers and a couple of guys dressed like mechanics eating sandwiches. Hungry as she was, she couldn't quite bring herself to order food. She continued nursing her drink and watched a couple more patrons come in, including an older man with bushy gray hair.

"You ready for another one?"

Caitlin raised her head at the sound of the bartender's voice right beside her, and realized she was slouching over her drink like an old bar fly. It was time to leave. "No. I'm getting ready to go. Thanks."

The darkness outside was a little disorienting as Caitlin made her way back to her Jeep. The only illumination came from a Budweiser sign in the window, and that produced little more than a low glow with very little reach. As she inched her way down the steps, she tried to decide her next move. There seemed to be no other alternative but to go home and crawl into bed.

Caitlin felt her stomach rumble again as she walked, but decided she no longer had the energy or desire to eat. The strong drink had calmed her nerves a little, but it certainly hadn't helped her feel any better. In fact, when she was halfway across the parking lot, her legs grew weak and wobbly. She kept walking, assuming it was just the alcohol going to her head, but then her whole body began to tremble.

Reaching her Jeep at the edge of the parking lot, Caitlin paused with her hand on the hood, trying to breathe deeply and gain control of her emotions before climbing inside. Overwhelmed with the past few months of torment, she failed. The feelings of emptiness, pain, and betrayal that she'd been fighting all day were suddenly too overwhelming to stop. They washed over her in an agonizing wave of anguish and suffering that left her shaky and unsteady. She moved one hand up to her palpating heart as if that would halt its rapid throb.

She had never felt so helpless, so alone, or so weak. They had beaten her. She had to admit it here and now. She had no one to turn to and nowhere to turn. She could take no more.

"I'm so sorry, Vince," she whispered into the night.

The admission that she would never find Vince's killer left her reeling, but she knew it went deeper than that. The knowledge that she'd lost Blake Madison's trust was a sucker punch that knocked the very breath from her lungs. She could not fully understand the emotions coursing through her—but she had a strong sense she had lost something special, something she hadn't even realized she'd possessed. Before she knew what was happening, she was bending over with her hands on her knees, vomiting into the bushes.

Struggling to catch her breath, she swiped her mouth with her jacket sleeve as she continued to sob and heave alone in the darkness.

"Hey. You okay?" The voice from out the darkness was strong and loud, but the next words were almost a whisper. "Don't turn around or act like you know me."

Caitlin nodded. She reached behind her to feel the hood of her Jeep again, and took a step back so she could steady herself. The sound of Blake's voice affected her deeply.

"Here." She heard rustling, as if he was getting something out of his pocket. "Here's a napkin." She didn't turn around. Just held out her hand and took it.

"Sorry I had to make that call." His voice was barely a whisper.

Caitlin closed her eyes tightly and swallowed hard. *Oh, dear God, he believes me.*

"I'm okay." Caitlin spoke as loudly as she could, while wiping her mouth with the napkin. "Thanks, mister."

"I'm taking the kids to my sister's in North Carolina. Lay low a few days."

Caitlin nodded once to show she understood, then opened the door to her Jeep and climbed inside. She forced herself not to watch him walk away, not that she could make him out in the dark anyway. Instead of starting the engine, she put her head on the steering wheel and took a few deep breaths.

The sound of a knuckle banging on her window startled her. Looking up, she saw two young men staring at her worriedly. *You okay?* One of them mouthed through the glass.

Caitlin put down the window.

"You okay?" the man asked again. "That old guy told us to check on you."

Caitlin turned her head and saw a vehicle pulling out of the parking lot. It wasn't a pickup truck, but she had no doubt it was Blake.

"I'm okay." She flashed them a thumbs up sign. "I just drank on an empty stomach."

"You sure you're okay to drive?"

Caitlin nodded. "I'm fine. I only had one." She glanced toward the hedgerow. *And it's all out there.*

How embarrassing that Blake had watched her puking her guts out after one drink. But she knew he understood it wasn't the alcohol that had made her physically sick. She could tell that from the tone of his voice.

Caitlin started her Jeep and waved at the two men. "Thanks for your concern, guys."

As she put her Jeep in reverse and turned to look over her shoulder, she noticed the napkin Blake had given her. There was something written on it. Putting her Jeep back in park, she switched on the dome light and opened the flimsy paper. The writing was uneven and scrawling, but was easy to read. *They're desperate. Watch your six.*

Even though the words were a warning, the fact that they came from Blake somehow made her feel better. The use of military slang for *watch your back*, reminded her she was dealing with a veteran who was not unfamiliar with defending himself and others. She found that strangely reassuring.

She knew he must be worried about her meeting with the Senator in two days. Just the thought of that important occasion made her sober up. She needed to pull herself together, concentrate on the task at hand, and put the past behind her.

As she drove away, Caitlin wondered how Blake had known she was here. Most of the day was now a blur, clouded by pain and misery. Had he followed her around all day to make sure she was okay? His sudden appearance taught her a lesson about staying alert and being aware of her surroundings. The risk was high and danger lurked everywhere.

She needed to learn how to play this high-stakes game of deceit.

Chapter 22

Caitlin was in the middle of an editorial meeting a few days later when she received a text from Mad Dog. As soon as the meeting concluded, she went outside and made the call.

"Hey. You're back?"

"Yeah. You hanging in there?"

"So far."

"You near anyone right now?"

Caitlin was standing in the alley outside the paper's loading dock. "No. I'm alone."

"You know where that little coffee shop in Grantville is?"

"Grantville? Is that even a town?"

"Well, it's a crossroads with a coffee shop. You know where it is?"

"I think so."

"Meet me there around four. We can figure out our next step."

"Okay."

"And Cait?"

"Yeah?"

"Make sure you're not being followed."

Caitlin wanted to ask him why he would say that, but the call ended.

Blake sat in a corner booth wearing a ball cap and tee shirt.

"Hey." Caitlin put her computer on the table and sat down. "How was your *vacation?*"

Blake was staring out the window and watching the shop's entrance as if searching for someone. "Great. Lots of fun." He waved for the waitress to bring Caitlin a cup of coffee. "Glad to be back though."

Caitlin noticed that his gaze never stopped moving. Even though he appeared relaxed, with one arm propped on the back of the booth, his head was on a swivel, his eyes in constant motion.

"You're sure you weren't followed, right?"

"Yes. No one was coming to this Podunk town."

His eyes went back to the window. "How did you make out with the Senator?"

"I thought you might ask me that." Caitlin opened her computer and searched for the file with her notes. "He was quite amiable, but it was more just talking points than anything substantive." She continued clicking through folders until she found the right file. "He's definitely looking forward to being the next president. Almost like it's a done deal."

Blake took a swig of his coffee as a waitress poured some for Caitlin. "Hate to break it to him, but he's got some tough competition with Calloway." He waited for the waitress to leave. "Did you talk about anything specific to the Kessler Affair?"

"I tried." Caitlin paged through her notes. "He called it a tragedy, a terrible misfortune that, quote, tore his heart out, unquote."

"Same quotes he's been saying for a year." Blake sounded

disgusted. "I believe the official statement from his office read: 'something went wrong,' so the hostage and two former special ops members were lost."

Caitlin nodded. "I asked him specifically about the rescue attempt, and he said..." She finally found the right page. "He said, quote, those who were involved knew the extreme danger of the mission, unquote."

She raised her gaze and saw that Blake's jaw was set and his eyes burned with raw emotion. He slowly opened his hand, which had curled into a fist, and took a deep breath, noticeably trying to calm himself.

"I wonder if he thinks they knew they were going to be left to fend for themselves for thirteen hours with no support."

"I tried to touch on that."

He raised his eyebrows. "And?"

"He said that in his communications with the State Department things were very chaotic because they didn't anticipate the rescue attempt." She looked up at him. "That confused me, since I would think they would be the ones orchestrating the release of an American citizen."

Blake sat back and crossed his arms, his eyes on the distant wall. "They never anticipated a rescue attempt because the rescue team was given a stand-down order."

"There was never a stand-down order in the testimony I've seen—at least not worded as such." Caitlin blew away the steam coming off her coffee. "What I've inferred from the State Department is that they ordered the rescue immediately. Yet the Senator seemed to confirm your theory."

"It's not a theory."

Caitlin raised her gaze at the tone of his voice.

"I have sources close to the case."

"Oh. Okay." She leaned back and thought about what he'd said. "So these guys hear a hostage release has gone wrong and that State Department employees are in trouble. They ignore orders not to respond, most likely thinking it's just bureaucracy that will work itself out at some point. They probably decided it would be better to get a jump on the bad guys and get into the fight than wait around until things really went to hell."

"Something like that."

Caitlin squinted at him again.

"I mean, from what I've heard."

"So either the State Department didn't think the private contractor guys would go to the extent they did to make the rescue a success..."

Blake's hand tightened around his mug and his eyes were focused in the distance. "Or they didn't give a damn."

"As usual, I've got more questions than answers." Caitlin picked up her coffee cup. "At least I've broken the ice so getting another meeting with him shouldn't be difficult."

Blake seemed preoccupied and pulled out his phone. "Damn. This is almost dead and I'm expecting something important. Can I check my email real quick?"

"Sure." Caitlin turned her computer toward him. "I'm going to the ladies' room. Be right back."

When she got back to the table, her laptop was closed and Blake was staring out the window.

"You okay?"

He looked over at her with a distant stare. "Yeah. Why?"

"I don't know. I guess you seem tired."

"I haven't gotten much sleep."

Caitlin gave him a sympathetic smile while glancing around the table. Even though he had been trying to quit smoking ever since she had known him, there was usually a pack of cigarettes within reach—as if it calmed him to know they were there. Today he seemed kind of irritable, distracted. "No cigarettes?"

He turned his head toward her. "Haven't had one for two weeks."

Maybe that explains it. He seems so detached. So distant.

But when he cleared his throat nervously, she knew it was something more than that.

"Are you sure you want to move ahead with this?"

"What are you talking about?"

His blue eyes blazed with intensity as he leaned forward. "They aren't playing games."

"Thanks for the newsflash." Caitlin bristled at the thought he would think she was going to quit searching for the truth. "Neither am I."

He studied her for a few long moments, then pulled his wallet out and stood to leave.

"I'll get it." Caitlin stood too.

"Okay. Thanks." He headed toward the door, seeming to be completely preoccupied, but he abruptly turned back toward her. "Stay out of trouble, Scoop. Okay?"

And then he was gone.

Caitlin got out of bed the next morning with a feeling she couldn't quite ground in thought. No matter how hard she tried, it remained just below the surface and beyond her reach. Something wasn't right.

Trying to stay positive as she got ready for work, she focused her thoughts on the Kessler Affair. She'd been waiting for so long for something decisive on it. Hoping for it. Counting on it. Maybe today would be that day.

She laughed at the thought that she would go to work and suddenly have a big break in the case, but at least the thought brought some brightness to her dismal mood. By the time she left for the short ride to the office, she was feeling a little better. And when deadline passed without a hitch, she had pretty much shaken off the shadow of discontent and was almost her normal self.

Following her habit of pulling an early-run copy off the conveyor belt, she stopped to talk to a pressman before heading back to the newsroom. She heard a commotion as she rounded the corner, and then noticed it was coming from her corner cubical. Three men wearing FBI jackets stood at her desk, intent on examining her computer.

"Can I help you guys with something?"

One of the agents turned around. "Are you Caitlin Sparks?"

"Yes."

"Is this your personal computer?"

Her attention shifted to the laptop computer he now held. "Yes."

She saw him nod to someone behind her.

"Can you put your hands behind your back, please?"

"What are you—?"

Someone from behind her grabbed her hands and twisted them forcefully behind her back. Before she could even react, she heard the snap of handcuffs closing on her wrists.

"What is this about?" She looked up at the man who held her by the arm.

"We found classified documents hidden on your computer, Miss Sparks."

"Classified? From where?"

"The State Department."

Caitlin felt her knees go weak. "I don't know what you're

talking about." She began to struggle, knowing she had been set up for a fall—a big and public fall. "Did you ever hear of the Fourth Amendment? What gave you the right to search my computer?"

"You have something to hide?"

"No, I don't have anything to hide." She tried to keep her voice from shaking. "But you don't have the right to search a private computer without cause or a warrant."

"We received a tip that you had classified documents. That's a federal offense, miss. A major federal offense."

"You can't search someone's computer based on a *tip*." Caitlin's voice grew louder as they began to lead her outside. "Where's your search warrant?"

No one answered. Caitlin realized they didn't have to answer—let alone produce a warrant—in this new, lawless government. What was she going to do about it? *They* had the power. She had nothing.

"Watch your head," one of the agents said after leading her outside and pushing her into an unmarked vehicle.

Caitlin put her head back once inside and closed her eyes, trying to figure out how classified documents ended up on her computer, if indeed they were even there. But then her mind drifted back to the preceding day. Blake hadn't seemed himself. And he had used her computer. Her thoughts drifted back to their conversation. Had he been asking her to stop for a reason? Giving her a chance to prevent this? Or was it all just a coincidence?

Her head went down to her knees and she choked on the bile rising in her throat. All of the desperation and despair she had been through with Vince's death was nothing compared to this. They'd finally gotten to Blake. She knew he had been on her side, but they must have pressured him with something—maybe threatened his kids. Yes, that was it. They'd somehow tracked him down in North Carolina and threatened his kids.

Blake knew the State's Department power. Their reach. He wouldn't put the kids' lives in jeopardy. She couldn't blame him for protecting them, yet that didn't lessen the pain—or the feeling that a long, serrated knife had just been plunged into her back.

Caitlin choked and swallowed, trying to control the emotions and thoughts racing through her head.

One of the agents banged on the window. "You okay?"

She didn't even bother to raise her head.

Chapter 23

Blake poured a fresh cup of coffee and sighed as he surveyed his desk. The stack of unopened mail was leaning precariously after almost a week away. Sitting down with a sigh, he grabbed his letter opener and began slicing through the paper with jabs of silent frustration. *Damn junk mail.*

His mind went back to the meeting with Caitlin at the coffee shop. He had failed to convey to her that his concern had gotten to the point where he thought it best for them to call it quits. Whoever—whatever—they were fighting was too powerful. They needed to turn this over to someone with more influence and more assets.

The only question was who? Who in this town could be trusted to find justice? The fact that Blake didn't have an answer for that was the only thing that had stopped him from pulling the plug on the investigation. He knew Caitlin would be devastated—not to mention angry—if he'd insisted they completely stop.

Still deep in thought, he continued tossing envelopes without even taking the time to open some of them, but he stopped his hand in mid-throw when he noticed a hand-addressed envelope with no stamp.

Blake examined the envelope addressed in crude, block letters. He tore it open and found it contained just one sheet of paper and one sentence. It read:

STOP WHAT YOU'RE DOING OR SPARKS WILL ~~FLY~~ *DIE*.

Blake grabbed his keys and ran for his truck. *Dammit, Cait. What have we unleashed?*

Caitlin sat in a holding cell trying to keep from bursting into tears. It wasn't fear that now had her in its grasp—it was humiliation and frustration. Everyone who questioned her or had any contact with her treated her like a criminal. She knew she needed a lawyer, but who could she call? She didn't know a single soul who wasn't part of this huge web of deceit. If Blake could succumb to this vast tangle of treachery, she knew anyone could.

Caitlin's stomach rumbled, making her realize she hadn't eaten a full meal for almost twenty-four hours. When they'd brought her something to eat last night, she'd refused it, and this morning, she'd only eaten a couple of bites of fruit—the only thing she could actually distinguish as being real food. The thought of eating another meal in this place almost brought tears with it, but she forced them down. What good would crying do? When—if—she ever got out of here, she wasn't going to have a job, so she might as well start thinking about what she was going to do.

Just for kicks, she tried to imagine the headline in today's paper and who had written it. No doubt there would be jubilation by Stan and Fred, and all of the others who would be glad to be free of the troublemaker in their midst.

Drawing her legs onto the bench, she hugged them and rested her forehead on her knees. A huge sigh—almost a sob—escaped her as she pondered her options.

"You ready to go home or do you want to hang around here?"

Caitlin's head jerked up at the sound of the voice, the tone of which she would never forget.

Blake stood gazing at her with a grim smile—and a look so full of concern it would have successfully disarmed her fear and anger on any other day. But Caitlin was not going to succumb that easily today. Her defenses had risen to a new level. She shifted her gaze to the man beside him, a handsome, distinguished man wearing an expensive suit.

"This is a friend of mine, Walter Snow. He's an attorney who's agreed to take your case. You're being released into his custody."

Caitlin swallowed but said nothing. For one thing, she wasn't absolutely convinced she wasn't hallucinating from lack of food. For another thing, she wasn't sure who she could trust anymore. She studied Blake with half-closed eyes, trying to figure out why he was here.

"You okay?" He took a step closer and talked through the bars in a low, serious tone. "You should have called me. It took me forever to track you down."

Caitlin fought the urge to reach out for the solid strength of his arm. Instead she succumbed to the pain and mistrust that consumed her and confronted him. "You used my computer yesterday."

Blake's head jerked back as if she had physically assaulted him. She watched his eyes turn from pure surprise to disappointment, then anger "You think *I* did this?" He choked the words out.

"Miss Sparks, if I may," the attorney interrupted, taking a step forward. "I've known Blake for more than fifteen years, and he wouldn't have the slightest idea how to do something like this. The file was deep in your hard drive, not just a saved file."

"Why would it be deep in my hard drive?"

He cleared his throat. "They are saying you wanted to hide it."

Caitlin remained silent as she allowed what he'd said to sink in to her weary mind. Then her gaze drifted over to Blake, who stared absently over her shoulder with a stone-cold look on his face. His eyes were an icy gray, a reflecting pool of intense gloom and disappointment.

She returned her attention to the attorney and examined him guardedly. "Then how would *I* know how to do it?"

"That's something we will have to ask when the time comes." He sounded composed and at ease, as if he handled this type of problem all of the time.

"If I didn't do it, and *he* didn't do it, who did?" Caitlin failed to keep an accusing and skeptical tone from her voice. When she glanced at Blake again she noticed a flicker of anger just beneath the surface. There was still a lethal calmness in his eyes, but he had failed to hide that slight but undeniable spark of emotion.

The attorney shrugged. "Does anyone else have access to your computer?"

"No." She answered, and crossed her arms defiantly.

"Have you had your laptop to a repair shop lately?"

Caitlin thought back. "Two weeks ago. It had a virus." She felt the blood drain from her face as her gaze drifted over to Blake. His expression was rugged and somber, but a raw hurt glittered in his dark, unresponsive eyes. She put one hand to her head and squeezed her temples. "I'm sorry. I can't believe this is happening."

Mr. Snow opened his briefcase. "Here's some paperwork. You may as well start reading it over. It may be a little while until they get to you."

Blake glanced at his watch "I have a hearing." He sounded distant and cold as he nodded at Walter. "Thanks again, buddy."

He didn't acknowledge Caitlin as he turned away, and before she could tell him thanks or ask when she'd see him again, he was gone.

A few hours later, Caitlin sat in an uncomfortable wooden chair at a large table in a stark, unfriendly room. She heard the door open and close behind her, but didn't turn around.

"Miss Sparks." She recognized the voice of Walter Snow as he walked into the room. "How are you doing?"

"Great." She still didn't bother to turn her head or look in his direction.

He laid his briefcase on the table, pulled out the chair opposite her, and took a seat. "You understand these are serious charges, right?"

Caitlin shrugged. "I would think if the government is going to trump up false charges, they would probably go ahead and make them serious. So to answer your question—yes."

He sighed heavily and opened his briefcase. "Well trumped up or not, they did a pretty good job of documenting things."

Caitlin's gaze finally met his. "What do you mean?"

"They have phone records verifying that you talked to someone from the State Department, as well as pictures of you meeting with her."

Caitlin's eyes widened. "Mary?"

"I believe that's the name." He scanned the paper, and then looked up at her over the rim of his glasses. "Yes, Mary Barto."

"Did they tell you she's dead?"

"Yes—only after I told them I wished to speak with her."

"Did they tell you the circumstances?"

"No. But they insinuated—quite strongly—that you were not above suspicion in her death."

Caitlin rested her head on her arms and rolled it back and forth, remembering Blake saying someone had witnessed a black SUV-type vehicle leaving the scene. No doubt, if pressed, they would come up with someone who could identify it as a Jeep. "Mary's supervisor ordered her to meet with me, took pictures, and now wants to implicate *me* in her murder?"

"They never said murder exactly," Walter corrected.

Caitlin raised her head. "Who is her direct supervisor anyway?"

"You don't know?" Walter never even blinked.

"I can guess."

"Well if your guess is Mallory Jarrett, then you got it right." He had pulled a tablet out of his briefcase and was scribbling notes as he talked.

Caitlin squeezed the bridge of her nose with one hand and then returned her gaze to Walter. She cleared her throat and, as casually as she could manage, asked, "Have you talked to Detective Madison?"

He kept writing. "Not since this afternoon." He stopped then and peeked up over the top of his glasses again. "Why?"

Caitlin looked at her hands on the table and then away. "I was just wondering."

He put his pen down and leaned forward. "It's none of my business what you think of Blake Madison, but I can tell you one thing. He's the most trustworthy, honorable, reliable man you'll ever meet."

His tone made it clear Caitlin was getting a scolding.

"So you think I owe him an apology." She said it as a statement, not a question.

"No, I don't think so." He picked up his expensive-looking pen and began writing again. "I *know* so."

Caitlin listened to the clock on the wall behind her tick away the seconds and considered her new attorney as he continued to fill out paperwork. His hair was silver, but still thick and plentiful. It was hard to guess how old he was because his face showed little signs of age, except for the lines of fatigue that appeared around his eyes. He appeared kind, fatherly and compassionate—not her usual impression of a lawyer.

"You've known Blake a long time?"

Walt slid a piece of paper over to her and laid a pen beside it. "Sign here." Then he sat back in his chair. "Yes, I've known him a long time."

Caitlin scribbled her name on the paper. "I hope he didn't call a favor in just for me. I mean I hope you'll let me pay you."

He laughed. "Nothing personal, but I don't think you can afford me on a reporter's salary."

Caitlin looked down. "Oh."

"To tell you the truth, I doubt Blake can afford me either. But he saved my life a long time ago." His eyes grew moist and took on a far-away look as if seeing visions from the past.

Caitlin wasn't sure if he meant that statement literally or figuratively, but his next words told her it was the former.

"I wouldn't be alive if not for him. I've owed him a debt for a long time." Walt stood and scooped up the papers, seeming to be embarrassed that he had said too much. "Well, that should be everything. You sit tight and someone should be in soon to get you out of here."

Caitlin shook his hand. "I appreciate your willingness to help me. Thanks so much."

"No. Thank *you* for giving me the opportunity to do something for Blake. All these years and he's never let me help him with so much as a ride to work."

His comment piqued Caitlin's interest. "Was Blake in the military when he saved you?"

Walter paused at the door. "He probably was, but it had nothing to do with military duty." He turned back to face her. "I guess I've made you curious now."

"Yes." Caitlin didn't know what else to say.

Walter walked back into the room, to the far window. He stood with his hands in his pockets, staring out for a long time before he spoke. "There was a workplace shooting in my office building about fifteen years ago. They tried to keep it quiet so it barely made the news."

He glanced over his shoulder at her and then shifted his attention back to the window. "Some lunatic was angry about losing a case. He came in and shot at the receptionist, but the bullet went through the wall and hit me."

Caitlin closed her eyes as she pictured the scene.

"I didn't know Blake at the time, but he was meeting with another attorney down the hall. I found out later he gathered people from other offices and herded them out a back door to safety."

Walter took a deep breath and let it out slowly. Caitlin could tell the memories still affected him today.

"All I heard was yelling, and gunfire moving from office to office on the other side of the hall. I was in so much pain I couldn't move. I just lay there and waited for it to be over. But all of a sudden someone was standing over me saying, 'Are you hit?'"

Caitlin imagined the scene. Imagined Blake going back *into* the office seeking other victims even while the gunman was still a threat.

"I told him to run. That I couldn't move. I could hear the shots getting closer."

Caitlin could tell by the tone of Walter's voice that he was seeing the scene as he described it. Her heart raced at the thought of the fear and terror of the moment.

"Well, he didn't listen. He picked me up and threw me over his shoulder. There were shots flying everywhere. How he got me out of there, I have no idea. I don't remember anything after that."

His eyes went back to her. "So, that's how it happened. He didn't know me from Adam, but he risked his life to save mine. That's the kind of man he is."

He walked back toward Caitlin. "I've done pretty well for myself over the years. I've told him over and over, anything he needs or wants, it's his."

"But he hasn't taken you up on it—until now."

"That's right. I know he had to jump through hoops to get that family house he can barely afford. Went through a nasty divorce. Sued to get full custody of the kids." Walt shook his head and started for the door again. "Never asked me for a minute of my time." He paused with his hand on the doorknob and turned back Caitlin. "So if there's a silver lining to this charge, it's that I get to do something for Blake."

He didn't wait for her to answer—seemed eager to get out of the room—because the next thing Caitlin heard was the door clicking shut.

Caitlin threw a tee shirt over her head after a twenty-minute shower and considered crawling straight into bed. She had never felt more physically, emotionally and mentally exhausted in her life. She could barely will her limbs to move or her brain to function.

Instead, she headed toward the kitchen and eyed her phone lying on the table. She had already delayed making the call by picking out her clothes for the morning. She knew the newspaper staff would not be expecting her to show up. They would think she was either still in jail or too embarrassed to show her face. But she wasn't going down without a fight. She was going to walk through that door like it was any other day, dressed to the hilt. She was going to make them look her in the eyes and fire her, if that's what they were going to do. And then she was going to walk out of there with her head held high, looking like a million bucks.

After that… Well, after that was still a bit unclear. She'd worry about that tomorrow.

Caitlin's attention went back to the phone, and the deed that was yet undone. It was after five, but there was a good chance Blake would be at work. He rarely left early and often stayed long after the regular day shift had gone.

She paced beside the kitchen table, biting a fingernail as she tried to figure out what to do. Should she call and apologize? He'd seemed so sincere. And without Walt's help, she'd still be sitting in jail. Caitlin picked up the private phone and then put it back down. Judging from the look on his face when he left, Blake might not answer if he knew who it was on the other end. She picked up her regular phone and called through the precinct instead.

"Detective Madison, please."

"One minute."

She heard the phone ring in his office and found herself breathing a sigh of relief when no one answered. Suddenly it stopped ringing.

"Madison here."

Caitlin almost lost her nerve at the sound of his voice.

"Hello?" He sounded impatient, like he was getting ready to hang up.

"Hey, um, it's me."

Silence.

"I just, ah, wanted to thank you for Walt, and let you know I'm home."

"Okay."

Caitlin couldn't see his expression, but she didn't need to. She could tell what he was thinking by the way he uttered that single word. His wariness and disappointment were clearly articulated. He wasn't going to add, "It's good to hear from you," or "Glad you're okay." Seconds ticked by. The apology she had rehearsed in her mind died on her lips. "Okay... well... I'll let you—"

"I need to talk to you." The tone he used sounded like an officer giving an order to a subordinate, but at least she would be able to see him face to face and apologize.

"When?"

"Mickey's at six tomorrow."

"Okay."

Click.

Chapter 24

Blake looked at his watch and decided he needed some air. He preferred the kind with nicotine in it, but he hadn't had a cigarette for three weeks and the smoke in the bar was killing him.

He glanced at his watch again as he stepped outside. She wasn't late yet, but Caitlin usually showed up ten minutes early. Maybe it was because of the circumstances of their last meeting—or the warning note he'd received—that was making him nervous. He knew the written message he'd received had been a warning, and the arrest had been a way to prove they meant business. He took it seriously. He wasn't sure she did.

As soon as he stepped outside, Blake heard the familiar sound of sirens. At first he didn't think twice about it, but as the minutes ticked by a shadow of doubt and concern started inching its way up his spine. He opened the door to his truck and turned on the scanner. Units were still being dispatched to an accident about three miles away. *Okay. She's probably stuck in traffic.*

But the warning voice in his head didn't stop—and neither did the sirens. They made him jump into the truck, put it in drive, and head toward the scene.

The road was closed, but with his blue lights flashing he was waved through by the fire policeman. Maneuvering his truck to the side of the macadam to avoid all the stopped cars, Blake was able to make it to within fifty yards of the crash. Emergency vehicles blocked the road from that point, but up ahead he could see a vehicle leaning on the guardrail, totally engulfed in flames. Black smoke still billowed through the smashed windows as firemen worked to connect hoses to a pumper that had just arrived.

Blake parked his truck, put on his four-ways, and started walking toward the fiery crash. Rigid with apprehension, he focused all his attention on the scene that lay before him. As much as he longed for a different conclusion, the vehicle appeared to be black—and was shaped like a Jeep.

His heart did a somersault and then thumped even faster as his gaze shifted to the first responders. Those who weren't directly involved in putting out the flames stood in small, solemn groups with their backs to the scene. Even the firemen with the hoses, didn't seem to be attacking the fire as if it were a rescue. They were more intent on keeping the flames from spreading to nearby trees. His attention turned to the ambulance sitting by the side of the road. The back door was open, and a medic sat inside staring idly at his cell phone.

A new and unexpected sense of urgency consumed now, causing a sense of dread that left him feeling sweaty and nauseous and weak. He stopped, put his hands on his knees and took a couple of deep breaths to calm his pulse and prepare himself for what he might find.

As he straightened back up, Blake noticed one of the police officers walking hurriedly in his direction. Hoping to avoid a confrontation, he continued to walk toward the vehicle, his eyes focused on the wreckage, but a few steps later, the officer caught him by the arm. "Sir, you can't go any closer."

Blake flashed his badge. "I think I know the driver." He cleared his throat. "What happened?"

By now Blake was close enough to see that a body remained in the burning vehicle. As accustomed as he was to death, this was a shock. Vivid images flashed through his head—images of a rosy-cheeked woman laughing with his kids, followed by the image of the weary, disheveled woman from yesterday who had eyed him accusingly. He tried to remember their last conversation. Had he been friendly? Or angry? And then he stopped dead in his tracks.

When she called him yesterday, it had been on his office phone—not the private cell. Was that phone bugged? Was it his fault they knew she'd be heading this way at this time?

"Detective Madison, you don't have any jurisdiction here. I'm going to have to ask you to leave." The policeman's voice jolted Blake back to the reality before him. "But maybe you can be of help if you have any contact info for next of kin."

Blake's eyes went back to the vehicle. He'd never heard Cait talk about family. He had no idea who to contact. He shook his head and tried to think coherently. "What happened here? I mean, it's a perfectly straight road. What could have happened?"

Even as he was talking, he saw the large dent on the driver's side door. Something had pushed the Jeep into the guardrail. Something big and heavy.

"We think she was texting or something."

The thought was so ludicrous it made Blake even angrier. He peered back at the cop, trying to decide if he had come up with that theory himself or been fed it by someone higher up. Caitlin barely texted at all. And she was certainly too responsible to do it while driving. He tried to control his voice because every nerve in his body was quivering with rage and remorse.

"Geezuz," Blake said. "Did you get her phone yet to check? Maybe there's an ICE contact." He hoped Cait had an *In Case of Emergency* contact on her phone, because other than her employer, he had no idea who to call.

"Not yet. Coroner is running late, and no one wants to disturb the body."

Blake's gaze drifted again to the Jeep, and once more he had to suppress the urge to gag. He'd been in war zones and thought he'd seen the worst there was to see—but this was shocking. Revolting. Agonizing. Paralyzing. He stared silently at the wreckage, and then turned to his pickup. He didn't look back. He couldn't.

Just as he was opening the door to his truck, his phone vibrated in his back pocket. Still shaking, he pulled it out and answered without checking to see who it was as he slumped onto the seat. "Madison."

"Hey. Sorry I'm late."

Blake pulled the phone away from the roaring din in his ear and stared with disbelief at the screen. He hadn't realized it was the private phone. Only one person knew the number. And that one person was speaking.

"Hello? You there?"

"Cait? Is that *you*?" He couldn't believe what he was hearing.

"Who else would it be?"

"Where are you?"

"Geez. I'm not deaf. You don't have to yell."

Blake took a deep breath and repeated his words more calmly. "Where are you?"

"I'm at a friend's house. Her battery died and she had to go pick something up, so I told her to take my Jeep. It was out that way—maybe I should have just ridden along."

Blake's mind was racing a mile a minute. Since he didn't speak, she further explained. "She helped me pack up my stuff at the office today so, you know, I thought I kind of owed it to her to let her borrow my car for a quick errand."

"Okay. Never mind that." Blake was thinking clearly now. "How far are you from your house?"

"I don't know. Two or three miles."

Blake considered going straight to wherever she was and picking her up, but discounted it almost instantly. He didn't know how much they knew, and was afraid they might put a tail on him immediately. He didn't want to be responsible for leading them right to her.

"Listen to me carefully, and don't ask any questions. Walk home. Right now. Or better yet, run."

"But—"

"No buts! Listen to me! Go home. Lock your door and don't answer it for anybody for any reason until I get there."

"Okay… but I'm wearing heels. *High* heels."

"I said no buts!"

"Okay." He could tell she was surprised by the commanding tone of his voice, and that she knew he meant business.

"Be careful." Blake hung up, not giving her time to do anything but follow his commands. He looked back at the burning car. There was still no movement as far as identifying the body.

Good. Time to get a few things done.

Blake started his truck, already going over the list of things he would need and the amount of time it would take to gather them. He had to move fast. Cait was safe at home as long as they didn't know they'd killed the wrong person. But once that discovery was made, the manhunt for the one they wanted would be redoubled.

The image of his ex-wife floated into his mind. Would she exterminate the father of her children with as much ease and little concern as the innocent victim in that car?

Caitlin did exactly what Blake had said to do, even though she
had no idea why. And where was Judy with her Jeep anyway? Did
she have an accident? She missed being in the newsroom already.
She'd always been among the first to know what was happening
anywhere in the county. Now she felt out of touch with what was
happening right down the road.

Although Caitlin would have preferred to call someone and
get a ride, Blake had ordered her to hoof it and to hurry. She'd
paused only long enough to go through Judy's closet, but couldn't
find a pair of shoes any larger than a size five—not even a pair
of slippers.

So here she was in her size nine wide heels, trying to concentrate on anything but the pain in her feet as she clicked down the
back road. A few cars passed by her, but amazingly none of them
showed any interest in a woman walking along in a dress and nice
shoes. Caitlin decided to shave even more mileage off her journey
by cutting across a field, but her heels sunk into the ground at
every step, making it almost impossible to walk.

At least the hike gave her time to think. Blake hadn't sounded angry on the phone, but his voice had been different. Loud.
Commanding. Concerned? What had caused the change in him?

By the time she climbed the steps of her porch, her shoes
were completely ruined and her feet were absolutely killing her.
The last light of the day was fading fast, so she took some solace
in the fact she'd made it home before dark.

Once inside she locked and dead-bolted the door as Blake
had instructed, then flung her purse onto the kitchen table with
such force that its contents spilled everywhere. She didn't care.
She was too busy kicking off her shoes. *Ahhh. Who knew it could feel*

this good to take off your shoes? She looked down at her swollen feet and the muddy mess of leather on the floor. *He'd better have a good reason for this. A hundred dollar pair of shoes ruined, and these blisters are going to take weeks to heal.*

After taking care of the next necessity—going to the bathroom—she did what she always did as soon as she got home. She unclipped her hair, ran her fingers through the braid to undo it, then bent forward and shook out the long strands.

Giving her head one last shake, she headed into the bedroom to change into a pair of jeans and her favorite comfy sweatshirt that had a big pouch pocket. Since she was waiting for Blake to contact her, she tucked the private phone in there, and then laid a pair of socks on the bed. She was getting ready to grab her sneakers from the closet when she heard someone knocking.

Assuming it was Blake, she headed to the door and was preparing to unlock it when the knocking became louder and more violent—so violent it seemed like the deadbolt was the only thing keeping the door from bursting open.

Why would Blake be trying to bang the door down? Standing in the middle of the room, unsure of what to do, she heard her work phone begin to vibrate on the kitchen table where it had landed when she'd come in. Ignoring the pounding, she walked over and picked up the phone. Caller ID reflected it was the police station. The text said OPEN THE DOOR. She turned toward the door. *Geez, Blake. I'm coming. You don't have to break it down.* She had her hand on the deadbolt when she felt the phone Blake had given her vibrate in her pocket. Pulling the phone out, she saw a message from Mad Dog that read *GET OUT NOW!*

Caitlin momentarily froze, unsure which way to go, or what to grab. Her frantic mind refused to function. Her throat went dry and her limbs turned stiff with panic. Noticing her Glock lying on the table where it had fallen from her purse, she stuck it into her back waistband then headed for the stairs. Halfway up, she turned around and ran back into the kitchen, grabbed a second magazine for the gun from a drawer and stuck that in her pocket.

With no back exit, her emergency plan was to go out the upstairs window to the porch roof, and then drop down into the yard. There was really no other choice. Even with her slight build, she didn't think she'd fit through the window over the kitchen sink, and the one in the living room had been painted shut years ago.

Sliding open the upstairs pane, Caitlin could hear movement and see lights reflecting from the front of the house, but saw nothing in the inky darkness to the rear. She crawled out onto the porch roof and remained still, half expecting to see the beam of a flashlight illuminate her hiding place. When the sound of the banging on the door began again, she closed the window and laid flat on her stomach in case anyone was watching.

Calm down.

After taking a few deep breaths, she pulled herself to the edge of the roof and tried to figure out how she was going to lower herself to the ground ten feet below. Why hadn't she practiced this during daylight hours?

Deciding it was now or never, she held her breath as if she were jumping into deep water and slid her body off the roof. Dropping like a brick, she collapsed onto the ground and lay still to catch her breath and listen for any sign of disturbance.

Nothing. All was quiet except for the whooshing in her ears from her pounding heart. She scrambled up and had just started to turn around to run when two hands grabbed her from out of the darkness in a vice-like grasp. One of them wrapped around her waist and the other covered her mouth, stifling the scream that rose in her throat.

Chapter 25

"It's me," a low voice whispered.

Caitlin nodded her head that she understood, even though she wanted to punch Blake in the face for scaring her to death. It was probably a good thing he didn't give her time to think about it. Grabbing her hand, he led her through the shadows, slowly at first, and then at a breakneck speed through the darkness. Caitlin had to bite her lip to keep from whimpering out loud, and almost fell down a number of times. Each time she stumbled, his strong hand held her up, even as it dragged her across logs and under low-hanging limbs. Although she was gasping for breath and struggling to keep up, there was no stopping him—or even slowing him down.

Her lungs felt like they were about to burst and her side felt like it was going to explode by the time they burst out of the woods onto a seldom-used dirt road. Caitlin looked up and noticed the black truck silhouetted in the darkness. Grabbing the door and flinging it open, she jumped into the passenger seat and gasped for breath with her head between her legs.

Blake was in the driver seat with the engine started by the time she closed the door.

"You're out of shape." Blake calmly put the truck in first gear and pulled out onto the road. He wasn't even breathing hard.

"And you're out of your mind." Caitlin knew she sounded hysterical—because she was. "What the hell was that about?" She took a few deep breaths before she was able to raise her head.

Blake looked at her sideways. "Calm down. *That* was about saving your life."

"What are you talking about?"

He shifted gears as they picked up speed, then reached down and turned on the scanner.

Car Four-One establishing a perimeter.

Caitlin turned to him. "Is that the police car-to-car channel?"

Blake nodded.

"Who are they looking for?"

The chatter continued. *Every available car, set up a perimeter at McCalister and Main.*

"Guess," Blake said as they sped past the McCalister Road sign.

"Geezuz." Caitlin sat back and gazed out the window. "What the hell did *I* do?"

"You lived."

"What does that—?" Caitlin stopped in mid-sentence when she caught a glimpse of her image in the side-view mirror. After letting out a small gasp, she pulled down the lighted mirror on the visor, then put her face in her hands.

"Cowboy up, Cait." Blake sounded irritated. "You said you knew this was going to be dangerous."

Caitlin viewed him through misty eyes. "I know, but look at my hair!"

Blake slowly turned his head toward her, his eyebrows raised at her unexpected meltdown. "Really? You're worried about your *hair?*"

Caitlin tried to run her fingernails through it, but they snagged on the tangles of twigs and leaves. "Well, look at it."

Blake returned his attention to the road. "Get a grip. Seriously. Tangled hair should be the least of your worries."

As he reached down and casually shifted gears, Caitlin assumed he was going to continue to scold her about not sweating the small stuff—especially when they were being chased by murdering maniacs. She couldn't have agreed more, but she didn't want to be lectured. All of the desperate despair, agonizing guilt, and paralyzing fear that had been a part of her life for the past year fused together in one upsurge of emotion, making it impossible to think rationally. She was tired of being strong and in control. She had never felt so overwhelmed and overcome in her life. Couldn't he just help her out and give her some sympathy? Let her be a girl?

"Seriously." His tone sounded almost sympathetic. "Why worry about something as insignificant as tangled hair when you have mascara running halfway down your cheeks?"

Caitlin's eyes widened as she inclined toward the mirror again. Sure enough, the makeup she had painstakingly applied this morning so she could get fired in style was smeared with sweat and streaked with dirt. She gasped, but stifled a sniffle, knowing she would get no sympathy from the man beside her.

"Don't worry." He reached over and pulled a twig out of her hair. "It could be a new trend—kind of a back-to-nature, raccoon-ee look." He held the twig up for her to see.

Caitlin stopped wiping the smudges from under her eyes with her shirt sleeve. "Stop making fun of me." Deep down she knew he was simply trying to lighten the mood and keep her mind off what had happened—and what they faced. His next words confirmed that belief.

"I'm sorry." Blake put his hand on her knee and patted it. "Are you okay?" His voice was low and full of concern now.

"I'm great." She turned her head abruptly toward the window.

Blake exhaled loudly.

Caitlin glanced at him and then back out the window. "Now what?"

"You know what pisses me off?"

"No." She didn't even bother to look at him this time.

"When someone says they're okay and they're really not."

That made her turn toward him. "Know what pisses *me* off?" She didn't give him time to answer. "When I say I'm okay and someone doesn't believe me."

Blake started laughing.

"What's so funny?"

"We sound like we're married."

Just then his phone in the console between them began to chime.

"Who's that?"

Caitlin squinted, trying to read it. "There's no name. Just a number." She leaned closer. "Uh-oh."

"You recognize it?"

"Yes." She swallowed hard. "Louie."

They looked at each other. Why would the former CIA agent be calling Blake at this hour?

"He's checking to see if I'm with you." Blake was all business again.

Caitlin reached over and touched his arm. "You gave him your cell number?"

"Now that you mention it, no. If I had, I would have put his name in my contacts."

"He called my cell once too—but I never gave him the number." She threw her hands over her head, and put it between her knees. "Geezuz, not Louie."

Blake slammed on the brakes and pulled off the side of the road, but his hands remained on the steering wheel. "Okay," he said in a calm voice, his eyes remaining on the road in front of them. "Time to go to Plan B."

"I didn't know we had a Plan A," Caitlin murmured with her head still between her legs.

"We didn't, but that's behind us now. You need to get a grip."

Caitlin's head jerked up. "Get a grip? Really?"

Blake put the truck back in drive and swung out onto the road.

"That was a quick Plan B."

"Yeah, I'm good like that."

"Care to share?"

"No."

"Somehow I didn't think you would." Caitlin stared straight ahead as the events of the last twenty-four hours settled on her shoulders like a lead weight. Something was wrong. Something infinitely worse than even her arrest had been. She couldn't see it, and she hadn't been told about it, but she could feel it.

"What happened today, Blake?" She didn't bother to change her gaze from what was in front of her, but she saw his hands tighten on the wheel out of the corner of her eye, confirming her suspicions.

"We'll talk about it later."

She turned her head to the window even though there was nothing to see but the darkness and the night. "Is Judy dead?"

Blake didn't say anything this time, but he reached for her hand, closed his fingers around it, and drew it protectively against his leg. The gesture was soothing, but his wordless answer brought pain. Caitlin put her head against the window and cried as quietly as she could.

When she looked out the window again to get her bearings, Caitlin saw they were cruising on I-95.

"Where are we going?"

"You'll see."

She took solace in his careless confidence and the fact that he seemed undisturbed, but they were now rolling down I-95, probably the most obvious place the police would search for them.

Sure enough, the scanner squawked to life again.

"All units be advised, suspect may be traveling in a black pickup truck with a law enforcement officer. Consider them armed and dangerous. Repeat, consider them armed and dangerous."

Caitlin sat back in the seat and closed her eyes. "Louie told them."

"So it appears. They're getting ahead of me." Blake still sounded composed and unruffled, as if this was nothing more than a little extra obstacle thrown into his path. He clicked on his turn signal and pulled into a rest stop. "You have your work phone on you?"

Caitlin patted her pockets, not remembering what she had grabbed on her way out of her house. She pulled the phone he'd given her out of her sweatshirt and then her work phone out of her pants' pocket. "Yeah." She held it up. "Habit I guess."

He pulled into a parking space. "Anything you want to keep on it?"

She glared at him incredulously. "Of course there is."

"Too bad. Delete all your contacts, texts, calls."

"Why? Someone can retrieve all that."

"Yeah, but why make it easy for them? Hurry up."

Caitlin groaned. "Are you kidding? It's taken *years* to gather these—"

"I'll do it." He grabbed the phone. "While we're at it, turn off the phone I gave you."

Caitlin continued to stare at him.

"Need to save the battery. We might need it later."

"Okay." Caitlin took the phone out of her sweatshirt pocket and pushed the power button.

"And if you need to go to the bathroom, do it now." Blake didn't look up as he concentrated on clearing contacts and messages from her phone. "We're going to be driving for a while."

"I'm good." Caitlin shrugged. "Anyway, I don't have any shoes on."

Blake stopped what he was doing and lifted his head. He turned slowly toward her, his gaze moving from her face to her feet, which he couldn't really see in the dark, and back to her face again. "Excuse me?"

"You heard me." She lifted one sticky foot off the floor mat and then the other. "I don't have any shoes on. And if you're wondering if they're bleeding, my guess is *yes*."

"Why the hell don't you have shoes on?"

"Because I walked three freaking miles in heels and had blisters on my feet. I was in the process of getting my sneakers when I got your text—*get out now*."

"*Damn*." Blake exhaled loudly. "Next time I'll be more specific and say, '*Grab shoes and get out now*.'"

"Ha. Ha. *Next* time—very funny." Caitlin shook her head in disgust while reaching around to the small of her back. "I figured this and an extra mag were more important than shoes."

Blake stared at the gun, then reached over and patted her knee. "You're right. Sorry about your feet." His look of approval faded as quickly as it had appeared. He turned around and grabbed a bag from behind the seat, and placed it on the console between them. After rifling through it, he pulled out a roll of duct tape, ripped a few long strips off, and opened the door. "Be right back."

Caitlin watched him walk discreetly to the other side of the parking lot where a tractor trailer was getting ready to pull out. Moving to the side in the shadows, he put his phone on the bumper and slapped a piece of tape over it, almost in one movement. Then he did the same thing with her phone on a pickup with Florida plates.

Hopping back into the truck, he watched the tractor trailer pick up speed as it moved toward the ramp and the highway. When the pickup began backing out of its space, he turned the key and began to back out as well. "That ought to keep them busy a little while."

"They'll be putting a BOLO out for this truck." Caitlin knew she was stating the obvious, and as the words were leaving her mouth the scanner came to life.

All units, Be On the Lookout for a black F350 Ford pickup, Virginia license plate NAV-ST6. Consider the subjects armed and dangerous.

Blake absently glanced at his watch.

"You late for something?"

He rested his hand on the gear shift. "Running behind. We need to make where we're going by daylight."

"We must be going far away. It's only about nine, isn't it?"

"Yup. But we need a new vehicle first."

After traveling a few miles, Blake whipped the truck off the highway again and drove slowly down a double-lane surface street lit with the soft glow of urban sprawl on both sides. Without warning, he turned onto a long, winding lane that led to a large hotel and drove around to the back.

As they rolled slowly around the corner, he looked at her and winked. "Perfect."

Parked off by itself, well out of the reach of any light, sat a navy blue, older model Jeep. Turning off the truck, he reached into the back for his bag again, and seemed to deliberate a few seconds over what tools to use. Then he opened the door and got out.

"You can drive a stick shift, right?" He turned around and leaned into the truck, his blue eyes, twinkling from beneath the rim of a ball cap, reflected a kind of boyish charm.

"Yes."

"Figured that." The way he said the words made her feel good. "If anyone comes along, just drive out of here like you're lost."

Caitlin nodded as she climbed over the console into his seat. Since she had no idea where they were, she figured that part of her assignment would be pretty easy.

By the time she had adjusted her seat, discovered where the headlights were, and figured out where first gear was, Blake was already in the other vehicle. His head disappeared under the dashboard, and a few minutes after that the Jeep turned over.

Caitlin slowly pulled the truck up beside him and he motioned for her to follow him. Instead of getting back onto the highway as Caitlin has expected, Blake turned in the opposite direction. The sprawl ended abruptly and the road narrowed. They traveled quite a few miles, and then Blake seemed to be slowing down, searching for something. From out the darkness ahead of her, she saw him put on his turn signal for a single blink, and then turn into an old dirt farm lane.

Where the hell is he taking me? For the first time, Caitlin realized she trusted this man with her life. The admission was dredged from a place beyond logic or reasoning, because in reality she barely knew him.

After they'd driven down a hill, around a turn and through a copse of trees, Caitlin had no idea what direction they were heading—but at last a farmhouse appeared in view. With no lights and a sagging roof, it showed definite signs of abandonment.

Caitlin followed Blake to the other side of the house, where he stopped beside an empty tractor shed and motioned for her to pull in. After getting out of the Jeep, he rummaged through the contents of the building until he came up with a piece of old, battered tarp.

Not sure what he was doing, Caitlin gingerly got out. Luckily grass had grown up over what was once a driveway and it was not too hard on her feet.

"Here, can you grab some of this stuff and put it in the Jeep?"

Caitlin limped to the back of the truck. She hadn't noticed how much stuff was packed in the back until now. There were duffel bags and a cooler, as well as large canvas bags of unknown contents.

Once everything was transferred, Caitlin helped Blake cover the back of the truck with the dirty piece of canvas. They took a step back and surveyed their work. The tarp covered enough of the truck that anyone just driving in—by mistake or otherwise—would perhaps be fooled into thinking a piece of old equipment was stored beneath.

Blake inhaled deeply. "Guess that will have to do."

As Caitlin turned to head back to the Jeep, he put his arm over her shoulder and gave it a squeeze. "You hanging in there?"

"Trying to." She couldn't help but feel a sense of contentment when she saw kindness and respect mingled in his gaze. "For justice."

A slow, purposeful smile spread across his face. "Yup. For justice."

As they rolled back out the long lane, Caitlin stared out the window into the darkness. "How'd you know about this place?"

"It was owned by the grandparents of a friend of mine from the Navy. I'd lost touch, but figured I'd give it a shot—as far off the beaten path as it is."

"Good call." Though she was glad the truck was hidden and probably wouldn't be found anytime soon, Caitlin couldn't help but wonder where they were going and how they were ever going to get out of this mess.

"Why don't you try to get some sleep?"

Caitlin shook her head. "No. I'm good."

"How are the feet?"

"They're good. No worries."

"I'll tell you one thing." He looked over and gave her a grin that almost sent her reeling. "You're a trooper, Caitlin Sparks."

Chapter 26

Mallory Jarrod smoothed down the front of her tailored suit and sat down at her desk. This was no time to panic. She needed to be stronger than she had ever been in her life. She could still make this work, still control the outcome, if she just kept her nerves in check.

An attorney for more than fifteen years, Mallory knew the inner workings of Washington, D.C., perhaps better than anyone. She had worked in the State Department while still in law school, and had become acquainted with the players and non-players, the scattered factions, and the heavyweights—all of whom were in a desperate fight to screw the other person before they got screwed themselves. That's just how the game was played in this town.

She found that game intoxicating. Once she had gotten her foot on the bottom step of the power ladder, she was hooked. She'd pushed and clawed her way up, rung by rung, until she met someone equally in love with the game—someone who made her see the possibility of moving to the top, perhaps to a level where no woman had ever gone. That thought weighed so powerfully inside her now she sometimes shook with the anticipation of it.

The two of them had been working on their plan for years,

and now that they were close enough to touch it, neither one of them wanted to stop. In fact, they would do just about anything to make sure their dream ended exactly as planned.

Mallory tapped her pen on the polished cherry surface of her desk as she waited for her phone to ring. She swiveled in her chair to stare out over the expansive cityscape view of Washington, before returning to agitatedly drum on her desk again.

"What is taking so long?" she murmured just before the phone rang. "Did you get her?" She answered without even saying hello.

"They didn't find her at the house."

"What do you mean, they didn't *find* her?"

"They think she was there, but she got away. They didn't *find* her." There was a long pause before the voice on the other end of the line spoke again. "You still there?"

"Yes, I'm still here. I'm trying to figure out who I can work with to take care of a job I thought *you* were handling."

"Well it gets worse."

Mallory stood and waved her hand in the air. "How can it get any worse than killing someone we don't even know and not finding the one we were trying to kill?"

"We think she may have hooked up with Blake."

Mallory sat down, hard, and fell silent again.

"Hello?"

"I'm still here. Why do you think that?"

"He showed up at the accident scene. An officer saw him get a phone call and he hightailed it out of there."

"Well, that makes it easy. Put a trace on his phone and *find* them."

"Don't you think I did that?"

"Well?"

"No call came in at the time of the accident on the phone we have for him."

"How can that be?"

"It means he's being careful and has another phone."

Mallory put her free hand to her temple. "Are you suggesting he knows what's going on?"

"You know Blake better than I do, I would think. Maybe he's just being careful."

"I don't like this. Do we have a BOLO out on his truck?

"Yes. For whatever good it's going to do."

"What's that supposed to mean?"

"He's a cop. He knows how we're going to track him." The voice sounded exasperated. "He's probably stolen a car by now."

"Well that will help us pin him down, right? We'll know where he is as soon a car turns up stolen."

"Cars are stolen every day. And knowing him, he'd steal one that's not being used and it isn't reported missing for days, or even weeks. Right now, we're pinging the cell phone we know about, and it's definitely on the move."

"Which direction?"

"South on 95. Moving fast."

"And you're on him?"

"We've got units on the lookout as we speak. The latest I got is he's already down in southern Virginia, getting ready to cross into North Carolina."

"We need to catch up with him *now*." Mallory tried to keep the agitation out of her voice, but it was impossible to miss. She pressed the phone closer to her ear when she heard whispering and some papers rustling on the other end.

"What's going on?"

"Standby, I just got handed something."

Mallory grew impatient when she heard a muffled conversation that sounded like a hand was being held against the phone to mute the discussion. "Did we find him?" She practically yelled into the phone.

"Umm …"

"Spit it out," she demanded.

"A unit just pulled over the vehicle the cell phone was pinging from."

"And?"

"It was a tractor trailer."

"Blake stole a tractor trailer?"

"No. Blake taped his phone onto a tractor trailer."

Mallory almost dropped the phone. For a moment, she was speechless. "He's trying to outsmart us," she said at last. "He's probably heading in the opposite direction."

"Or he could be thinking that's what we would think, and he's watching the truck get pulled over in his rear-view mirror."

"Dammit!" Mallory stood and began pacing. "I told Louie it was a mistake to let him nose around in this. He's too smart."

"Don't worry, we'll find them."

"Don't worry you'll find them? The police haven't had much success so far! I feel like I'm working with the Keystone Cops."

"He's going somewhere to lie low for a while. We'll just have to wait him out."

"You think the reporter's with him?"

"Most likely, since she hasn't surfaced anyplace else."

"He doesn't like reporters." She drummed her long finger-nails on the desk. "Despises them. I can hardly believe they're together. Are you sure you're not going down the wrong path?"

"I'm sure. They're together." The voice faded at the end of the sentence, and then was quiet. "We're working on tracking down the reporter's phone. That might lead us to them."

"You know what this will mean if they go public, right?" Mallory's voice was cold and threatening. "If they find someone who will listen to them, you know—"

"That isn't going to happen." The voice on the other end of the line sounded calm and in control. "Anyway, we don't even know what they know—if they know anything."

"They wouldn't be running if they didn't know *something*. At the very least, they know the woman in the Jeep is dead. Blake is smart enough to know it was supposed to be the reporter."

"Don't worry. Even if they do try to go public with whatever it is they've found, who is going to believe them?" The voice on the phone laughed. "I mean really—a rogue reporter and a cop ranting about a huge conspiracy involving a Senator and a general counsel to the Secretary of State? No one's going to listen to that."

Mallory remained quiet, but she had to agree.

"I've already touched bases with all my contacts at the networks telling them I might have a juicy leak for them." He laughed. "They're salivating right now to get the story, so if Blake turns up he's going to find himself the focus of a major media story—and it won't be complimentary."

"I hope it doesn't come to that."

"Why not? You want to protect him?"

"No. I want to protect *you*. You're underestimating him if you think he's going to go down without a fight."

"You worry too much."

"And you don't worry enough."

"No. We're golden, Mal. I'm going to be the next president, and you're going to be the first female vice president. It's our destiny. We've come too far and done too much. Nothing can stop us now."

Chapter 27

The night was dark and a little misty, but Caitlin could see they were on a winding country road that rose and then fell away almost out from under them. She held her breath every time the Jeep descended and rounded a turn, her stomach lurching. It wasn't just the road causing the butterflies, but the speed at which Blake was driving—like in-a-car-chase-fleeing-from-police fast

A red traffic signal appeared in the darkness ahead and Caitlin felt the truck slowing. Almost as soon as they stopped, the light turned green.

"Wait. Is this a covered bridge?" She gawked at the craftsmanship as they traveled through the old, canopied structure.

"Yep."

"I know we've come a long way, but did we travel back in time?"

Blake laughed. "Kind of. We're in Pennsylvania." He looked over at her. "Near Gettysburg."

"Oh."

"We're getting close."

"To where?"

"Where we're going."

Caitlin shrugged and tried to content herself with staring out the window. It was obvious she wasn't going to get much out of him, so she didn't bother trying.

The road wound through a small village with large, old houses, and then they were back into countryside with only a house here and there on either side of the road.

Blake slowed down and leaned forward as he looked for a turn. At last he flicked on his signal and turned onto a secondary road. "Hold on. If I remember right, this road is bumpy."

Caitlin nodded, but the road, unlike the ones she was accustomed to in Virginia, was paved. There was a pothole here and there, but for the most part this one was smooth. After about a mile though, she understood what he meant. The surface turned to stone, and was so washed out that it was little more than a tractor path through the woods. She was glad she was wearing a seatbelt to keep her in her seat.

Blake made one more turn onto another dirt lane and maneuvered the vehicle over an overgrown driveway, mowing down tree limbs and shrubbery as he went. Finally the headlights picked up the sight of an old, forlorn-looking cabin.

Caitlin surveyed the surroundings—what she could see in the darkness anyway. "What's this?"

"It's home, for now." Blake pulled a backpack from the seat behind them. Then he got out, walked over to her side of the Jeep and opened the door. "Hop on. The rocks are sharp here. I don't want you to cut up your feet any more than you already have."

Caitlin laughed and looked at him incredulously. "I can walk."

He ignored her and turned around. "Hop on. That's an order."

Seeing she had no choice, Caitlin stood in the Jeep's doorway and was helped with a strong hand onto his back. Her weight didn't seem to faze him in the least.

When he got onto the porch, he put her down and examined the door, which was locked.

"You have a key? Right?"

"Kind of." Blake took a step back and gave the door a swift kick. Then he stepped aside and motioned for her to go in. "After you."

Caitlin entered the one-room cabin and tried to see in the dark. Behind her, she could hear Blake digging around in the backpack he had brought in. Warm light soon illuminated the room as he found the lantern he was seeking.

"What is this place?"

"My sister's husband owns a hunting cabin a few miles from here. I ran across this place while out hunting with him one time. It's been abandoned for years."

"I can see that." Caitlin's gaze roamed the room. There were some cabinets and a sink—but she noticed the sink had no faucet. *No running water. No stove. No refrigerator.* Her eyes drifted over to the large stone fireplace, and then to the small, single bed in the corner of the room.

"Small problem." Caitlin stood motionless. "I'm a four-star hotel type of girl."

Blake laughed. "You're lucky we have a roof over our heads." He pushed her into the room. "Make yourself at home. I'll go get the other things."

Caitlin walked in and started examining the cabinets. The basic necessities as far as dishes seemed to be there, but the cobwebs hanging in the corners of the cabinets demonstrated they needed a washing, and sent a shiver of revulsion down her spine.

When she heard Blake coming back up the steps of the porch,

she glanced over her shoulder. Her jaw dropped open when he appeared in the doorway.

"What are you staring at?"

Caitlin snapped her mouth closed. "You look like freaking Rambo or something." She continued to gape at Blake, who had what appeared to be an M-4 slung carelessly over one shoulder and a pistol holstered on his hip. Slung over his other shoulder was another holster and pistol, and a heavily loaded ammo bag. He also carried a rifle in each hand.

"I only had room for a couple of things. You ever shoot a rifle?"

"Not lately." Caitlin examined the guns in his hands and the bulging veins in his forearms. "With scopes like those though, I should be able to hit something."

Blake turned to stack the guns along the wall.

"I guess it pays to be on the run with a highly-decorated Navy SEAL."

Blake whirled around. "What did you say?"

Caitlin froze at the tone of his voice and the look in his eyes. She bit her top lip, but a quiet "ohh" escaped when she realized what she'd said.

"Where did you hear that?" he demanded, before she even had time to answer. When she remained speechless, he repeated the question again, slower and louder. "Where. Did. You. Hear. That?"

"I-I'm a reporter." Caitlin stumbled over her words.

He exhaled loudly and returned to unloading his arms. "That doesn't answer my question." He sounded angry and disgusted.

"It's not like I ran a background check on you like you did on me. Remember—"

"That's different," he interrupted, turning back to face her.

"No it's not, Blake."

"I have some other things to bring in." He turned abruptly to leave.

"I'll give you a hand." Caitlin followed him to the door.

"No. Sit." His voice was sharp and authoritative as he pointed to the table in the middle of the room. "Stay off your feet until I get them cleaned up. There might be broken glass in here."

Caitlin pulled her pistol out of her pants and lay it in front of her before she sat, then watched him bring armload after armload of things through the door, including the cooler.

"Are you sure I can't help?"

"That's the last one." He reached down for a canvas bag he'd brought in earlier and threw it on the table. Then he sat down on the remaining chair and rummaged through its contents. "Give me your right foot."

Caitlin moved her chair to face him and raised her foot, which he promptly plopped onto a towel on the table. "Geezus." His brows were knit and his jaw set as he evaluated the cuts and bruises.

Removing a small bottle from the bag, he squirted something soapy onto the bottom of her foot and wiped it clean with a small medical pad. Then with seemingly practiced hands, he probed some of the deeper wounds to make sure there was nothing lodged in them before applying some type of ointment. Finally, he wrapped the foot in a bandage and taped it securely.

"Give me the other one."

Caitlin obediently lifted the other foot, and watched him repeat the procedure without speaking. His face was grim and determined as he worked, but when he was done and was returning the medical items to his bag, he finally spoke. "So what do you know about my work?"

Caitlin swallowed hard. "You mean about your involvement in the Kessler Affair?"

He stopped, raised his gaze to meet hers, and then went back to repacking the bag. "Yeah."

"I know you were there."

He stopped again, his blue eyes seeming to burn brighter than usual as they reflected the lantern light. "That information has all been sealed. My job was classified."

Caitlin swallowed hard. "I know. But I talked to Jimmy... Podge."

Again he lifted his gaze, his eyes lit with anger. "You talked to Podge? Why?"

"He gave me his card at the legislative open house. Remember?" She looked away from his penetrating expression and stared at her foot. "I called him for some information on the latest surveillance..."

"I told you not to do anything illegal."

"I didn't. I just wanted to get an idea of what's out there with new technology."

"And then, because you're a reporter, you grilled him about me. Do I have it right?"

Caitlin could hardly stand to hear his accusatory tone. "Not exactly." She paused, choosing her words carefully. "He thinks a lot of you. Admires what you did."

"So?"

"So, he said some things—just little things about your service—that made me curious."

Now his attention drifted from her face to somewhere over her shoulder. Caitlin wished she could see what he saw during those silent moments of remembrance; that she could learn a little more about the man who had overcome so much.

He didn't say anything for what seemed like an eternity, but his expression spoke volumes. "So that's when you started digging."

Caitlin inhaled deeply. She felt like she was sinking into an abyss, and the more she talked, the deeper she sank. "I read everything I could on it, and after talking to Jimmy, put two and two together on who the unnamed private contractor survivor was. That's all." She tried not to blink or look away from his intense scrutiny, but could barely take the bleak expression in his eyes.

"How long have you known?"

"Not very long."

"What does *that* mean?" he snapped.

"What difference does it make?"

"I like to know when people are digging into my life."

"I wasn't digging into your life." Caitlin defended herself. "I was digging into the Kessler Affair."

Blake nodded while staring at the wall again, obviously trying to control his emotions. He stood abruptly and turned to set the bag along the wall. "So do you have any questions?" He spun back toward her, his jaw set determinedly again, as if bracing himself for what was to come. "I'm sure the reporter in you has some sort of burning question that wasn't answered by the testimony."

"Well… now that you've asked." Caitlin hesitated. She knew he'd heard the wobble in her voice, the nervousness. He was a man who missed nothing.

"Go ahead."

"When are you going to stop blaming yourself for something that wasn't your fault?"

"You weren't there." He stepped toward her and jabbed his finger in her face. "You don't know what you're talking about."

"I know you did everything you could… more than most thought was humanly possible."

He turned away, but not before she saw the silent sadness of his expression. "If only *that* had been enough."

Caitlin tried once again to reach him, desperate for him to listen. "You did what you felt you had to do—there's no fault in that."

He gave a choking laugh as he turned back around. "Yeah... did what I felt I had to do." He took a step closer and leaned down. "How would *you* feel if you were the one who made the decision to go in without orders?" He pointed a finger at her. "And no one but you came out alive?"

The raw agony in his voice cut Caitlin to the bone. And when she looked up at him, the grief and regret glistening in his eyes almost made her weep. He'd been good at hiding the pain of his past behind a tough exterior and unemotional demeanor, but it had all been an act. This was a man who was hurting.

"They went in willingly." She reached for his arm. "To help save American lives. You know that."

He shook free from her grasp and gave her a blank stare. "They went in because *I* went in. *I* was the one who countermanded the stand-down order."

It wasn't so much the words that he said, but the tone that struck Caitlin to the core. And when she gazed up at him, his dark blue eyes were suffused with a tortured expression of guilt and pain that had obviously not diminished over the years. She could feel him pulling away, distancing himself from her. She wanted to help him, but felt powerless to ease the weight of responsibility that burdened him. "You did the right thing. You saved a lot of lives."

"But not *all* of them." The words were said curtly, angrily.

Caitlin had never felt so helpless in her entire life. "Blake, I read the testimony. No one blamed you then... or now."

"You never told me you read the testimony." His tone was calm now, but underneath there was a razor's edge.

She raised her gaze to meet his. "I guess you never asked."

His jaw tensed noticeably and his blue eyes turned dark and cold—unemotional. There was not an ounce of compassion in his unyielding stare. But Caitlin now knew what lay behind the mask of stoic solidity—the torment, the pain, the anguished remorse he could not let go.

"Dammit." He clenched his hands into fists by his side. "We need to trust each other if we're going to get through this."

"I trust you, Blake. With my life. Completely."

Her words were said sincerely, but his were hostile and grim. "But can I trust *you*?"

Caitlin's breath caught in her throat. "Why wouldn't you?"

"Why didn't you tell me you knew?" His fist hit the table, sending a cloud of dust into the air.

"What was I supposed to say?" Caitlin threw up her hands. "'Oh, by the way, I know about the seven gunshot wounds you received, and that you were still able to drag your two mortally wounded buddies into a safe room so their bodies wouldn't be mutilated by Islamic extremists. How exactly do you start that conversation?'"

"I've never seen you at a loss for words." His expression was set in an irritated scowl. "I'm sure you could have figured out something."

"I thought you knew I knew." Caitlin shook her head. "If you didn't know I knew, then you must think I'm a pretty lousy reporter."

"Oh, so now this is *my* fault?"

Caitlin turned her back on him. "I'm sorry if you don't believe me." When she heard no response from behind her, Caitlin closed her eyes and summoned her strength. "If you don't trust me, I don't want to stay. Just show me the way to the main road."

Again there was silence, and she assumed he was going to

take her hand, lead her to the door, and point her in the right direction. But finally he spoke. "Yeah. Right. You don't even have any shoes."

He sounded so disdainful and condescending that, despite her exhaustion, Caitlin jumped into action. "Never mind. I'll figure it out." She turned to pick up the Glock she had placed on the table—the only thing she had brought in and the only thing she intended to leave with.

She gasped when his hand locked onto her wrist, keeping her from picking it up.

"I don't think that will be necessary." His voice had a hard edge, strung tight with emotion.

She jerked her gaze up to meet his, amazed at the strength in that single-handed grip.

"We're in this together." He seemed more pensive now than angry or annoyed. His tone was mild and controlled, his eyes a lighter shade of blue.

"But you said you don't trust—"

"I didn't say that."

The intensity of the moment flared through her. "But you—"

"Just forget it. Okay?"

Caitlin nodded, her eyes still locked on his. She didn't try to move. She couldn't. She was held in place as much by the potency of his expression as the physical restraint of his hold.

"We're a team, Cait." The pressure on her wrist increased as he drew her toward him. "We've got to be, or they'll win." As his hold tightened, his expression softened but remained somber and serious.

"I'm glad to be working with you, Blake. I mean that—even if you don't trust me."

"I did not say that."

Caitlin looked up at him and tried to blink the tears away so she could see more clearly. She could feel his chest rising and falling against hers, could feel the race of his heart as he moved his other hand to the small of her back and applied more pressure. A surge of unexpected contentment spread through her at the feel of his strong arms holding her captive.

"I trust you, Cait." His voice was deep and throaty. She waited expectantly for him to elaborate as he stared into her eyes, but instead, he cleared his throat and turned away. "You hungry?"

She stood there, practically shaking, in the middle of the room. "Um, no. Just tired."

Blake glanced at her over his shoulder as he went through his gear. "Okay. There's an outhouse out the door to the right, and a hand pump for water if you want to wash your face." He nodded toward the counter. "There's a flashlight."

Caitlin didn't move. "Excuse me? Did you say outhouse?"

He stopped what he was doing. "Okay, outdoor *restroom*. Does that sound better?"

"But…" She shifted her weight and rubbed her palms on her legs. "Things probably live in there, don't they?"

He kept a straight face, but barely. "If by *things*, you mean spiders, then yes. But I cleaned most of them out already."

"*Most* of them?"

He picked up the flashlight and handed it to her. "Do you need me to go along, Miss I'm-A-Big-Girl?"

The glimpse of amusement she thought she had caught in his eyes before was glimmering there now with no restraint. "No. I don't need you to go along." She turned on the flashlight and pointed it on the wall to make sure it worked—and to stall for time as she tried to gather her courage.

"You know, in the Navy we had a saying for situations like this."

Caitlin eyed him quizzically, waiting for him to reveal some important knowledge that would help her go to the bathroom surrounded by eight-legged creatures of horror.

"Embrace the suck."

Caitlin was half-angry at his callous humor and half scared to death. "Okay. Got it." She tossed her head, pretending a courage she did not feel. "Excuse me while I go *embrace the suck*."

"Don't worry, Cait," he said, just as she put her hand on the door latch. "They're the kind that mostly don't bite."

Caitlin stopped and took a deep breath, then opened the door and slammed it shut behind her.

When Caitlin returned, there was a sleeping bag, a pillow, and a small cotton blanket neatly placed on the cot. Blake bowed and waved his hand toward the bed. "Welcome to the Hilton, Miss Sparks."

She raised her eyebrows innocently. "No chocolate for the pillow?"

He clicked his fingers. "Damn. I knew I forgot something *important*."

Caitlin got the hint. "I'm sorry. It looks wonderful. Thanks." She walked over to the cot and sat. "Where are you going to sleep?"

"I have another sleeping bag. I'll hit the floor."

Caitlin's brow wrinkled. "You sure?"

"I've slept in worse places, believe me."

Caitlin frowned and nodded. "Thanks, Blake." She swallowed hard, and felt tears welling. "For everything."

"Goodnight, Cait."

"Night." She laid back, pulled the cover over her and remembered nothing else.

Chapter 28

Caitlin awoke from the drowsy warmth of the bed feeling an odd twinge of confusion. It was pitch-black around her, but something had roused her from a deep sleep—a sound or a feeling, she wasn't sure which. Lifting her head, she strained her eyes, trying to figure out where she was. As memories of the preceding day began to infiltrate her groggy mind, she discerned the form of a man standing near the foot of the bed. Holding her breath as she watched him move closer, she let it out slowly. *It must be Blake.*

But as the image materialized more firmly in front of her, she could tell it was not Blake at all. Her heart thumped hard, then skipped a beat altogether as he took a step closer. His figure and build were vaguely familiar as he moved even closer with his hand outstretched.

"You're getting close, Caitie."

Cait threw the blanket off and struggled to reach out to him. Only one person ever called her by that name. "Vince!"

"Don't look back." The form shimmered, and the voice had an echo to it now, like it was being reverberated back and forth in a steel tube. "Put the past... behind you..."

"No, don't go!" She lunged toward the end of the bed as the image began to dissolve into a distorted mist, before melting away completely. Even though she could no longer see him, she kept reaching and probing the darkness trying to find him. "Come back. I need you!"

Two strong arms grabbed her and held her back. "Cait, wake up." The voice was gentle and soothing. "It's just a dream."

"No!" She pushed the hair out of her eyes and struggled against him, seeking the form at the end of the bed that had seemed so real.

"There's nothing there. See?" Blake relaxed his grip a little and allowed her to scan the room.

Caitlin sucked air in and out, feeling like she had just run a race. Her clothes were soaked with sweat despite the coolness of the night.

"Take a deep breath for me."

Caitlin did as she was told, and then, realizing it must have been a dream, collapsed against him, crying. "I saw him. Vince... he... talked to me."

Blake stroked her hair. "It's okay, baby. Just a nightmare."

"It seemed so real." Caitlin felt his arms tighten around her, felt the power in them, and appreciated the comforting peace they provided. She had never felt so exposed, and yet so safe and secure. She turned her head and strained to see into the darkness again. "It felt like he was really here."

"Dreams have a way of doing that." He rocked her for a few more minutes in his soothing embrace, and then whispered in her ear. "Better?"

Caitlin took a few more deep breaths, and then tried to draw away, embarrassed. "Yes. I'm all right." Again, she peered over her shoulder into the darkness to see if the figure would reappear. "Sorry if I woke you."

Blake did not release his grasp. "Don't worry. You didn't wake me."

Caitlin knew it was useless to struggle so she rested her head against his chest again and tried to relax. Her mind drifted back to a time when she had been intimidated by this man. Now his mere presence was reassuring. His touch, his voice, brought security and a sense of peace.

"That's better." He cleared his throat, but it still sounded hoarse when he talked. "I wish you would put the past behind you."

Caitlin's breath caught in her throat. That's what Vince had just told her. She pulled away and regarded Blake with a troubled look. Had Vince been trying to tell her something from the other side that was merely being echoed by Blake? Was it time to move on with her life? Was she ready for that?

She lay her head down again before answering. "I'm not sure I want to yet."

Blake's chest rose against her cheek as he sucked in a deep, slow breath, but he didn't speak and his grasp was unrelenting. She savored the sensation of being held by him with her head against his heart, keenly aware of the solid strength of his arms and the warmth of his skin. His embrace was powerful and tender, strong and gentle.

She allowed herself to bask briefly in the peaceful, shared moment, but then feared she was being selfish. *He's probably uncomfortable and wants to go back to bed.* "I'm okay," she murmured into his chest, trying to reassure him. "You can let me go now, Blake." She opened her eyes when he didn't answer.

"I'm not sure I want to yet." His voice was soft, soothing, and carried a trace of possessive desperation in it. His protective arms pulled her even closer.

Now it was Caitlin's turn to inhale a deep breath and let it out slowly. She felt the pace of her heart begin to race and warmth surged through her. The touch of his hand was suddenly almost unbearable in its gentleness.

"When we get justice, Blake, I'll be able to put the past behind me." She returned his steady embrace, soaking in the comfort of his nearness. "I promise."

Steel blue eyes, heavy with emotion, regarded her with a thoughtful, wistful look. She thought she saw an invitation within their smoldering depths—but maybe it was just the simmering light reflected from her own eyes. She waited, not knowing what to expect, and then Blake lowered his head, his iron self-discipline seeming to succumb to overwhelming forces as he brushed his lips against hers in an action that was breathtakingly tender. "I hope so, Cait."

Her heart stopped. Time stood still. And then a loud sigh—almost a moan—escaped from him and the moment was gone, carried away by his strong will and sense of respect. He released her and walked away. The door squeaked open and the latch clicked shut. Groggy and tired, and alone in the dark, she couldn't help but wonder if she had just dreamed the whole thing.

Caitlin woke up slowly from her deep sleep, thinking she smelled coffee. She opened her eyes and turned her head toward the kitchen.

"I thought that might wake you up." Blake laughed. "Fresh instant coffee."

Trying to wipe away the sleep that remained, Caitlin took in the scene. A small camp stove sat on the table, and something in a frying pan was sizzling. "Are you making bacon?"

"Bacon and eggs. We need one good meal before we go to MREs. This is the only perishable food I grabbed."

Caitlin swung her feet out of the bed and surveyed her surroundings, still disoriented from the cobwebs of sleep that remained.

"You remember Meals Ready to Eat from the military. Right?" Blake dug around in a backpack and pulled out a little package. "Doesn't that look delicious?"

"I remember them." Caitlin rubbed her eyes. "But as for delicious, actually, not so much." She tried to run her fingers through her hair, but gave up.

Blake must have noticed her agitation. "Oh, I bought you a few things." He flipped the bacon over and nodded toward the corner of the room. "In that bag over there."

Caitlin saw a grocery bag sitting on a small stand. "Bought them? When?"

"Last night."

Her eyes drifted from the bag to the rifle leaning against the wall in the corner. "Did you stand guard duty?" She turned her gaze back to him. "I would have taken a shift."

"You needed your sleep." The way he said the words made it clear the conversation was over.

Cait walked over to the bag, picked it up, and almost screamed in delight. The first thing she saw was a comb. The second thing was a pair of sneakers. They looked big, but they would be better than walking around on bandages.

She turned to him. "There's a store near this place?" She didn't say it, but she appreciated how he always took charge, made decisions without asking for a second opinion. Got things done. She wasn't accustomed to such efficiency.

"About ten miles."

"That's funny; I never heard the engine start."

"Oh, I didn't take the vehicle. Figured it's been reported stolen by now."

"You walked?"

He laughed. "No. I *borrowed* a car from a house a couple of miles down the road."

"You borrowed it?"

"Returned it before they knew it was gone."

She put her hands on her hips. "That's not legal is it?"

He stopped what he was doing. "No. But I put gas in it to make up for the transgression."

"You wouldn't make a very good crook." Caitlin laughed as she turned back to the bag and found a clean shirt in it as well.

"Had to buy men's stuff. I didn't want to raise suspicion."

Caitlin started combing the tangles out of her hair and laughed. "You're right. A man buying women's clothes might stick out."

Blake cracked some eggs into a bowl. "Well, I couldn't see you lasting another day with tangled hair and walking around in bandages."

She snorted at his comment. "Hope they didn't have security cameras."

"One in the parking lot, but it was dark, and I wore a gray wig."

Cait's eyes jerked up to his. "*Bushy* gray hair?"

By the warm smile that Blake shot her, Cait knew it was him who had entered the bar that night she had gotten physically sick by her Jeep. He'd been protectively watching over her without her even being aware it was him.

"About that day. How'd you know where—"

"I pinged your phone."

"Pinged my phone?"

"I'd written down the serial number when I bought it, so all I had to do was call the phone company. They got a signal that gave me the approximate location, and from there I took a wild guess you were sitting in a bar drowning your sorrows."

Caitlin's thoughts drifted back to that night as she continued yanking the tangles out of her hair. When she was able to get the comb all the way through, she began absently braiding it to the side. "Hey, do you have a—"

A rubber band hit her in the hand. "One of these?"

She bent down and picked it up. "Yeah, one of these." She wound it around the bottom of her braid. "Don't do that any-more, okay?"

"Don't do what?" Blake went back to cooking. "Throw something at you?"

"No. Read my mind."

"Oh that." He laughed. "Sorry. I guess we're getting to—"

"Know each other too well," Caitlin interrupted.

He shot her a cockeyed grin. "I promise I'll stop reading your mind, if you stop finishing my sentences."

"Deal." Caitlin sat down at the table and watched him scram-bling eggs with practiced ease. "You sure they're not going to track you back here?"

"By the time they figure out we're here, we'll be gone."

"We will?" Caitlin's brow creased. "Where?"

He scooped the eggs onto a plate beside two pieces of bacon and handed it to her. "That's what we have to decide after break-fast."

Chapter 29

Caitlin reclined back in her chair. "That was honestly the best bacon and eggs I have ever eaten in my entire life."

"You were just hungry."

"No. They were delicious. Thank you."

She stood and picked up a small bucket. "I'll do the dishes since you cooked."

"Fair enough."

Caitlin took the bucket to the hand pump outside. After filling the bucket halfway, she splashed some of the ice cold water on her face. By the time she entered the cabin again, Blake had the plates and pan stacked on the table.

"Can't say I've ever washed dishes like this before." Caitlin dipped the plates into the bucket, wiped her hand over them a few times and laid them on the table to dry."

"Maybe I'll convert you yet." Blake sat down at the table.

"Convert me?" Her brow wrinkled in confusion.

"From a four-star hotel girl to a pioneer woman."

Caitlin laughed. "Maybe you will."

After sitting the dishes back in the cupboard, she noticed his sleeping bag rolled up in the corner of the room near the rifle.

"Did you sleep at all or are you bionic?"

"Don't worry. I got some sleep."

"Good. I need you." Caitlin cleared her throat when she realized what she'd said. "I mean, to get me out of here. I'm completely lost."

Just then the phone Blake had laid on the table vibrated once before stopping. He stared at it as if it were bad news.

Caitlin stared at it too, then at him. "I thought I was the only one with that number."

"I called my sister last night and gave it to her."

"Why didn't you pick it up?"

"Because I know what it meant."

Caitlin waited.

"I told her to call and let it ring once if she was contacted and questioned."

"They tracked her down in North Carolina?"

"Mallory would have told them." Blake said the words matter-of-factly, but he had a grim expression on his face. "They're moving fast."

"Then we need to move fast too." Caitlin rubbed her temples as she sat. "You have a plan?"

He laughed at that. "Do you think I have a magic wand or something? I'm not *that* good."

"Well I have an idea." She shook her head. "I mean, it might be crazy. But I'm not sure we have a choice."

Blake leaned back and crossed his arms. "I'm all ears."

"It would mean getting into DC without being spotted."

"That's doable—it's the last place they'll be looking for us." He put his arms on the table, an intent expression on his face. "But this needs to be done in a legal manner. If they can find any loopholes or missteps, it will mean they'll walk free."

Caitlin exhaled. "You're killing me. We have to play by the rules and they don't?"

"That's how it is." The look he gave her revealed a steadfast determination, telling her he would not divert from his code of conduct.

Caitlin took a deep breath and weighed their chance of success. He possessed operational instincts that would give them an edge over even the savviest of enemies. If she gave him the bare bones of her idea, he would be able to turn it into a tactical plan, dissect it, perfect it, and come up with a way to carry it out. This was a man who had kept fighting while getting the living hell pounded out of him, all the while knowing there was no help coming. She took a deep breath. "Okay. You're the boss."

Blake stood and went to one of his backpacks. "Here's some paper." He threw a writing pad on the table, along with a couple of pens. "Let's do it."

They sat together hashing things out, talking in low tones even though they were miles from the nearest house. Sometimes they bowed their heads together over a map or a sketch; a few times they balled a piece of paper up and threw it on the floor; or stood to stretch their legs. When the basics were in place, Blake made a single call with Caitlin's phone, then turned it off again and pulled the battery.

"Okay. The ball is rolling on that end."

"But can they do what we need them to do?"

"That's the six million dollar question." He ran his hand over the stubble on his chin. "And we won't know the answer until we're in too deep to stop."

The sound of a helicopter flying low overhead caused them both to stop talking and listen. Caitlin held her breath as she searched Blake's face for any sign of fear or concern. He just tilted his head and stared into space, as if doing calculations in his head about the type of aircraft and its possible origin and destination.

"Do you think they're searching for us?" Caitlin whispered, as if the chopper's occupants could hear.

"There's a helicopter business up the road outside Gettysburg." Blake looked at his watch. "They're probably just returning from checking power lines or something."

Caitlin studied his eyes to see if he was lying or trying to hide something from her, but it was a lost cause. He was so stoic and stone-faced, and always so calm in the face of danger anyway, it was impossible to tell.

She decided to probe him anyway. "Do you think they're using infrared heat sensors to check abandoned cabins or something?"

He threw his pencil down on the table, crossed his arms over his chest, and tilted his chair back on two legs. "I think you've watched too many Hollywood suspense movies is what I think." He said the words in a joking manner, yet she got the distinct feeling he had been pondering the same thing.

"It's possible, right?"

"I suppose it's possible, but we're as safe here as anywhere." He let the chair fall forward again, and picked the pencil back up. "And as soon as we get this plan into a workable strategy, we'll be out of here anyway."

Caitlin nodded and tried to turn her attention back to the map on the table, but she was still listening to the sound of the chopper fading off into the distance. When the helicopter didn't turn around and circle over them as she half-expected it to, she felt a little more secure about accepting Blake's theory.

"Here. Have a drink."

Caitlin contemplated the energy drink Blake was shoving toward her. "Thanks. I think."

"It's good stuff." Blake emptied his in one swallow and set the empty container on the table. "Restroom break. Be right back."

Caitlin twisted off the black cap. As she lifted the drink to her lips, an idea struck her and a smile rose to her lips. How enjoyable would it be to use Alinsky's Rules for Radicals against those who had used them against her? Rule #1 popped into her mind: *Power is not only what you have, but what the enemy thinks you have.*

"Hey, you have some black tape with you?"

Blake paused in the doorway and pointed. "There should be some in that bag there. Why?"

"Just thought of something, that's all."

When the door closed, Caitlin examined the bag's contents and found a variety of odds and ends, like scissors, pins, tweezers, zip ties and the tape. As she was replacing the contents, she noticed a small piece of coated wire. *That might add a nice touch.*

She had just completed her task when Blake came back through the door, whistling like he didn't have a care in the world. She shook her head, amazed at his cool composure and confidence. It made her feel more at ease—she wondered if that was his intent.

"Miss me while I was gone?" He winked at her before sitting down, then became all business again. "You find what you were looking for?"

"Yep. Just needed a piece of tape. I'm good to go."

He rubbed his hands together. "Okay. Let's get back to work."

With the short break behind them, they continued their work, running possible scenarios by each other and continually refining and improving upon their plan. After developing a solid Plan A, Blake insisted on a Plan B, and then alternative contingency procedures in case both of those fell through.

All morning and afternoon they consulted with one another, relaxed in the intimacy of mutual fatigue and consumed by the significance of the task at hand, until gradually the sounds of day were replaced by those of night.

"You sure you're good with your end?" Blake dug a couple of MREs out of his backpack. "You haven't told me your exact line of attack."

"I'm good."

"I'd kind of like to know a little bit more than that." He appeared taken aback. "Like what you're going to say."

Caitlin's breath caught in her throat. She wouldn't be breaking any laws, but she wasn't sure her strategy would line up with his strong ethical and moral values. If he shot it down, they would be back to square one. "It's complicated, but I got it. Don't worry."

"Oka-a-y." Blake looked at her quizzically and shrugged. "If you're *sure*."

"I'm sure. You don't need to micromanage me."

"It's not micromanaging. I don't want any surprises." His brow was creased and his expression intense. "I'm your backup in case things go south. Remember?"

"Yes sir, I remember." She saluted him, causing him to shake his head. "And I also remember your words of advice from the first night we were on the run."

He cocked his head and squinted, trying to remember what he'd told her.

"You told me I had three choices. *Give in. Give up. Or give it your all.*"

"I said that?" He grinned out of the side of his mouth. "That's good advice. Glad you haven't forgotten it."

"I got my end, dude." Caitlin picked up the MRE on the table and opened it. "Roast beef. Yummy." She could feel him continue to scrutinize her, but she ignored it as she dug into her food. "Hope you didn't spend all day cooking this just for me." She thought she could rouse a smile from him, or at the very least, change the subject. She failed at the former, but succeeded at the latter.

"It doesn't taste like anyone spent much time in the kitchen as far as I'm concerned." He grimaced as he took a bite and then washed it down with water.

They ate the rest of the meal in silence. When they were finished, Blake stood and stretched. "We better try to get a couple hours of sleep."

Caitlin stood too and yawned. She was tired, but wasn't sure how much rest she would get. She understood the significant implications of the next twenty-four hours. There was a good chance they would end up in jail—or dead—if things did not go as planned.

"We'll plan to break camp about 0400. That should get us to the Metro in plenty of time."

At the words "break camp" Caitlin had a sudden feeling of intense loss. It sounded so firm and final. The end. No matter what happened tomorrow, good or bad, her time with Blake would be over. He would go back to his life, and she would go back to hers. She gazed up at him and forced her lips upward. "Sounds good."

"You okay?"

She nodded. "Um-hmm."

Blake put his hands on her shoulders and gave them a gentle squeeze. "You're sure you're comfortable with the plan for tomorrow?"

Caitlin was almost afraid to look into his eyes. She was too tired and exhausted to fight the magnetic power they held. But she knew he was questioning her preparedness and was waiting for an answer.

"It's not going to be easy, Cait," he said, before she could think of a reply. "But it's doable." He seemed composed and confident, as if facing some of the most powerful and dangerous people in the world tomorrow would be just another day at work. But it was his voice that struck her to the core—so concerned and kind that it made her heart flutter and kick.

"Got it." She nodded and smiled indifferently, but a nerve in her cheek twitched at the effort to appear unaffected. His hands—strong, firm, protective—still rested on her shoulders. *How does he expect me to think straight when he's standing this close?*

Caitlin forced herself not to look away from the encouraging glint in his eyes and the reassuring expression on his face, even though the combination was pure seduction to her. She wasn't expecting this reaction to him—maybe that's why she was finding it so hard to control her response. Taking a deep breath, she attempted to mask her inner turmoil with light-hearted humor. "Not exactly probable for success, but possible. I'm good with that."

"This is going to be dangerous. Don't take it lightly."

Caitlin nodded to show she understood, but in reality all she wanted to do was to fall into his arms. He was her security, her protector—and the attraction she felt for him was suddenly undeniable. It wasn't just his rugged good looks and principled past that made him so alluring. It was so much more. He had shown her the value of someone having your back, and taught her how to overcome disappointment when someone didn't. She could no longer pretend that his voice, his touch, his very presence did not affect her.

"We've done the inconceivable by surviving this long. There's no reason we can't do the impossible by exposing their crimes."

She was proud of how calm and poised she sounded—because the effort of trying to control her emotions was making her dizzy.

"But a lot of things have to go right." He increased the pressure on her shoulders. "Things that are out of our control."

She nodded, not trusting herself to speak. The only words she heard, and the ones that kept replaying in her mind were, "out of control." *Is he reading my mind again?* She clenched her teeth to keep them from chattering. Her legs began to shake.

"Are you okay, Cait?"

She swallowed hard and nodded, knowing he must feel her trembling. Reluctant to face him, yet unable to turn away, she tried to hide her emotions from his probing stare by lowering her chin and closing her eyes... tight.

"Not afraid about tomorrow?"

She shook her bowed head, her eyes still closed. "No."

"Look at me." His tone was soft, but commanding.

Cait opened her eyes and then gradually lifted her head. His blue eyes glistened in the beam of soft lantern light, and the probing intensity in them threw her even more off balance. She reached up to hold onto his arms for support. "I'm not afraid about tomorrow," she murmured. "Really."

Slowly, and she thought seductively, his gaze slid downward to her fingers wrapped around his forearms, before leisurely lifting to meet hers again. "Then it's me you're afraid of?" His eyes bore into hers in silent expectation.

"No." Caitlin shook her head emphatically and swallowed hard again as she watched a smoldering flame of yearning begin to build in his eyes. Her fingers reflexively dug deeper into the flesh of his arms. "I mean...it's not fear," she whispered.

She felt his chest rise and fall with increased intensity against hers, felt her own heart hammering in her ears. Caught on the fragile edge of control, things began moving in slow motion—yet still too fast for her to comprehend.

Her breath caught in her throat as one strong arm wrapped possessively around her waist while the other moved to the back of her neck. His thumb left a burning path of heat on her cheek as he stroked it, sending forth a surge of sensations that both confused and overwhelmed her. She clung to the folds of his shirt and waited for him to speak, half in anticipation and half in dread.

"This wasn't supposed to happen." His voice was husky as his eyes probed hers with need.

Caitlin closed her eyes and nodded. So he was feeling it too. *Fighting* it.

Her arms, seemingly of their own accord, lifted and wrapped around his neck—tight, like she was drowning and he was a life preserver. With her head against his chest, she could feel his heart pounding in her ear, could feel liquid heat pulsing through her veins. She didn't know what was going to happen tomorrow. She didn't care. She needed this now—to touch him. To feel him. To know he shared her desire and need.

She waited for what seemed like a lifetime before she heard him inhale a deep, ragged breath, and then exhale in a way that sounded like a groan. "Not here." His deep voice simmered with barely controlled passion and she thought she felt him shudder with suppressed emotion. "Not now."

When Caitlin looked up at him, the tenderness and resolve in his expression were almost more than she could bear. He was a professional. A warrior. Trained to be alert, disciplined, calm, and prepared. They both needed to concentrate on the tasks at hand—not each other.

She nodded, and watched with wide eyes as he leaned down hesitantly, and pressed his lips against hers. The kiss was slow, gentle—sensual—like he was savoring every second. But all too soon he loosened his embrace and inhaled shakily, as if to regain control. "We have a big day tomorrow, Scoop. Try to get some sleep." He bent down and kissed the top of her head.

Caitlin pressed her lips together so no sound would come out, and listened to the throb of her heart in her ears. Standing in the middle of the room with her eyes closed, she winced when the door slammed shut.

Chapter 30

Blake walked confidently into the Senator's reception area and smiled at the secretary. "How ya doing?" He put one arm over the top of the counter and relaxed against it. "I'm Patrick Donahue. I have an appointment to see the Senator."

The woman appeared confused, but turned to her computer. "I'm sorry, Mr. ..."

"Donahue," Blake repeated. "Patrick Donahue. I should be on the schedule for nine." Lifting his hand, he pointed to his watch. "See, I'm right on time." He winked at the woman to throw her off guard, and leaned in closer to make sure her view of the senator's door was blocked.

"I'm sorry, I don't see any appointments for nine." She seemed flustered and unsure of herself. "The Senator is busy preparing a very important speech and isn't taking visitors."

"Are you sure?" Blake interrupted. "I've had it on my schedule for more than a month. I traveled all the way from western Virginia."

"I'm sorry. Give me a minute here to check his other calendar." She turned her back and walked to another computer on a table against the wall.

"Damn it. I told my wife to call and confirm." Blake hit the countertop with his fist to cover the sound of the Senator's door opening and clicking shut behind him. "Just like her to drop the ball."

"Senator Wiley. Nice to see you." Caitlin walked into the office, startling the senator as he sat at his desk. He glanced in confusion at his phone as if questioning why he hadn't been forewarned of a visitor, but Caitlin pretended not to notice. She strode toward him with her hand extended. "You remember me, don't you?"

The expression on the senator's face changed from confusion and anger to one of recognition, and then suspicion. "Of course I do. How could I forget?" He shook her hand. "I'm surprised you got by my receptionist." His eyes flicked from her face to the large flannel shirt of Blake's she wore over her tee shirt, and finally landed on the oversized men's sneakers on her feet.

"Oh, I think she was busy. And you told me to drop by anytime." She folded herself as casually as she could into one of his plush leather chairs, adjusting her shirt as she did so. "Remember?"

"Well, actually, Ms. Sparks—it is Sparks, right? Actually, today is not a good day. And now is not a good time." He started to reach for his phone and gave her a condescending look. "But I'm sure I know some people who would be interested in talking to you."

"Oh, I won't take too much of your time." Caitlin stood back up, took the phone from his hand, and placed it back in the cradle. She was enjoying this more than she thought she would.

"Then what can I do for you?" He no longer tried to sound calm or act courteous.

"There are still a few things that aren't adding up in my mind."

Instead of sitting back down, Caitlin began pacing in front of his desk. "I mean, even after that interview I did with you, the facts just don't seem to be fitting."

"I'm sorry about that." The senator stood as well. "But today is not a good day to get into a lengthy discussion over questions you may have." He moved toward the door to show her out. "I'll have my receptionist make some calls. Like I said, there are a number of people who would like to talk to you."

Caitlin took a quick step and blocked the door. "But I'm here, and I promise it won't take long. We might as well get it out of the way."

Senator Wiley threw up his hands and walked back to his desk. "What are your questions about?" He shook his finger at her. "Not the Kessler case. Surely you aren't still chasing your tail over that Kessler mess."

Caitlin laughed. "That's a good analogy, Senator, because I have indeed been chasing my tail... thanks to the runaround I've been getting from you and your cohorts in crime."

The senator placed both hands on his desk and inclined toward her. "That's just about enough." He went for his phone again, but Caitlin anticipated the move and stepped forward, putting her hand on his before he could pick it up.

"I don't think you want to do that. I think you want to hear what I have to say."

"I think what I want to do is call security—and they can be here in about two seconds," he said threateningly. "Do you have any idea how many people are searching for you at this very minute?"

Caitlin took a deep breath to control her voice and heart-rate. She knew she had to sound calm and in control. There would be no re-dos.

"For me? Why would anyone be searching for *me*?"

"You're in a lot of trouble, young lady." He smiled like he had a secret, but his eyes reflected evil intent. "A lot of trouble."

"I'm sure it's all a misunderstanding." Caitlin was surprised at how utterly calm her own voice sounded. "If it will help clear things up, I'll turn myself in once we're done talking."

That relaxed him even more, bringing an expression of confidence and satisfaction to his face. But it didn't last long. "Okay. Get on with it. What do you want?"

Caitlin took a deep breath. "Remember when I visited you a few weeks ago?"

The senator sat back in his chair with his arms crossed. "Of course I do."

"Well, I've discovered a few things since then."

Wiley regarded her with a look of suspicion mixed with anger. "You're wasting your time—and mine—if you think you're going to implicate me in something."

"Really?" Caitlin pretended to be surprised by his reaction. "What if I have evidence?"

The senator did not even blink. "There is no evidence because I've committed no crimes. Anything you think you've found will come down to your word against mine." He laughed. "And who do you think they will believe? A sitting senator who is favored to be the next President of the United States, or a low-life news reporter—excuse me, *former* reporter—who's been trashed in the media and possesses not a thread of credibility."

Reminded of the scorn and ridicule heaped upon her by false media reports almost made Caitlin wince. She decided to change tactics. "To tell you the truth, this has more to do with me than anything about you." She looked down at her hands, and then up at him with just her eyes. "I'm here because my conscience is killing me."

Now the senator seemed interested. "About what?"

She squared her shoulders, lifted her chin, and boldly met Wiley's suspicious stare. "When I was here last time I did something I shouldn't have done."

The senator absently brushed some lint from the sleeve of his dark suit, unconcerned, and seemingly indifferent to her solemn declaration. "What did you do?"

Caitlin stood and walked over to a credenza. With her back to him, she reached under the lip and then turned and held out her hand. "I planted this."

She watched the blood rush out of the senator's face, just before it turned beet red. "What is that?" he demanded.

"It's a recording device." Caitlin brought it closer and pretended to examine it before holding it out for him to see. "They really make these things small these days, don't they?"

The senator stood and banged his fist on the desk. "That's against the law! I'll have you arrested!"

"You're right. It *is* against the law." Caitlin closed her hand around the device and held it close to her. "I was told not to do it, and I feel badly about it." She shook her head before continuing, trying to sound remorseful. "But then again, I have a feeling that what's recorded on here might reveal something else against the law." She looked him straight in the eye. "So the question is, which crime is worse?"

Wiley appeared uncomfortable, but he spoke calmly enough. "I don't know what you're talking about."

"Seriously?" Caitlin extended her hand, revealing the device. "You're not worried about what might be on this?" She had to work hard to keep her voice from quivering. His calm exterior worried her. Was he really that unconcerned?

"Who says there's anything on there?" The senator crossed his arms and leaned back in his chair as if he were completely at ease, yet Caitlin noticed beads of sweat had begun to form on his temples. She reminded herself he was an expert at lying under pressure. She had to be careful.

"I'm glad to hear you don't have anything to hide." Caitlin walked closer to his desk. "Because I'm willing to go to jail and serve my time for an illegal recording. In fact, like I said, I will turn myself in—right after I turn this over to the media."

"This is blackmail." His voice was low, an angry whisper, but there was a twinge of fear in it now as well.

"That's how this system works, isn't it?" Caitlin's voice was equally low and angry. "Any means to achieve the desired ends?"

"What do you want?" His effort to sound unconcerned failed miserably this time.

"I want to know how Vince died." She leaned forward for emphasis. "And *why*."

"What for?"

"So I can get on with my life."

"This is a personal thing? You're not trying to screw me?" He laughed without smiling. "You expect me to believe that?"

"I don't give a damn what you believe, Senator." She held the device out again. "This gives me the upper hand."

Wiley pulled a handkerchief out of his pocket and swiped his head. After putting it back, he moved his chair closer to the desk and crossed his hands in front of him. "Let's be reasonable here."

Caitlin sat down. "Of course."

"How much do you want for it?" He bent down and began unlocking a drawer on his desk.

Now it was Caitlin's turn to laugh. "You think this is about *money?*"

The senator seemed confused. "Of course. I mean, there's probably nothing on there, but I want to put it behind me. How much?"

"Oh, that's right. There *is* an election coming up, isn't there? I almost forgot about that." Caitlin shot him a grim smile, letting him know she hadn't forgotten at all. "At the very least, I'm sure there are some interesting conversations with your mistress on here that might not sit too well with your wife and your constituents." She paused to let that sink in. "But I have a feeling your love life is the very least of your worries."

Wiley slammed his hand against his desk. "Look here. I've had just about enough of this."

Caitlin could see he had indeed had just about enough. A blood vessel running along his temple appeared about to burst. She put her hands on the arms of the chair, trying to look relaxed and in control. In reality, it felt like her heart was coming out her throat. "Like I said, I want to know what happened."

"Why?"

Caitlin exhaled, starting to get agitated, but then centered herself again when she thought of Blake. War had taught him how to dig deep for courage when he needed it most. She needed to do the same, to mask her inner turmoil with deceptive calmness and composure. She had to get through this. She had assured Blake she had this part under control. "So I can put it behind me."

"You'll give me that recording device if I tell you what happened?"

"That's the only rule." Caitlin nodded. "You talk, it's yours."

Wiley squinted his eyes and studied her. "You can't be serious. Once I have that in my hand, it will be your word against mine. What kind of game are you playing?"

"My only interest is knowing the truth so I can get on with

my life. You tell me here and now what happened, and the device is yours. Pretty simple. Otherwise…"

"How do I know *you're* telling the truth?" The senator remained skeptical. "I need some assurance that you're going to give me that thing."

"Not everyone is as corrupt and immoral as you," Caitlin replied with narrow-eyed scrutiny. "You'll just have to trust me."

"I don't trust anyone in this town," he replied. "Least of all an obnoxious, overbearing small-town reporter."

"And you think calling me names is going to help your case?" Caitlin contemplated him with a look of contempt. She held all the cards, and she knew he knew it.

The two sat eyeing each other until at last Caitlin stood and set the device on the very edge of the desk, close to her. The senator was portly and the desk was wide. There was no way he could grab it.

"It's yours if you tell me everything."

He glanced at the gadget and then shifted his attention to her, seeming to measure the sincerity of her words. "Okay, what do you want to know?"

"Everything."

Caitlin's heart started beating wildly. The time had arrived. This was what all of the pain, fear, humiliation and digging had led to. He was starting to crack. Her mind began whirring out of control, yet was still fully aware that the next few minutes were going to dictate her entire life. This was it. Success or failure was on the line. "Start at the beginning."

Seconds ticked by. Caitlin could feel beads of sweat sliding down her temple, but she didn't want to move. She stared at the senator, and he stared back.

At last he shifted in his chair and cleared his throat. "Okay.

Deal. I'll play."

Caitlin let her breath out slowly, keeping a detached look on her face so he would not see her relief.

"I guess I should start at the beginning…" He paused and his eyes fell upon something over Caitlin's shoulder. In the split second that she turned her head to see what had caught his attention, he stood, lunged across the desk and swept the device off with all the force he could muster. She watched it fly across the room—seemingly in slow motion—until it made contact with the far wall and exploded into pieces.

Senator Wiley laughed loudly and triumphantly. "Whoops. There goes your evidence."

Caitlin clenched her jaw to kill the sob in her throat, and then sat in silent disbelief at her blunder. The device had been *her* idea, her leverage, to use to discover the truth. It took a moment for her to recover from the spark of hope and expectation being extinguished so abruptly. She had been so close, but now the justice she thought within her grasp was once again unreachable.

Her next thought was that she had failed, not just herself and Vince, but Blake. Everything the two of them had endured while on the run would be for nothing if she didn't get Wiley to talk. Covering her face with trembling hands, she felt a stab of guilt bury itself deep in her breast. She had assured Blake she had this part under control. She could not fail.

"Now, what are you going to do?" The senator stood behind his desk with his arms crossed, seeming to enjoy her struggle to recapture her composure.

Get a grip, Cait. She knew Blake would have no trouble reacting to this turn of events. He would have a new plan in a heartbeat and carry it out with composed authority. But could she be that strong, calm, and resourceful?

Beneath Wiley's steady scrutiny, she found it hard to think. But when she recalled Blake's desperate struggle in Renoviah, she resisted the urge to give up in despair. Instead, she drew strength from what he had endured, and convinced herself to emulate the resolve and fierce determination that had brought him through it. Somehow he had fought for thirteen long hours, then dragged his two mortally wounded buddies to a safe room despite being dreadfully wounded himself.

She squeezed her hands together and remembered an old saying: *Your setbacks don't define you, your determination does.* Determination is one thing she had in abundance. She never wanted to see regret or disappointment in Blake's eyes because of something she had done to let him down. She would do anything to prevent that. *Anything.*

At that moment, she could almost hear Blake's voice. It sounded loud and clear, as if he were standing right beside her— *Embrace the suck. Never, never quit.*

Chapter 31

Caitlin took a long, slow breath, reached deep inside, and relied on her instincts even though she was more shaken than she cared to admit.

She no longer had the device, but she had her brain. And the plan she and Blake had devised was still viable if she stayed strong and pulled herself together. All she had to do was outwit and out-maneuver the senator, and the way to do that was to use his arrogance and overconfidence against him. *You can't prevent problems and crises—but you can control your response to them.*

Here goes Plan B.

Giving the senator a look of pure agony, she sat down, put her face in her hands and began to sob in mock resignation. "All I wanted to know was the truth. I didn't want money."

"Really? You want the truth?" The senator came out from behind the desk, but the expression he wore wasn't one of sympathy for her pain. It was triumph that he had beaten her. "Sorry, honey. You're way too trusting to make it in this town." He laughed as he surveyed the pieces of the device scattered on the floor.

When Caitlin didn't respond other than to keep sobbing, he

spoke again. "Okay. Stop your bawling."

Her sobbing became hushed as she tried to quiet the roaring din in her ears. *Don't throw me out. Talk to me. Please.*

"I'm not the bad guy you think I am."

Caitlin sat up slightly and readjusted her position. She stole a glance at the senator from between her fingers as she slowly slid her hands from her face. The expression he wore was still jubilant—if not downright smug. "Really?" She took an exaggerated sobbing breath. "You're not doing a very good job of... of proving that."

"Like I said, you don't know how this town works. Sometimes things have to be done to achieve the right end result."

Caitlin's heart raced. She had to be careful. *Go slow. Don't spook him.* "What do you mean by *things?*"

"You know. Exploitation. Manipulation. Persuasion."

Murder?

Caitlin bit her lip to keep from saying what she was thinking out loud. Instead she said something else. "So you mean like running guns?" The gunrunning scheme was the least of the crimes she wanted answers to, but it is what started the whole sordid affair.

"If you're talking about Operation Flintlock, then yes." He waved his hands in the air as if that was completely irrelevant. "I had to get that gun control bill passed in order to satisfy my donors before the election. That's just how the system works. If it weren't for that damn journalist getting involved, everything would have been fine."

Caitlin stopped wiping her eyes. Stopped breathing. "Kessler?"

"Yes, that damned nosy bastard Kessler was about to report the details on how Operation Flintlock had failed. We had to do something to keep that from happening. It would have meant the end of my campaign."

"We?"

The senator laughed sardonically as he paced, his voice taking on a boastful tone, proud of the things he'd accomplished without getting caught. "The Secretary of State, of course. Well, it was all planned by Mallory in such a way that it wouldn't raise eyebrows. I'm not sure how much the Secretary actually knew about what was going on."

"Mallory who?"

He stopped pacing and regarded her with a quizzical expression. "Mallory Jarrott, of course. Isn't that the mistress you were referring to?"

Caitlin tried to keep all emotion from her face but wasn't sure she was successful. She had only mentioned a mistress because everyone in D.C. had one. She didn't have any facts to support the matter—and certainly never dreamed the senator had been having an affair with Blake's ex-wife.

She went back to the subject at hand, hoping she could keep him talking. "So Mallory planned the capture of the journalist?"

"Of course. Mallory thought of it, planned it." He turned around and smiled. "She's good with things like that. She'll make a great vice president."

Caitlin's mind was moving a hundred miles a minute as she tried to absorb all of the details and not appear too stunned. "What about the rescue attempt?"

Wiley pulled a cigar out of a drawer and proceeded to light it before he answered. "Well, that didn't go exactly as planned."

"Didn't go as planned? Three men lost their lives." Caitlin blinked, trying to understand how this man could be so cold and callous; so absolutely unfeeling and unremorseful.

"But we didn't get caught, darling. In this business, the end always justifies the means."

"What about Vince? What did he do?" Caitlin closed her eyes, afraid she would hear what she feared all along—that it had been the phone call to her and their relationship that had caused the series of events that followed.

"Vince ran across some private emails he shouldn't have seen."

Caitlin grabbed the arm of the chair for support, but said nothing.

"And the first thing he did as a conscientious employee was call and tell me he wanted to testify in front of my committee." The senator laughed. "That was the end of that."

Caitlin tried to keep from trembling with rage. "And the two State Department workers killed at the weekend retreat?"

"They were told not to talk. Frankly, they asked for it."

Caitlin could barely comprehend that she had really just heard a sitting senator say two people deserved to be killed because they were going to blow the whistle on a government that already had a string of dead bodies behind it.

She cleared her throat. "You had them killed because they wanted to tell the truth." She stated it bluntly and confidently, with no tremor or noticeable fear in her voice.

"I guess you could put it like that if you want." He shrugged and tapped his cigar on the side of the ashtray. "But like I said, they were told not to talk. In fact, they signed agreements to that effect. Of course, again, they called me to let me know they intended to break the sanctity of that agreement."

Caitlin wanted to stand, but feared her legs would not hold her. "What about Mary? What did she do to deserve to die at your hands?"

"It wasn't at my hands exactly. She was on her way to see you."

"About what?"

"Not sure about that," he said offhandedly, "but it wouldn't have been good. Anyway, I told a friend of mine to stop her. I didn't tell him to run her down."

"So you accept no blame." Caitlin said the words as she was thinking them. She could not stop them.

"Of course not." He gave her an irritated glare. "Why would I?"

Caitlin felt almost nauseous. She took a deep breath to control her emotions. "What about my friend, Judy?" She shot him an accusatorial look. "She didn't do anything to you."

"Oh, sorry. That one *was* my fault. We'd warned you and warned you, but you wouldn't stop digging. How was I to know she would borrow your vehicle that day?"

"You ordered a hit on *me?*"

"You could say it was a mutual understanding between Louie and me."

Caitlin's heart did a somersault. "So Louie is in on this too." It was a statement, not a question. Of course, she had known he was a part of it ever since the first day she and Blake were on the run. But it was still hard to accept as fact. "I thought he was a friend."

That made the senator erupt into laughter. "Old Louie. Just shows how good he is at his job. The best, really."

"But he's retired. What do you mean good at his job?"

Again the senator laughed as if she had just told a good joke. "He's retired in the sense that he no longer does what he used to do for the CIA."

"What does he do now?"

"He's what I call a Master Manipulator. His specialty is PSYOPS, you know."

Caitlin studied the senator warily. Louie had never told her he did PSYOPS—that he was trained to conduct operations with the intention of influencing and changing motives and behaviors.

"Manipulator?" she questioned. "But I met him by chance."

Wiley laughed. "See how good he is?" He sat down at his desk and tapped his cigar ashes again. "No, honey, there was no *chance* about it."

Caitlin remembered very clearly the first time she had met Louie. It had been on the Metro. "I don't think you know what you're talking about."

"Let me tell you how this town works." The senator paused to relight his cigar and then relaxed back in his chair. "About eighty percent of the people will fall for whatever we feed them through the media. We call them sheeple." He grinned. "Know what I mean? Ba-aa-a. Like sheep to slaughter."

Caitlin remained quiet, listening, taking it all in.

"Then there are the ones like you, who try to buck the system, gather their own facts, make up their own minds." He blew a smoke ring into the air. "For people like you—and Madison—we use Louie."

"So he knew I was going to be on that Metro. How?"

"Tapping into your phone calls or digital calendars. Maybe he knew your regular routine. I don't know what all he does. I just know he's good at it."

"And he pretended to just run into me and befriend me, why?"

"Two reasons, really. One was just to have the ability to keep his eyes on you, know what you were working on and where you were going to get your information."

"And the second reason?"

"That's a bit more complicated." He took a long, slow draw on his cigar. "It was his idea to keep you off track, steer you in the wrong direction whenever he could."

"I guess it surprised him when Detective Madison and I showed up on the same day."

"Well, your arrival wasn't a surprise. You know they never did find a cause for that darn barn fire."

Nothing could have prepared Caitlin for that statement. Her mind returned to that day when the editor had assigned her to the fire story. Louie had called soon after, knowing she wouldn't turn down the offer to stop since she was going to be going right by. It was a small crime in comparison to the murders, but it had cost a hardworking farmer his livelihood.

For some reason this tidbit of information struck her more forcefully than the others—maybe because it wasn't something she had foreseen. This one was so hurtful, manipulative, and far reaching that it stunned her.

"But to answer your question," the senator continued, "Detective Madison was not expected that day—just like you were not expected today." It was not so much the words as the tone of his voice that carried evil intent.

She nodded, even though her mind was spinning. She could hardly believe that everything she had suspected or envisioned, and more, was indeed fact.

The senator interrupted her thoughts. "If that's everything you wanted to know, then it's time for you to leave. I have work to do."

Caitlin stared at the floor where the recording device still lay in pieces. "Yes, I guess you told me what I wanted to know." As she turned toward the door, she heard a drawer open behind her.

"You may think you're smart, but you're not."

Caitlin turned back around to answer and found herself staring into the barrel of a pistol. She instinctively raised her hands. "What do you mean?"

"Did you really think I was going to let you walk out of here, knowing what you know?"

Chapter 32

Caitlin stared at the end of the gun and then at Senator Wiley's finger on the trigger. "I told you I only wanted the truth. And like you said, it would be my word against yours. Who's going to believe me?"

Wiley's tone indicated both confidence and rage. "Nevertheless, it could create a scandal, and I can't afford that this close to the election. It's not just for me, you understand." He lowered the gun, but then steadied and aimed it once again. "I promised Mallory she would be the first woman vice president. She's counting on that."

Caitlin remained quiet, not wanting to irritate him further. She was not sure he was rational at the moment—or even sane.

"Move over here." He motioned with the gun. "I've come too far to let you stop me now."

Caitlin's breath caught in her throat as the door crashed open and Blake stepped into the room holding a gun of his own. "Put the gun down, Senator Wiley." His stance and tone revealed a ferociousness she had never seen.

The senator continued to point the pistol in Caitlin's direction. "She threatened me. I need to hold her until the police arrive." His finger remained on the trigger of a gun that trembled violently with agitation and rage.

"Don't make any sudden movements or I'll blow a hole through you." Blake's voice was calm—too calm, as if he were hoping the senator would ignore his command.

Wiley appeared to notice the insinuation and his nervous gaze shot over to Blake. "I need to call the police. She broke into my office. I want her arrested."

"Don't worry, the police are on their way."

No sooner had he said the words, when two uniformed officers charged into the room.

"Arrest her!" Wiley shouted, pointing at Caitlin with his gun. "We've been looking for her. She's dangerous."

The officers ignored Caitlin and went toward the senator. "Put down the gun, sir."

"Of course, of course." Wiley laid the gun on his desk. "No need to be alarmed, gentlemen. She broke into my office. I want her arrested."

"Please put your hands behind your back, Senator." One of the officers kept his gun trained on the senator while the other pushed him roughly into the wall. Wiley looked at him over his shoulder, then at Caitlin and Blake, with confusion. "What are you talking about?"

Once the cuffs had been clicked on the struggling man, Blake walked over to the smashed device and picked up a piece, turning it over in his hand. "I told you not to plant anything in here. What is this thing anyway?"

"The bottle caps from two energy drinks and a piece of wire I found in your bag."

Wiley's head jerked around. "You lied? That wasn't real?"

Blake merely shrugged at the disclosure, but his tone revealed a hint of admiration. "Not only was it not real. It was never in your office until today. She literally had it up her sleeve."

The officers started to push the senator toward the door. "It's still your word against mine," he spat. "They'll never believe you. Just wait until we launch a media campaign against you." His face turned red with rage. "You'll never work again in this town. Or anywhere. I promise you that!"

Blake crossed his arms and turned to Caitlin. "Shall we tell him?"

Caitlin's legs were shaking so much she had to sit down. "Sure."

Blake nodded toward the officers, who turned the senator around and walked him to the window. "See that white van down there?"

The senator stared with a confused expression at the simple white van and the handful of men around it. One of them waved and pointed to the large antenna sticking out of the roof of the vehicle.

Blake moved toward the window and waved back. "That's my buddy, Jimmy Podge."

Everyone watched as the senator began to understand what was happening. He struggled against the officer holding onto him. "She was wired?" He literally shook with fury. "She was wired?"

Caitlin lifted her shirt just enough for him to see.

"That's illegal!" His face was beet red and he appeared to be shaking.

"Actually, it's not illegal in D.C."

"And definitely not with a warrant." Blake stood with arms crossed.

"Who would give you a warrant against me? That's impossible!"

"There are still a few good judges around, Senator."

Wiley continued struggling against the officers. He turned violently around to face Caitlin. "We had a deal. You tricked me!"

"The rules of the deal were simple." Caitlin appeared somewhat shell-shocked by all that she'd heard. "You talk, you get the device." She nodded toward the floor. "I'll make sure you get every piece."

Blake bent down and picked up some of the pieces. "Here you go." He walked over to the senator and stuck them in his shirt pocket, then gave it a pat for good measure. "All yours." He nodded to the cops. "Get him out of here."

"Do you know who I am?" Wiley's voice could be heard booming down the hall. "I'm going to be the next President of the United States and Mallory will be my running mate. You'll regret this. Both of you!"

Blake listened to the senator's voice continue to echo through the halls and then disappear. A knock on the frame of the door made them both turn.

Walter Snow stepped through the battered doorway. "Appears as though everything went as planned."

"Thanks to you, Counselor." Blake grinned and held out his hand. "Couldn't have done it without the judge."

Walter grasped Blake's hand and put the other on his shoulder. "My pleasure. The judge and I went to school together. He owed me a favor."

"So in other words, you had plenty of college material to blackmail him with."

Walter winked. "Something like that." Then he got serious again. "I just stopped by to tell you they picked up Mallory as well. It will be hitting the news soon."

Blake nodded. "Thanks."

"There'll be a congressional investigation of course. They'll want to see how much the Secretary of State knew." Walter turned his attention to Caitlin, who was staring in their direction but did not appear to really be seeing. "She okay?"

Blake slid his gaze over to Cait. "She will be." He talked to Walt in a low voice. "We're even now. Right?"

Walter gave him a questioning look.

"I saved your life and you saved mine." He nodded toward Caitlin.

That made Walter smile. "If you say so, Blake." He shook his hand again and headed toward the door. "Glad to hear it. If you say so."

When Walter's retreating footsteps could no longer be heard, Blake turned to Caitlin. "Good job, Scoop."

She remained quiet, a confused expression on her face. "It's over," she said, as if she couldn't quite believe it.

Blake put his hands on her shoulders. "It's over. And you did what you set out to do—you got justice."

Caitlin took a long, deep breath and let it out slowly. "Finally. Justice." She looked up at him for the first time. "But now what?"

"What do you mean?" Blake tried to keep any disappointment from showing in his eyes.

"It's been so long since anything's been normal, I'm not sure I know what to do."

A long silence ensued before Blake spoke again. "Get on with your life, maybe."

Caitlin stared at him, uncertainty visible in her eyes. When he increased the pressure on her shoulders, she stepped into his embrace and wrapped her arms tightly around him. "Get on with *our* lives, you mean?"

"Yes, that's what I mean." He pulled her away and studied her face. "If you're ready."

Something flickered far back in her eyes, while something passionate and emotional replaced the dazed, overwhelmed look.

"I'm ready." She wrapped her arms around his neck. "If you are."

He drew her back in, both arms wrapped tightly around her. "I've been ready for quite some time, Miss Sparks. Actually, I've been ready for quite some time."

Epilogue

B lake parked his truck in front of the house and walked in the front door, expecting to be greeted by his family.

"Anybody home?" He looked around, but no one appeared. "Glad everyone missed me so much," he said to himself. The meeting he'd attended had taken longer than he'd thought, but still, he thought Cait would be anxious to hear how it went.

Glancing around the foyer, he had to smile at what she had accomplished since becoming his wife not quite a year ago. She had not only turned this house into a home, but also created a cohesive, loving family after the chaos caused by the disclosures uncovered in the Kessler Affair.

Any direction he looked, he saw signs of Cait's devotion and style—from the Indian corn and gourds decorating the mantle in the dining room to the homegrown pumpkins sitting on the wide windowsills and the front porch. With a look of contentment on his face, he closed his eyes and inhaled, then followed his nose to the kitchen where he found more evidence of her domestic touch. *I am a lucky man.*

Although tempted to give the freshly baked pie a try, Blake continued through the house to his office in the back. As he threw the folder he was holding onto his desk, a small handwritten note taped to his stapler caught his attention. He bent over and read the words. *Missed you—much.*

Blake smiled out of the corner of his mouth. Even beyond the tangible things, Cait had brought a light and warmth that had been missing in this house… in his life. Before meeting her he was only going through the motions—existing—not really *living*. She'd taught him to take pleasure in the simplest things in life, and to be thankful for every day they had together.

The sound of laughter coming from outside drove Blake to the window. *There they are.*

He watched Drew race through a huge pile of raked leaves, followed closely by a squealing red-cheeked Whitney. Caitlin and their dog, Max, ran through the scattered remnants that remained. As wide as their grins were, he couldn't tell who was having more fun. Even the dog appeared to be laughing.

Blake had added the highly trained German shepherd to their security mix six months ago, hoping he would serve as another deterrent to anyone who wanted to harm his family. But even though Max had been purchased as a last line of defense, it hadn't taken him long to move from protector to pet.

Cait's pet, that is. Max followed her everywhere, including their bedroom. With a wife and two kids ganging up on him, Blake had found himself on the losing side of the argument that dogs don't sleep in beds. He'd consoled himself with the knowledge that the connection between Cait and Max meant no one was going to get out of their house alive if the dog thought her life was in danger.

As Cait picked up the rake to resurrect the pile, Blake mused about the preceding year. There had been lots of changes since their marriage—some had tested their relationship, others had strengthened it. Perhaps the most trying had been Cait's transition from having a successful journalism career to being a stay-at-home freelance writer. Even though her old job at the newspaper had been offered back, she'd decided not to accept, wanting to concentrate on becoming a wife to him and a mother to his children. She appeared content and happy, but he knew the choice to give up a challenging career she loved had been a tougher adjustment than she'd let on.

Blake, too, had quit his job, deciding to fulfill a dream of starting his own personal security and weapons training business. He and two of his former military teammates created Top Tier Tactical, which had already inked contracts with a handful of Fortune 500 companies. The meeting he'd just returned from was with a government agency, and it seemed promising. If they got that contract, Top Tier would have the footing to compete with just about any personal protection and security agency in the country.

Relaxing against the window frame with his hands in his pockets, Blake watched Cait intently. Joy bubbled in her laugh and shined in her eyes as she held hands with the kids and jumped into the pile. She appeared blissfully happy and fully alive, as if the dark shadows that had brought the two of them together had never crossed her path. He exhaled a long sigh of contentment before grabbing a blanket from a chest near his desk and heading outside. Tossing it on the hammock as he walked by, he continued to the quaking pile of leaves where his family had disappeared. "Keep it down out here. You'll annoy the neighbors."

"We don't have any neighbors, Daddy." Whitney popped out of the pile and shook her hand at him, then turned her attention to shaking the leaves from her pink mittens.

Cait stood and wrapped her arms around his waist. "Welcome home. Now make yourself useful and grab the rake."

Blake looked at his watch and then over her shoulder at the

sun that was getting low over the hills on the horizon. "I would but your show's about to start."

"Oh?" Cait's eyes grew wide. "You have time to watch my favorite show with me?"

"Yep." Blake glanced at the kids, who were already busy raking the leaves to run through again, and then nodded toward the hammock and winked. "Saved you a seat."

The smile of pure delight that crossed Cait's face almost made Blake weak in the knees. She took immense pleasure in the simplest things—like watching the sunset from their hammock. He opened the blanket and stretched out on the hammock, then held out his arms for Cait, who practically dove in on top of him.

"I was beginning to think you wouldn't get back in time." She snuggled against him as he wrapped the blanket and his arms around her. "How'd it go?"

"Great." He took a deep breath of contentment. "Don't want to count my chickens, but it looks really promising."

They both fell silent as the laughter of the kids playing in the leaves drifted across the yard and the setting sun turned the sky ablaze.

"Are you happy, Blake?"

The question from out of the blue surprised him. "Happiest I've ever been in my life. Why?"

"Me too."

"Except..." He lifted his head and peered down at her. "You don't sound like it."

She remained silent a moment before looking up at him with an expression that appeared more apprehensive than happy. He noticed a vague uneasiness had crept into her expression.

"It's just scary."

"Wait. Why is being happy scary?"

"It seems too good to be true." She snuggled in closer. "You know, like it will end."

"That's silly. You know that, right?"

"Yes. I know."

The shadows grew longer and longer as they watched the sun hit the top of the mountains in the distance then begin to sink.

"Life is strange, isn't it?"

Blake lifted his head again. "What are you talking about now?"

"If someone had told you fifteen months ago you were going to marry a reporter, what would you have thought?"

He laughed. "That they were absolutely, positively, completely, and categorically crazy."

She poked him in the ribs with her elbow. "You don't have to be so emphatic about it."

Whitney interrupted their conversation. "Daddy, it's getting dark."

"Tell Drew to take you inside. We'll be there in a minute."

Blake listened to their footsteps and then the sound of the door banging shut. "Stop worrying." He kissed the top of her head. "You hear me?"

"That sounds like an order." She sat up and watched the last trace of light disappear over the hilltops.

"Yes, that's an order." Blake draped his arm over her shoulder as they stood. "Let's go get a piece of that pie you baked."

"You found that already?" Cait put her arm around his waist and leaned into him as they strolled toward the house.

"How could I miss it? The whole house smells like apple pie."

When she remained quiet, Blake sensed something still wasn't right. "You're still worrying."

She smiled up at him. "No. I'm not worrying. I was just wondering something."

"What's that?"

"When did you first know?"

"Know what, babe?"

"That you loved me."

Blake pondered the question while wondering why his wife was being so reflective. Maybe she was thinking about their up-coming first anniversary. It was only five days away, and he too was agonizing over what to do to celebrate.

"I don't think there was a specific moment." He pulled her to a stop and looked down at her. "You just kind of grew on me."

Her eyes twinkled with amusement, but she didn't say any-thing.

"How about you?" He started walking again. "It was love at first sight, right?"

She gurgled with laughter at the comment, which threw him off guard. Just knowing he was the one who'd caused the joyful outburst was enough to flood his heart.

"No, I don't think so." She grew quiet until they reached the porch. "I think it was the first time I saw you in a pair of jeans."

The humorous retort calmed his fears about her melancholy mood. He stopped in front of the door and wrapped his arms around her. "No more worrying. Right?"

She didn't respond other than to lay her head on his chest and squeeze him tightly, as if she didn't want the moment to end.

This is not the end of Blake and Cait's story. Read the first chapter of FINE LINE, coming July 2016.

Coming in July

FINE LINE

A Phantom Force Tactical Novel

FINE LINE

Chapter 1

Blake Madison reached for the alarm at the first ding so it wouldn't wake his wife.

"It's Saturday," Cait said sleepily, reaching for his arm. "Sleep in."

"I'm going for a quick run." He crawled out from under the covers, carefully moving their dog, Max, off his legs. "It's a lot of pressure having a young trophy wife. I have to stay in shape."

She threw a pillow at him, but then reached over and ran her hand over his abs. "You're doing a pretty good job of staying in shape."

The comment made Blake smile. He had gotten back into a training and running routine shortly after getting married, and was in almost as good shape now as he had been when he was a young Navy SEAL.

Then again, Cait was pretty fit herself. She'd taken over most of the barn chores, and actually enjoyed hauling, splitting, and stacking wood. She was always amused when other women saw her toned arms and requested the contact information for her personal trainer.

Dressing as quietly as he could in a pair of sweatpants and tee shirt, Blake headed toward the door.

"You forgot something," he heard from beneath the covers.

He came back and bent over Cait. "I know. But I was afraid I'd be tempted to crawl back into bed."

"Good answer." She reached up, grabbed a handful of his shirt, and pulled him down for a kiss, causing him to linger.

Sitting on the side of the bed, he leaned down with his hands propped on each side of her pillow. "Do you know how much I love you, Mrs. Madison?"

She grinned sleepily and pulled him close again. "Show me."

"I just did that a few hours ago. Remember?"

"Umm hmm." She drew the words out with her eyes still closed and a contented smile on her face. "But that was last night."

He glanced at the door, then back at the bed.

She must have sensed his hesitation. "I'm just kidding. We have all day. Go for your run."

Blake lifted her hand off the covers and kissed it. "We've been married almost a year. We need to start acting like an old married couple, not newlyweds."

"Are you saying you want me to become a nag?"

"Only if you nag me about getting back into bed with you."

He gave her another long kiss, and then stood and stared down at her in the dim light. She was wearing his NAVY tee shirt—or as she called it, her favorite negligée—with one arm lying on top of the blankets. His gaze fell on her wedding band, and then drifted to her tousled hair spread out on the pillow and her long lashes resting on her cheeks. He reconsidered his need for outdoor exercise.

"Bring me a cup of coffee when you get back," she murmured, pulling the covers up and rolling over.

"I won't be long, baby." He headed toward the door and patted his leg for the dog to follow. "I'll take Max so you don't have to get up and let him out."

"Love you."

His heart flipped. "Love you more."

Just as he started to close the door, she spoke again. "Don't miss me too much."

He grinned as the door clicked shut. She always said that when he left, even if they were only going to be separated for a few minutes. It had become a routine. Even the kids said it now when they left for school or went to visit a friend. *Don't miss me too much, daddy.*

Heading down the stairs he turned off the security alarm and went out onto the porch, taking a deep breath of the cool morning air. After doing a few stretches, he sprinted down the lane with Max trotting along beside, his heart bursting with happiness and contentment.

Until recently he had been blind to the beauty of the scenes that surrounded him—now he felt like he was seeing the world through new eyes, enabling him to notice the gifts that had always been right in front of him.

As he listened to the cadence of his feet hitting the dirt road and the sound of his steady breathing, Blake's mind drifted to his upcoming anniversary. He wanted to come up with something really special to celebrate—something that would show Cait how much she meant to him and the kids. It had been on his mind for weeks, but now the milestone loomed just days away and he still didn't know what that something was.

Moving to the side of the lane to avoid a large mud puddle without missing a stride, his mind continued to drift and wander. He thought back to the day he'd proposed, causing the vivid memories to replay through his mind like a movie.

Cait had just finished testifying at a congressional hearing, and was waiting for him by the Washington Monument. He'd snuck up behind her and grabbed her around the waist with one hand and the shoulders with the other. Drawing her up against him, he'd whispered in her ear. "Come here often?"

She'd tried to turn around and look up at him, but he held her firmly with her back pressed against him. "If that's your best pick-up line, you're going to be a lonely man," she'd said.

"Really? It works in the movies."

"Sorry. But, no."

"Okay. How about this?" He'd leaned down and whispered in her ear. "Hey, baby. Wanna ride in my truck?"

"Now you sound downright creepy," she'd said. "That's a definite no."

"Okay. Let me see… Close your eyes this time."

"All right. They're closed."

"Hey, sweetheart." He had let go of her then and backed away. "Are you free?"

"I don't know." She'd laughed, but continued to stand with her back to him. "When?"

"The rest of your life."

Whether it had been his words or the seriousness of his tone he didn't know, but she'd turned around with a perplexed expression on her face—and found him down on one knee with his kids, Drew on one side and Whitney on the other. All three held onto a sign that said, Will you marry us?

Blake smiled at the memory. Her surprise and the children's pure delight at being a part of the occasion had forged a memory he would never forget as long as he lived.

Bypassing the security gate he'd installed, Blake turned left at the end of their long driveway and continued toward the main road. His breath came faster now, creating short bursts of steam in the chilly morning air. The gate had been installed after he and Cait had exposed a scandal at the State Department that had involved a sitting senator and his ex-wife. They'd tried to keep a low profile and return to their private lives, but the press reports and social media campaigns from political fanatics made that impossible.

There had been lots of intimidating communications and a few death threats immediately following the hearings, so despite the home's isolation, Blake had taken the extra steps of installing the electronic gate to stop vehicles, and upgraded the security system in the house.

The addition of Max and the fact that his house was a sort of informal headquarters for his fledgling security firm, made him feel pretty secure and confident that his family was protected. There was rarely a day when at least one former Navy SEAL or special operations veteran did not stop by or spend the night, and depending on deployments for his company, there were often half a dozen or more.

Blake inhaled the musty smell of dying leaves and contemplated the gold and red colors splashed like a painter's canvas all around him. It was Cait's favorite time of year, and was beginning to be his as well. They'd harvested the last of the vegetables and pumpkins from the garden, and spent any free time together stacking wood in preparation for the coming winter. Somehow it wasn't work when Cait was involved. It was pure pleasure.

Passing the two-and-a-half-mile mark he knew by heart, Blake slowed down. The image of Cait lying in bed turned him around before he'd made it to the main road. If the kids were still asleep, maybe he'd take a quick shower and re-join her.

Sprinting the last hundred yards, Blake was surprised when Max didn't follow him up the porch, but continued around the side of the house with his nose to the ground. The dog usually had a hearty appetite after a run and wanted fed immediately.

"Where you going, boy? Smell a raccoon or something?"

Blake let him go and entered the house to find Whitney walking slowly down the stairs, looking disheveled but wide awake.

So much for going back to bed. "What are you doing up so early, young lady?"

He didn't hear her answer as he continued into the kitchen to make a pot of coffee. With the coffee starting to brew, he stood in the glow of the open refrigerator door, trying to figure out what he could scrounge up. Maybe he'd surprise Cait with breakfast in bed as an early anniversary gift.

Whitney shuffled into the room behind him and noisily pulled out a chair at the small kitchen table. "When is Cait coming back, Daddy?"

"What, honey?" Blake continued staring into the fridge. Having just turned four, Whitney talked a lot, but didn't always make sense.

"When are they going to bring her back?"

Blake closed the refrigerator door slowly as a twinge of alarm crawled up his spine. He turned to Whitney and knelt down beside her. "What men, honey? What are you talking about?"

"The mean ones." Her eyes brimmed with tears.

Blake didn't ask any more questions. He stood and turned in one movement.

Racing to the stairs, he took them two at a time and headed at a full sprint down the hallway to the master bedroom. He tried to open the door quietly, intending to find Cait still sleeping, but he almost tore the door off its hinges in his urgency.

The bed was empty.

FINE LINE

Will be available July 30, 2016

Other Books by Jessica James

Suspense:
MEANT TO BE

Historical Fiction:
SHADES OF GRAY
NOBLE CAUSE
ABOVE AND BEYOND
LIBERTY AND DESTINY

Non-Fiction
THE GRAY GHOST OF CIVIL WAR VIRGINIA
FROM THE HEART: Love Letters and Stories from the
Civil War

Dear Reader: Thank You!

I am honored that you took the time out of your busy schedule to read this book. If you enjoyed the journey, would you consider sharing the message with others?

Write a review online at your favorite retail store or goodreads. com.

Recommend this book to friends in your book club, church, school, workplace, or class.

Go to facebook.com/romantichistoricalfiction and "like" the page. Post a comment about what you enjoyed most.

Mention this book in a Facebook post, Twitter update, Pinterest pin, or blog post.

Pick up a copy for someone you know who would be impacted by the story—or send a copy to a soldier serving our country.

Visit the author's website at jesssicajamesbooks.com and sign up for the newsletter to keep up on giveaways, new releases and special events.

About the Author

Jessica James is an award-winning author of military fiction and non-fiction ranging from the Revolutionary War to modern day. She is the only two-time winner of the John Esten Cooke Award for Southern Fiction, and was featured in the book 50 Authors You Should Be Reading, published in 2010.

James' novels appeal to both men and women, and are featured in library collections all over the United States including Harvard and the U.S. Naval Academy. By weaving the principles of courage, devotion, duty, and dedication into each book, she attempts to honor the unsung heroes of the American military—past and present—and to convey the magnitude of their sacrifice and service.

Connect with her at www.jessicajamesbooks.com.

Contact the Author

Email Jessica@JessicaJamesBooks.com

www.JessicaJamesBooks.com
www.Facebook.com/romantichistoricalfiction
Twitter: @JessicaJames
Pinterest: www.pinterest.com/southernromance

Discussion Guide

1. What is the significance of the title *Deadline*?

2. List five words that describe the emotions you felt when you read this book.

3. Did you learn something you didn't know before?

4. How do you feel about the way the media is depicted in this book? Do you think it is accurate?

5. Do you feel as if your views on a subject have changed by reading this novel?

6. Which character do you like the most and why? The least and why?

7. What passages strike you as insightful, even profound? Perhaps a bit of dialog that's funny or poignant or that encapsulates a character? Is there a particular comment that states the book's thematic concerns?

8. Is the ending satisfying? If so, why? If not, why not...and how would you change it?

9. If you could ask the author a question, what would you ask? Have you read other books by the same author? If so how does this book compare. If not, does this book inspire you to read others?

10. Has this novel changed you—broadened your perspective? Have you learned something new or been exposed to different ideas about people or a certain part of the world?